Which Promise This Time?

Chrissy Garwood/Chrisolite Books
email: chrissy@chrissygarwood.com
29 Weston Hill Road,
Sorell, Tasmania, Australia, 7172
www.chrissygarwood.com

Direct quotations from Scripture are taken from the World Wide Bible (WEB) and are available in the public domain. Other verses are written from memory and are not direct quotes.

Book Layout ©2017 BookDesignTemplates.com

Cover Design: Belinda Pollard

Which Promise This Time?/ Chrissy Garwood —1st ed.

ISBN: 978-0-6485434-6-6 paperback

ISBN: 978-0-6485434-7-3 eBook

Which Promise This Time?

A River Wild Romantic Suspense Novel

Chrissy Garwood

Chrisolite Books
Sorell, Tasmania, Australia

ಉ ☼ ಞ

I dedicate this book to my sister-in-law Sharyn,
a compassionate defender for those in need.

ಉ ☼ ಞ

Contents

CHAPTER 1
(Thursday 26th April)

Past Meets Present

ॐ ✹ ॐ

Isaiah 16:4b WEB - The extortionist is brought to nothing.

ॐ ✹ ॐ

Today, she was Jezebel.

Someone once told her she changed her name as often as her hair colour. Vixen, Mystery, Salome, Delilah...

She blended into the crowd outside the shopping centre in the Melbourne suburbs. Forgettable; an ordinary suburbanite with mousy-brown hair.

Her vantage point gave Jezebel a good view of the street in both directions. Right on schedule, a group of children emerged from the train station two blocks away. She stubbed out her cigarette as she stepped away from the other social outcasts.

The children were in no hurry. They reached the two-storey mechanics workshop across the street, which stretched halfway along the city block. Shadowy figures visible through the gaping portals into the workshop called greetings to the children as they passed. Jezebel held her breath. She knew that black building could transform into an impenetrable fortress.

A massive figure stepped onto the footpath: Romano, the owner of the business. He spoke with the children. Jezebel lit another cigarette. Last year, she had helped kidnap his fiancée. Of those involved, only she had escaped his retribution.

Jezebel refocused on her quarry. Often, the boy entered the building. Today the bulky teenager barely paused. The group continued on their way. Jezebel took another puff as

1

she approached the nearest set of traffic lights. A pedestrian voiced his disapproval. She sneered, blowing smoke at him. Smoking was a misdemeanour; if the lights changed in her favour, what followed would be a serious offence.

Jezebel tapped her foot on the pavement. She needed to be ahead of the children before they reached the intersection. The cars stopped across all four lanes, and the green walk signal flashed. "Ahh!" Her modest heels made a satisfying noise as she stepped off the curb. The traffic-light gods were on her side.

Unbidden, she heard her *"husband's"* voice chastising her for praising dead gods. Samson Davidson insisted there was "one true God" willing to care for her. She spat on the road. When he learned of her actions today, Samson would disown her. Good riddance! She needed neither him nor his God.

When Jezebel reached the other side, she didn't glance towards the children. By now they should be waiting at the set of traffic lights closer to Romano's workshop. She walked around the final corner. Here they would dash across the side street towards the white apartment building, where fresh paint gleamed in the afternoon sun. Romano's sister-in-law, Sofia, had recently bought the building – and made her home there. Jezebel had no intention of poking a stick into that wasps' nest.

Her mission was to ensnare the boy or his sister.

It wouldn't matter if the other children raised the alarm. She would be gone before help arrived.

Her hand shook. She scowled, dropping the smouldering cigarette to the gutter. She wrapped her arms across her body, her fingernails digging deep. The pain helped. But then she remembered the concealed needle-marks. A bitter taste filled her mouth.

This was not the future she had foreseen. Nine months earlier, Jezebel had escaped from Melbourne with enough money to establish a new life. She had dreamed of independence, of choosing when and where she worked. Financial freedom guaranteed a safe supply to feed her craving. Without that money, she now risked the streets. Endured the unpredictable side-effects of cheaper, contaminated stuff.

The gangsters waiting for her in Sydney had ruined everything. She only escaped from them by latching onto Samson. She stamped her foot. Why was she thinking about *him* again?

The children's voices announced their approach. Jezebel watched them out of the corner of her eye as she slipped a hand into her pocket. The boys walked ahead, leaving the two girls unprotected. Didn't they know the streets were a dangerous place? The boys passed without giving her a second glance: three younger ones and two tall teenagers.

"Excuse me," Jezebel said, catching the smaller girl by the arm. "Can you tell me where I can find Second Avenue?"

The little brown-haired girl tried to shake herself free. She wore an expensive-looking silver bangle. Jezebel fought the temptation to snatch the trinket and run.

"Let go of her," the other girl said, tugging at the victim. "Come on, Lilly!"

"I'm sorry," Lilly said to Jezebel. "I don't know where Second Avenue is." Then she turned to her companion. "Nikki, you're hurting me!"

"I'll hurt you *more* if you don't come with me," Nikki hissed. She shouted towards the boys. "Hey, Marco! Hey, Butch! Make this woman leave us alone."

The boys hesitated. The dark-haired teenager must be Marco. He spoke to the younger boys who scampered towards the apartments. Butch was the one she wanted. He was taller than she remembered. When Butch turned, Jezebel withdrew her hand from her pocket. His eyes widened when he saw the blade.

The two girls screamed.

"Shut up!" Jezebel pressed the knife against Lilly's neck. "I won't hurt you unless you annoy me."

Lilly burst into tears, but Nikki recoiled in horror.

"I know you," Nikki cried, bolting towards the teenage boys. "Butch, Butch, run! Get away! It's Delilah! She's come to kill us."

Jezebel smiled. It would aid her escape if they only knew her by that alias. Sometimes it was useful to have many names.

Butch pushed his hysterical sister towards Marco. "Here, take 'er inside. I'll deal with this. Tell Sigrid. She'll know what to do." Butch ensured his sister went with Marco, before he turned to meet his foe.

Jezebel watched his approach. When he was a metre away, she spoke. "Stop there. Don't come any closer unless you want to see this girl bleed."

"Let Lilly go," Butch said. "She ain't done nothin'. I'm here. What do you want?"

Jezebel shook Lilly. "You know what I want," she snapped. "You took my money and I want it back."

"I didn't take yer money," he said, shaking his head. "I jus' moved it so Ma didn't steal it. Uncle Sam knows where it is. Ask him to show yer."

"I don't want to ask him. You tell me," she insisted, glancing towards the apartment building. One of the younger boys emerged from the main entrance and pointed across the road. The woman who appeared beside him was heavily pregnant. Jezebel went pale. What was *she* doing here?

Romano's woman sent the boy back inside and stepped forward.

Butch glanced across the street. His shoulders slumped. For the first time, he seemed afraid. Other women appeared in the apartment doorway.

"Tell me," Jezebel hissed, as the blade pierced the girl's skin.

Lilly screamed before she fainted. Jezebel caught the child in a smooth movement.

Butch turned to the approaching woman. "Evie! Don't come any closer."

"Do as he says," Jezebel shouted, but Romano's woman showed no fear.

"She's more frightened than dangerous," Evie said to Butch with a gentle smile. She stepped past him and stopped before Jezebel. "Put down the knife and pass Lilly to Butch. Then we can talk about why you're here."

Jezebel looked beyond Evie. The other women were approaching. "Tell them to stay back." The knife slashed empty air. Butch turned with his arms wide to slow their approach.

"Look in the loft in the ol' tractor shed," he shouted over his shoulder. "I've told yer – now let Lilly go."

There was no time to rejoice. One of the women slipped past Butch. Jezebel decided this small brown-skinned interloper was harmless. What was it with these people? Didn't they know any fear? The second woman stood beside Evie.

"Ruthie," this stranger said, regarding Jezebel with strange blue eyes. Every hair on Jezebel's body bristled.

"Don't call me that!" Jezebel cried, flinging the child away. The knife dropped to the footpath.

Time slowed as the consequences of her actions unfolded. The blue-eyed woman caught the child and staggered against Evie. They all fell. A jumble of bodies lay on the footpath. A blood-red puddle slowly spread beneath them. Cries of alarm rang out as the other women rushed to their aid.

Jezebel turned and fled. She almost made it to the corner before anyone gave chase. Shoved from behind, Jezebel landed face down on the pavement. Something heavy prevented her from rising. She waited for the blows that didn't come.

"You hurt Evie!" It was Butch who had caught her. Why did he sound so terrified? "Romano's gonna kill yer when he gets here. Why did yer hafta come?"

As Jezebel puzzled over his response, the blue-eyed woman knelt beside them. "Butch, let her go."

Jezebel lay quiet and still.

"Alixanda, no!" Butch cried.

"You have to let her go. Ruthie is one problem too many right now. Romano's on his way. If she's still here, there'll be trouble. Evie needs him. Sigrid's called an ambulance. The babies are coming, but there's too much blood."

"But you don't know who she is!" Butch protested as he eased himself upright. "Not even Uncle Sam dares to call her Ruth."

As soon as the weight lifted, Jezebel sprang to her feet and ran. She was already two metres away when Alixanda spoke again.

"I knew her when Ruth was her only name..."

Jezebel reeled and almost turned back. Then the voice in her head took over. *Keep running!*

ೞ✿ଓ

Five hours had passed since Jezebel fled. The fugitive stood at the top of the escalators in the Sydney airport domestic terminal. Her fellow passengers were hurrying past to retrieve their luggage.

Jezebel swayed. Raising the money for the airfare had come at a cost. It would take time for the bruises to heal, but she had repaid the offender by stealing his trousers along with his wallet.

"I've been here before," she whispered, clutching the handrail. "This can't be happening."

"Are you alright?" a woman asked. "You don't look well. Is someone meeting you here?"

"Samson—" Jezebel cried, her eyes searching for him on the concourse below. Her knees buckled as the crowded airport faded into darkness.

NINE MONTHS EARLIER

CHAPTER 2
(Saturday 5th August)

Back to the Beginning

ॐ ☼ ෴

*Isaiah 32:2 - A hiding place from the wind,
and a refuge from the storm.*

ॐ ☼ ෴

Stepping off the early morning flight from Melbourne, Jezebel carried two bags. She followed the other passengers streaming towards the exit. Her eyes continued to search for potential enemies. Across the hallway lurked a man in a dark suit. He smiled in her direction and spoke into his phone.

Jezebel veered into the ladies' restroom and joined a queue. Immediately behind her, two young women were talking.

"We have to hurry. We don't want the boys to see us dressed like this."

Jezebel turned and saw two girls wearing full-sleeved shirts buttoned to the throat, ankle-length skirts, and flat shoes. "I couldn't help overhearing," she chuckled. "I wish I'd thought of that. My mother's waiting downstairs. She'll have a fit when she sees my miniskirt and these heels."

"We're about the same size," one girl said with a grin. "Why don't we swap? I've always wanted a pair of those shoes."

Jezebel considered her expensive blue stilettos, a favourite pair. She slipped them off. "It's a deal."

Ten minutes later, Jezebel accompanied the two girls back towards the hallway. She mumbled a farewell, bobbing to adjust the shoelaces on her newly-acquired joggers. The girl wearing her clothes strutted away with her friend. Jezebel smiled as the man in the suit followed them.

9

Returning to the restroom, Jezebel whipped off the dark wig. Her short blonde hair was quickly tamed, and then she removed her heavy make-up. Smiling at her reflection, she smoothed the collar of the conservative floral shirt. Then she straightened the below-the-knees brown skirt. No-one would recognise her.

Alert to the conversations around her, she strolled onward.

"Did you see him?" a passing voice said. "He's been here all week with that sign. He's been the centre of a Twitter storm."

"Hang on, I was checking my boarding pass," a second voice replied. "Okay, we've got time. Let's go back to the escalators, and you can show me."

Jezebel identified the speakers and stayed close. Two girls stopped at the safety barrier, and one pointed downward.

In the middle of the lower concourse stood a rugged man in his late forties. He held a large handwritten poster which read "Waiting for Delilah". His reddish-blond hair was untidy. The short beard softened his weatherworn face. In his checked shirt, jeans and brown boots, he stood like an immovable rock. A divided stream of travellers surged past him. People threw him glances, some shaking their heads.

"His name is Sam," one of the girls said.

"He could have stepped out of an old Western," the other girl replied. "He doesn't look like a Samuel; more like Mitch or Jack."

"Not Samuel," the first girl replied, "Sam-*son*. That's why he's waiting for Delilah. He's named after that Sunday School hero. This Samson believes God sent him to collect Delilah. He says he's going to stay until she arrives."

"How do you know all this?"

Her informant waved her phone. "It's hot news. Some girl tried convincing him she was Delilah, but he asked for ID."

"Delilah's not a common name. He'll be waiting for a while.

If he's here when we come back, we should point that out to him. But now, we have a flight to catch..."

Jezebel studied Samson as the girls' voices faded. She grinned as she slipped her hand into her bag and retrieved her wallet. She had switched her cards in the restroom. This was an essential part of discarding her Jezebel identity. Scanning the crowd, she rubbed the leather thoughtfully. The girls were right, Delilah wasn't a common name.

☭

Samson shuffled his feet. How long did God expect him to wait? The tide of new arrivals ebbed and flowed, without a sign of the one he sought. He scrutinised each face, offering a secret prayer for those who looked at him. A few stopped to speak a word of encouragement or ask a question.

A big man in a dark suit came down the escalator. He signalled to two men loitering near the baggage carousel. They passed Samson without acknowledging his presence. Snippets of their conversation reached him.

"Sorry, Rick... can't find..."

"...looked everywhere..."

He wasn't alone in seeking someone among the crowd. As Samson began a silent petition for their success, cold fear gripped him. What if their presence meant his mission had failed? His shoulders tensed, and his hands held the sign more firmly.

The men stood behind him now. "...we've covered all the exits. She must be here somewhere."

"What do you want us to do?"

"Guard these doors. Question every solitary woman. I've got someone checking the security cameras. She went into that restroom, and she must have come out again."

The big man strode past Samson and returned upstairs.

"What's so important about this woman?" the voice behind him asked.

"Rick had plans for her, but now it's personal. He doesn't like losing to a woman. He's already sent the finder's fee to Valentino in Melbourne. Asking for a refund's not an option."

Samson shuddered, scanning the crowd.

> Lord, I need help. You made sure I heard these men talking, which suggests they're hunting Delilah. Either show me what she looks like or send me a sign? Otherwise, she's going to walk into their trap while I'm standing here like a fool.

Wave your poster and step forward to meet her.

The words echoed around the large space, but only Samson heard them. He took a deep breath, mustered a smile, and stepped forward. The hand waving the cardboard was clammy. His heart raced as the heat rose in his face. He closed his eyes, took another step then hesitated.

Running feet announced her arrival. Samson dropped the poster as a woman threw her arms around him, smothering him with kisses. Caught off guard, he embraced her.

"Men are waiting for you at every exit," he whispered.

"They're looking for a woman on her own," she replied, kissing him again.

He pulled back to gaze into her brown eyes.

"If you get me out of here," she whispered, "I'll give you whatever you want." She followed that declaration with a kiss that buckled his knees. Her strong embrace was all that kept him standing.

Samson reeled. He hadn't felt this helpless since that steer had tried to knock him into tomorrow.

A Moment to Breathe

ౚ ☼ ౛

Isaiah 41:10 - Don't you be afraid, for I am with you.

ౚ ☼ ౛

"I'm in trouble." Samson spoke quietly into his phone as he leaned against the taxi. His troubled eyes remained fixed on Delilah. She was across the street, talking with a group of young men.

"So you found her." His friend Caleb's voice chuckled in his ear.

"She found me."

There was a long pause at the other end. "So what's she like?"

"Her eyes are as dark and cold as midnight, and her kisses are like an anaesthetic. I'm still numb."

"Whoa! You've kissed her already? What happened to taking things slow?"

"She didn't give me a chance," Samson confessed. "She skipped hello and went straight to 'take me to your hotel'."

"Where are you? Are you at the hotel?" The steel in Caleb's voice signified a switch from friend to his pastor and spiritual advisor.

"Not yet. Delilah had to pick something up on the way. I think she's buying drugs."

There was another long pause. "Are you coming home? Your stepfather asked me when you'd be back."

"I don't know. I was wrong to criticise my namesake for falling into Delilah's trap. If she was anything like my temptress, he was already lost when she wrapped her arms around him."

"Don't concede defeat."

Samson laughed bitterly. "I'm out of my depth. It feels like I've forgotten all God taught me, and the darkness is consuming me."

"Don't trust your feelings. Listen for the Holy Spirit's guidance and stay focused on the light. God will steer you through this challenge. And remember you're nothing like our Bible hero. He already had a shameful reputation, while you've kept yourself pure. That's why you're not blind to the temptation now."

"Recognising the temptation doesn't make me immune." Samson sighed as he straightened. "I have to go. She's coming back. Pray for me."

Delilah hurried towards him. "Who were you talking to?"

"My friend Caleb. He wanted to know if I'm coming home now I've found you."

"You can do whatever you like, once we've concluded our deal." She reached for him, and he stiffened. Delilah's dark eyes studied him. She planted a kiss on his lips while she stuffed his wallet into his pocket. Then she retrieved the bag wedged between his feet on the footpath. Whatever was in the bag had been too valuable to take to her negotiations across the street. His wallet had been her insurance in case he tried to "ditch her and run with the loot".

৪০✿ଓ

Jezebel's mental transition to Delilah was almost complete. She patted her skirt pocket to confirm her recent purchase. She was seated on a sofa in the hotel lobby, while Samson stood at the reception desk. He was definitely an inexperienced country boy. When she was finished with him, she expected a declaration of eternal devotion. How long would she keep him on the leash?

As she tapped her toes, regret over parting with her favourite heels brought a cruel reminder. They were not her only loss. Less than twenty-four hours earlier, she had left one stiletto abandoned in the street. The expensive mate lay in an isolated nature reserve.

She closed her eyes to block the painful memories, but the injustice and betrayal were too strong. Those stilettos had been a gift from Loki, a man she once trusted. He styled himself as a criminal mastermind, and his rich rewards had bought her loyalty. As his prized lieutenant, she had been familiar with his brutality. The bruises on her arms were stark reminders of how easily he had turned against her. How dare Loki question Delilah's loyalty and treat her with contempt?

It was not her fault Loki's latest scheme had left him empty-handed. He knew Romano, a wealthy businessman and the kidnap victim's lover, had connections with Melbourne's criminal elite. Romano's far-reaching power was the logical explanation for the woman's disappearance from the hotel room. Delilah and her accomplice had only left their unconscious victim for a few minutes.

Nor was Delilah to blame for her accomplice's treachery. He had snitched to Valentino Horatio, the legendary cartel enforcer. Valentino had supplied her plane ticket to Sydney, but he was responsible for the men who were waiting when her flight arrived.

All these men had used her and thrown her away.

The bag at her feet held her future. She must guard it carefully. Delilah was through with trusting anyone.

She closed her eyes, clenched her fists, and her fingernails dug into her palms. She opened her eyes, turning her anger towards Samson.

She noted the way other women watched Samson as he walked towards her across the hotel lobby. Her smile broadened as she remembered the hard muscles beneath his shirt. Perhaps she wouldn't abandon her new pet just yet.

Samson stopped in front of her, cautious and alert.

"What took you so long?" she asked.

"The card reader wasn't working. Checkout's at ten. That gives us a couple of hours. I've ordered you breakfa—"

Slap.

How dare he make decisions for her! Delilah's hand smarted from the impact with his cheek. She prepared to defend herself. An expression appeared in Samson's eyes that she had rarely seen on a grown man. He blinked back tears. Without a word, he leaned forward, grabbed her bags and retreated. His long strides took him to the first-floor landing before she could catch him.

Samson did not acknowledge her presence until he placed her bags outside Room 205. He unlocked the door, and waited for Delilah to enter. When she passed, he followed with her bags.

In a single movement, he dumped her luggage on a narrow bench and kicked the door closed. He put the key card on a round table beside the door, on top of an open book. The budget room was small, without a window. She stood in the narrow passage between the bed and the bench. Delilah held her breath. When he retaliated, she would show him her dominance. Her heart-rate increased as he approached. Instead of the expected attack, he seized her around the waist and lifted her out of the way. Delilah was speechless.

Samson disappeared into the bathroom at the other end of the room.

He slammed the door. Delilah rattled the doorknob – locked! She heard running water.

Delilah scanned the room. On the bench beside her bags sat an electric kettle, two cups and a tray of coffee sachets. The kettle was cool to touch. Her shaky hands splashed water into a cup. She took a few sips before retrieving the packet of pills. Her fingers struggled with the seal, and she tipped the coloured assortment into her palm. She rolled them over, examining the maker's mark. Each one bore a black stamp that looked like a bishop's mitre.

"A cocktail of delight," the dealer had said.

"What kind of delight?" She had never seen this maker's mark before.

"The good kind," he had laughed, caressing her arm. "I could show you."

Delilah had grinned and brushed his hand away, indicating the waiting taxi. "I've already selected my next entertainment. My last one didn't last very long."

He had taken a step back then, and his companions joked about whether she was dangerous. She pretended to whip them into line.

"Is there anything else I should know?" she had asked as the dealer counted her money.

"I've explained the colour code," he said. "Experiment with different combinations until you work out which you prefer. Then I'll customise your next order."

"What makes you think I'll come back?"

"I'm exclusive for the reds."

"Red ones are that good?" She had felt the weight of the pills in her hand. The two red ones cost more than the others combined.

"Mm-hmm! But don't be greedy. You only need one of those."

Now she eagerly swallowed a red one. The bitter taste awakened a wave of unexpected anxiety. She chased the pill with the remaining water.

Delilah sat heavily on one of the chairs. She only had the assurance of strangers that these tablets would deliver what she needed. Her restless fingers drummed on the table. Why did that sound extra loud?

She stroked the smooth tabletop, beginning to understand. Next, she feathered the pages of the open book. She lifted the book and caressed the leather cover without registering the title. She glanced at the text. Halfway down the page was the heading "Samson and Delilah". Nausea rose within her, whether from the tablet or forbidden memories, she wasn't sure. She dropped the Bible with a bang. Delilah began to tremble, and she ran her hand down her arm. With a sigh, she closed her eyes.

Time to Talk

ଅଠ ✿ ଓଌ

Isaiah 41:10 - I will strengthen you and help you.

ଅଠ ✿ ଓଌ

Frozen in the doorway, Samson fought the urge to rush across the room. He wanted to prevent her from taking that poison. He'd tried that once with his younger sister and still bore the scars. The battle with addiction was not won that way.

His face still stung where Delilah had slapped him. Was violence another of her addictions?

While the drug distracted her, could he snatch his possessions and escape? He acknowledged his ownership of that thought and dropped to his knees.

"Lord, I can't do this," he whispered. The habit of praying aloud came easy. "I don't have the heart for another struggle with an addict. I've achieved nothing trying to save my family, except helping my brother Freddie escape. So why have you sent me this woman?"

He lifted his eyes heavenward. "I still don't understand why you let Mum marry Jack Kidman. She knew he was an alcoholic, but she thought she could redeem him. Now she's lost her faith, her health and her mind. Lord, why didn't she leave him before he ruined her?"

Samson stood and paced his side of the room. Delilah was watching him, but he could not stop now. He kept his voice low. "Mum made excuses for Jack. She said he needed someone to love him, but she made the situation worse by making allowances for his abuse. I don't want to be like her."

Delilah emphasised her curves with her hands. Samson turned his back on her. "Mum refused to admit their toxic relationship was hurting her children. Jack Kidman is the reason my sister's an addict, and he made life impossible for Freddie. You know how worried I am about what's been happening at home while I've been here..."

"Why go back?" Delilah asked.

Samson jumped with surprise. Did she have super-sensitive hearing?

She appeared in front of him. "Your brother got away."

"What kind of a man would I be if I left my mother to suffer alone?" What kind of man would he be if he abandoned Delilah?

"What kind of man are you, Samson?" Delilah reached for him, her dark eyes wild. "Isn't it time you showed me?"

"Don't touch me." Samson backed out of her reach.

Delilah laughed and sat on the bed. "Why don't you want me to touch you, Sammie-boy?" She patted the space beside her, as she unbuttoned her shirt. "Are you afraid you'll find out you're not a saint?"

Samson averted his eyes and headed for the door. With a whoosh, her shirt flew across and hit his head. He tossed it aside, reaching for the doorknob.

Tap, tap, tap!

"Room service!"

He already had the door open before the announcement registered with him. Samson leapt back, not realising he was giving the waitress permission to enter the room with the tray. Before he could correct his mistake, Delilah appeared beside him, kneeling on the bed. She wore only the briefest underwear. The temptress draped her arms around him. Samson's face flushed red.

"This is his first time," Delilah laughed. A knowing look passed between the women.

The waitress put the breakfast tray on the table. When she turned back towards them, the hotel employee's smile had intensified into a grin. "Enjoy your breakfast."

"I'm sure we will," Delilah said.

Samson pushed the door closed after the waitress left. "Why did you do that?"

"Just having a little fun." She giggled and selected a piece of toast. "Nobody's ever ordered me breakfast. I slapped you to remind you I'm in charge. Are you going to eat, or are you saving your appetite?"

He frowned, selecting a cup. "I didn't know if you preferred coffee or tea, so I ordered both. Which do you want?"

"Coffee," she said, "black, no sugar."

He poured from the coffee pot and placed the cup before her. She playfully stroked his hand. "Why are you being nice to me? Especially when it's obvious I'm going to be so-o-o bad for you. I'm not going to let you leave until I've given you everything I promised."

"Actually, that wasn't our deal," Samson said firmly. He retrieved a folded document from his Bible. "You promised to give me whatever I wanted. Before I can accept your offer, I need you to sign this." He unfolded the paper. "Make sure you read it carefully."

Her eyes widened. Delilah choked on her coffee.

"Is this a sick joke?"

"That's the same question I've been asking God for weeks. He told me to collect my bride from the airport. I told Him I didn't need a bride, but He insisted. She'd be Delilah to my Samson. And here you are. For you to be my bride, we need a marriage licence. I've already filled out my section and the minister has authorised the application."

"You expect me to marry you?"

"First you have to fill in this form. The choice is yours. There's no wedding if you leave before when the waiting period for the licence is up."

"How long is the wait?"

"A month. If you sign today, we can marry on the fifth of September."

"You said God told you to marry Delilah. That's not my real name."

"It doesn't matter what you call yourself. For all I know, you were Jezebel yesterday."

Delilah jumped to her feet, her eyes wide. "How did you know?"

She started to shiver. He handed her the discarded shirt. She struggled to put it on, then snorted in frustration and gave up on the buttons.

It was Samson's turn to laugh. "You were Jezebel yesterday? That explains everything. You'd make a fiendishly wicked Jezebel. No wonder you're so sure you can control me. And now you're trying your hand at Delilah, the beautiful temptress."

Delilah sank slowly to her seat, watching him.

He could almost read her thoughts. Had he called her "beautiful"? He looked at her closely. She was too thin, and through the open shirt, he could see bruises in multiple hues.

"You think you know me?" she growled. "If you make me sign this form, you're going to regret asking me to marry you."

"No-one is making you sign. You've made it clear what you expect from me but I've promised God I'll save myself for my wife. If you don't like those conditions, then get dressed and walk out the door. Or tell me to pack my bags and I'll leave.

But if you want me to help you get out of Sydney before those men from the airport find you, then sign."

"They'll never find me..." Her voice faded.

"I heard them talking," Samson said. "They have access to the airport security cameras. By now, they know about your new disguise. They'll also remember your performance when you found me. They're probably already on their way."

Delilah stared into space for a moment, before looking back at him. "Give me a pen."

"One final thing," he said as he held out the pen. "It has to be your real name, not one of your aliases. This application has to be legal, or it doesn't count."

"How will you know I'm not lying to you?" she whispered, as she filled out the form.

"The same way that I knew you were both Jezebel and Delilah. God will tell me."

ଔ ✿ ଓ

Delilah studied Samson as he folded the document. He seemed to dismiss her presence. She nibbled her toast and plotted her countermove. He opened his suitcase. The document disappeared into an inner pocket before he stepped to the wardrobe. She idly examined the items already in the case.

Under the jeans, she could see a pair of black dress pants and a silk tie. She glanced towards him and noted the shirts draped over his arm. With military precision, he began to fold them. The first three were practical and inexpensive. An unsuitable match for the formal pants. Her eyes lingered on the only plain shirt. She stretched out her hand, and he gave the white one to her. She examined the pearl buttons and the detailed stitching on the collar. A quick check of the label confirmed her assessment.

"This will do nicely," she said, as she threw off the shirt she was wearing and slipped into this designer one. After folding the sleeves to shorten them, she examined her reflection in the mirror. The lower hem came almost to her knees. The luxurious fabric was cool as it brushed against her skin. This reminded her she had expected more from this encounter. She raised her eyes and caught Samson heading towards the bathroom.

Her mind flooded with curses. If he refused to provide her with entertainment, it was time to take another pill. She stepped to the table where she had left the small plastic packet.

"No!" Samson strode towards her as she tipped pills into her hand. She gulped two blue ones before he reached her.

His fingers closed around her wrist and the contents of her palm scattered across the floor. Blind fury overwhelmed her. She visualised herself as a tiger as she sprang at him with her claws extended. In the narrow space, his head connected with the wardrobe as he fell.

Samson's eyes rolled back in his head.

Losing Track of Time

ೞ ☼ ಛ

*Philippians 2:4 - Consider the interests of others
ahead of your own.*

ೞ ☼ ಛ

Samson clenched the steering wheel. The GPS on the dashboard confirmed the date and location. He shook himself and checked the rear-view mirrors.

It had been ten years since his last blackout.

Heavy traffic surrounded his battered vehicle. He heard angry voices and honking horns. He refocused on the city street. His weathered Toyota LandCruiser was stationary at a green light.

He accelerated forward, his eyes searching for somewhere to park.

He didn't remember leaving the hotel.

He checked the time again: eight-forty-eight am. He should be at the airport.

Had he already found Delilah?

A flash of recollection made him flinch. The hatred in her eyes—

In confusion, he turned to the seat beside him. He was alone—

The realisation hit him hard, in the centre of his chest.

Finding the hotel took too long. At last, the familiar facade! Was he too late?

Three familiar men in dark suits stood outside the main entrance. Samson's vehicle crept past.

After rounding the corner, he zoomed into the underground car park.

He abandoned the LandCruiser in a disabled parking space, and ran for the stairs. Out of breath, he arrived at his second-floor room and banged on the door.

He didn't have a key.

He knocked again, calling her name.

Lord, why doesn't she answer?

He leaned his head against the wooden surface. No sound came from within.

Samson slid to the floor, his back pressed against the door. He dropped his head into his hands and groaned. Every movement hurt. He touched a tender spot on his head and then stared at his blood-stained fingers. His whole body began to shake.

Lord, what happened? Why can't I remember?

A band of pressure wrapped around his chest. His heart skipped.

Lord, I need to remember!

Whoosh! A roaring wind, louder than a freight train, rushed along the empty hallway. The force thrust his head against the door frame. Like a flood, the memories returned. Now he understood why he had forgotten. Delilah was an expert at inflicting pain.

Quiet footsteps approached. Samson jerked his head, flinching in agony. Then he sighed. It was the room service attendant carrying another tray. She glanced at him as she passed him to knock at a room further along the hall. The door opened, and the unseen recipient took the tray from her.

When the attendant retraced her steps, her eyes flew to the security camera in the ceiling.

"Please?" Samson croaked, standing to intercept her. "Could you unlock my room?"

He focused on her nametag: Macy.

"Of course," Macy said, slipping a key card from her pocket and tapping the sensor. "I'll collect your tray while I'm here."

He followed the hotel employee inside the room, and she shut the door. Delilah was unconscious on the bed. Macy frowned at him.

"Samson, what are you doing here?" Macy asked. "Dangerous men are asking for you downstairs. Your parking space was empty, so the manager told them you'd left."

"I came back for Delilah."

"What happened here?"

Samson stared at the floor. He picked up a coloured dot near his foot. Why were these pills scattered everywhere? When he straightened again, Macy was holding a clump of his hair and an almost empty packet of pills.

"How many did she take?"

"I don't know," Samson said. "I tried to stop her..."

"And?"

His hands went to his bruised neck. "Sh-she tried to kill me."

Macy stepped closer and studied him. She nodded as if making a decision before approaching the bed.

She shook Delilah while confirming she was breathing. There was no response.

"Get ready to leave," Macy said. "Make sure you pick up all those pills."

"Wh-a-at?"

Macy repeated her instructions before grabbing Delilah's breakfast tray. She paused at the door.

"Expect housekeeping. They'll move Delilah and tell you where to go. Don't trouble them with your questions, and don't lose those pills."

The door closed. Samson crawled across the floor, scouring the textured carpet. He was still there, checking that he had all the pills, when the door re-opened. He staggered to his feet.

Two women entered the room with a narrow laundry trolley. The first one was stocky, with dark hair and eyes. She ignored Samson, going towards the bed. In a few deft moves, she wrapped Delilah in a linen cocoon.

The second woman was taller, with red hair and a powerful muscular physique. She snatched up the bags from the bench, dumping them into the deep trolley. In a continuous movement, she went towards the bed.

Samson's mouth fell open. He took a faltering step forward. Delilah's limp body followed the bags into the trolley. The other woman tossed in the remaining bed linen before heading to the bathroom. Together, these women erased his presence from the room. The whole process took less than two minutes.

The tall woman pushed the trolley out of the room.

"Where—" Samson began.

The short woman glared at him. She put her hand in the centre of his chest. He froze. She held out her other hand.

He stared at it in confusion, as the room began to spin.

The woman frowned. She shoved him onto the edge of the bed, with his head between his knees.

He could hear her talking to someone. "He's in no state to go anywhere."

There was a pause.

She pulled him roughly to his feet. "Change of plans. Give me your keys and your phone."

He was helpless to deflect her fierce hands as she searched his pockets. She snatched the pills and his keys before activating his phone. After she tapped on the screen, a ping sounded beside him. A second phone lay on the unmade bed. The message notification read:

Samson

"Now I have your number, and you have mine."

"Who are you? What's happening?"

"Call me Xanda. There's no time to explain. They mustn't find you here. Go to room six-three-four and let yourself in."

Xanda thrust a key card into his pocket and pushed him out the door. She hustled him towards the elevator. His hand dragged along the wall until his feet delivered him to the elevator.

When the metal doors closed with him inside, Samson sagged against the wall. Numbers flashed above the door. The elevator sped to the sixth floor, where he stumbled out.

He struggled to find Room 634. Then he dropped the key card. His vision blurred when he bent to retrieve it. As soon as he was inside Room 634, he shoved the door closed and hurried to the bathroom.

Much later, he stared at his ashen face in the mirror. He could not remember the last time he had been so ill.

He stepped back into the main room and stared at the twin double beds. The closest one seemed to rise to greet him. He knew he should pray, but he was asleep within seconds.

Time to Dream

ॐ ☼ ॐ

Isaiah 18:7a WEB - In that time, a present will be brought.

ॐ ☼ ॐ

Samson shielded his eyes from the blinding light. He lay in a sun-bathed clearing surrounded by a mighty forest. The trees were home to brightly coloured birds, their music demanding his attention. The cloudless sky was the most intense blue he had ever seen. He lifted his head. The nearby undergrowth was thick with leafy green saplings and tall ferns. Unseen creatures set the foliage astir. Insects buzzed. In the background, he recognised the roar of distant water.

The grass was soft beneath him. Samson pushed himself upright. Beside him lay his favourite broad-brimmed hat. He frowned as he shoved it on his head – he was sure he had left that at home.

His phone was gone. Where was he? Was this still Sydney? How had they managed to transport him here without rousing him? He was a light sleeper – he had to be, to keep his confused mother from escaping at night. He wondered how his sister was coping, and then he remembered he had bigger worries now. He checked his recent injuries. The bruises and the headache were gone.

His only discomfort was a raging thirst. He needed to locate that river.

ॐ ☼ ॐ

Delilah awoke in a clearing. Dark clouds pressed down on her small sanctuary, promising rain. A chill wind rustled the leaves. She imagined the trees' twisted roots lifting from the soil as they walked—

Springing to her feet, she scanned the clearing. Delilah knew this was a dream, a familiar nightmare. Her mind had betrayed her again. She had only two fears: being alone in the Australian bush, and having that weakness used against her.

She spat on the ground. She refused to play the victim in her own fantasy. No matter how real this seemed, nothing in the nightmare could harm her. She knew how to speed up the process to bring about the inevitable conclusion.

Her body trembled as she tried to keep warm. Her skin was exceptionally sensitive to touch, and every noise too loud. She swore, remembering the red pill and the promised delight.

Delilah examined the flimsy, tattered garment that covered her. Mud concealed the many scratches and bruises on her bare arms and legs. Some of the injuries were weeping sores. She shook her head in dismay, and her hair fell loose. That was a new detail! The tangled brown locks reached almost to her waist. She hadn't worn her hair long since—

No! She mustn't let her thoughts go there.

Determined to master this dream, she searched the clearing. Her mind always provided an escape route. Was that a path over there in the shadows? Delilah trod carefully. The spiky grass was strewn with rough pebbles and her sensitised feet found every one.

She peered through the overhanging branches. A well-worn path led into the gloom. A vicious wind roared through the clearing. It whipped the trees into a frightful dance. Heavy rain began to fall. Lightning flashed, and thunder shook the ground. Delilah dodged a flying branch and dashed into the shadows.

Delilah ran until she was breathless, then paused. The noise from the storm faded here. The canopy was thick. Low hanging leaves dripped onto the path. The closest branches extended their cruel fingers towards her. The urge to flee was strong. The path ahead plunged into darkness. She fought for the strength to take another step.

Cra-aaa-ck.

What was that?

Cr-ree-ea-ak.

Where was that noise coming from?

Whoo-ooo-OOO-OOOSSS-shhh!

C-r-r-ASH!

The ground shook. Delilah fell to her knees.

Wooden shrapnel peppered the path. Within arm's reach lay the quivering upper branches of a fallen tree. Ominous creaking and groans erupted in all directions. Another forest giant fell towards her. Delilah ran screaming into the forest.

ଧ ✿ ଓ

Samson stepped from the forest to find himself beside a river wild and free. From his left, the water danced towards him. The opposite bank was distant. The trees grew too close to the river for a clear view. To follow the river's downstream progress, he had to push through the undergrowth. Abruptly, his progress ended at the top of a mighty waterfall. He grabbed an overhanging branch to keep from falling.

Rainbow spray rose hundreds of metres into the air. Thundering water surged over the rocky precipice at his feet. He dropped to his knees. Far below, the river plunged into a pool before it flowed through a green valley.

Lying on his stomach, Samson reached out to capture the spray to quench his thirst. The water was sweet and refreshing. He lay there, content.

Samson.

Yes, Lord.

ଧ ✿ ଓ

Delilah pressed through the low hanging branches, desperate to escape the dream. Her fingernails ripped, her knees bled. The pain was real. She could see light ahead. She cried with relief, using the last of her strength to reach it.

Dropping to her knees, Delilah closed her eyes. Her chest burned as she sucked in air. Between gasps, she could still hear the storm. *Swoosh!* Something lashed against her face. She put up her hands to defend herself.

"Wake up," she shouted as she fought the flailing branches. She crawled forward into a clearing. The storm had brought down another forest giant. It was not safe here. Then she heard the ominous sound again.

Whoo-ooo-OOO-OOOSSS-shhh!

This time, the branches smashed around her, pinning her to the ground. Her scream mingled with the violent crash that echoed among the trees. Delilah swiped at her eyes. She scolded herself for letting the fantasy distress her. Only a larger branch, broken from the main trunk, restrained her. She wriggled forward, fighting the branches until she was free.

Delilah shuddered, haunted by the horror of what might have been. *Wake up! Keep moving!* She couldn't move. *Idiot! Keep standing there and the next tree will get you!*

That message got through to the dreamer. In desperation, she ran around the clearing. *Look! A way out!*

She peered through the branches.

No. A fallen tree blocked this path—

Delilah jerked back. Snagged on a branch was a scrap of fabric. It matched the tattered garment she was wearing. She examined her surroundings. She was back where the nightmare began. "No! No! No-oo!" she cried.

An Appointed Hour

꙰ ☼ ꙯

*Isaiah 25:9b WEB Behold, this is our God!
We have waited for him, and he will save us!*

꙰ ☼ ꙯

Samson, awaken.

Thrust from the dream, Samson sat up. Delilah was lying on the other bed. An unknown man sat at the table. He nodded to Samson and continued talking on his phone. "He's awake. I'll report back when I'm done here."

"Who are you?" Samson asked.

"Nelson Felmingham; I work for Piper Maxwell." He watched Samson for a response. "*Maximum Security*?" Samson shook his head. "*Operation Phoenix*?"

"Those names mean nothing to me."

Before Nelson could respond, the door opened. Xanda entered, followed by her companion who brought in a large black suitcase.

"You've already met Xanda and Sigrid," Nelson said.

Samson watched a wordless exchange between the trio. "How much trouble am I in?"

"What do you know about your friend?" Nelson countered.

Samson glanced towards the sleeper and shivered. "Until I met her at the airport, all I knew was her name."

"Who sent you to meet her?"

Samson sighed. "God."

"That's the story on social media. Is that the truth?" Nelson asked.

"Yes."

"Why would God send you to collect a stranger from the airport?"

"I've been asking Him the same question," Samson confessed. "He said I'd been obedient with the things He'd given me. It was time to test the depth of my faith."

"God is testing you?" Xanda asked, stepping forward to check his eyes. She frowned, turning back to the others.

Suddenly, Delilah shrieked in terror. "No! No! No-oo!"

Sigrid strode to the bed. Delilah was unresponsive. After a restless moment, the sleeper resumed her silence.

"When will she wake?" Samson asked.

Nelson turned to Xanda, who brought out the bag of pills.

"I won't bore you with the chemistry," Xanda said. "These bear the Black Bishop mark. They're new, and the product range is still undergoing refinement. Each colour has a different chemical signature. I haven't seen some of these before. There are too many variables for me to give you a definitive answer."

"Is that why you're here?" Samson asked. "Are you investigating these drugs?"

"That's just a distraction," Nelson said, "which could jeopardise our mission. We're going to help you, but keep quiet about our involvement."

"What happens now?"

Sigrid unzipped the suitcase. She lifted Delilah from the bed, and folded the body into the suitcase. Samson thought this an impossible task, but Sigrid achieved it with ease. After fastening the zipper, she turned towards the door.

"We moved your LandCruiser to a car park where we control the security cameras," Nelson said. "Xanda and Sigrid will deliver the suitcase there, and help you transfer her to your vehicle. After you leave, we'll make sure no-one follows you. Whatever happens, don't stop until you're clear of the city. Expect a message when it's safe. Then forget you've seen us."

Samson frowned. "What if she doesn't wake?"

"You should be more worried about *when* she wakes," Xanda muttered.

"Don't take her to a hospital," Nelson added. "They'll notify the police. You want to stay out of any official reports. We don't know why these men are after her, but it can't be good."

"If you're worried," Xanda said, "find a sympathetic GP who does house calls. In the meantime, give her sips of water and let her sleep off whatever's in her system. She's now wearing incontinence pads, which gives you one less thing to worry about."

৪০ ☼ ৫৪

Samson turned onto Kidman Road, his mountainside destination only a few kilometres away. He had left the bustling city traffic behind hours ago, passing through towns and villages, each one more remote, stopping only for fuel. The low-lying pastureland had gradually given way to the wilder foothills as the roads became windy and narrow. Now, as the late afternoon sun had dropped below the tree line, he glanced towards Delilah.

Memories from a similar journey haunted him.

Sixteen years ago, it had been his half-sister beside him.

Kim had screamed at him for hours, but his combat-hardened heart had seemed immune. He'd had orders, and nothing would have prevented him from delivering Kim to her mother.

Samson could still visualise fourteen-year-old Kim in the passenger seat. The pretty girl had been emotionally exhausted and heavily pregnant with his nephew Butch. He blinked away a tear. Now almost thirty-one, Kim's drug habit fuelled a restlessness that threatened to destroy her.

A twinge of doubt pinched at his temples. Why was he bringing Delilah and her lifestyle choices anywhere near his sister? He thought of the old homestead and wondered what welcome he might receive.

After eighteen months away, Kim had come home with her children three weeks ago. She always blamed Samson for her troubles, yet this didn't stop her from demanding his help.

The familiar gravel road wound its way high into the forested hills. He needed to exercise caution on the hairpin turns, as he watched for wildlife on the road. He pressed his hand to his aching head.

Samson would never have left *Mountain Rise* if Kim and her two children hadn't been there to watch his mother. Grace needed constant supervision. Having another three people in the house had eased his burden. During the drama all those years ago, the seeds of his mother's forgetfulness had sprouted. Samson wrenched his thoughts away.

Kim's son Butch had grown into a tall, self-assured fifteen-year-old. No-one had expected Old Jack to make the teenager welcome, but they had become kindred spirits allied against Samson. Yet Samson bore Butch no ill-feeling.

He was grateful that his stepfather had finally made a connection with someone. Not even his half-brother Freddie – three years younger than Kim – had been able to find favour with the weathered mountain man.

The decisions made long ago – when he brought his pregnant half-sister home – continued to define Samson's role in the family. That was why he had helped Freddie to escape to Melbourne ten years ago. Old Jack seemed to have forgotten he had another son. Samson continually prayed for them to be reconciled.

As he navigated another sharp corner, Samson's mind drifted to Kim's daughter. Twelve-year-old Nikki was an unexpected blessing. The tiny girl resembled her mother in looks, but not in temperament. Nikki loved spending time with her grandmother, Samson's mother Grace. He smiled as happier memories awakened. It was good to see Grace at peace with the girl. His stepfather must have agreed. Old Jack had looked across the table ten days ago and ordered Samson to take a holiday. If only he had known the trouble that would follow—

The next corner was on him before Samson was ready, and he narrowly avoided disaster. He exhaled angrily. He had trouble enough without adding to it by being reckless. Too many people depended on him...

The full weight of his responsibilities hit him like an avalanche and his mind retreated to the past again. Back then, the death of his stepbrother Jack Junior had acted as a catalyst. His mother's broken heart had made it inevitable that Samson would need to retrieve fourteen-year-old Kim, who had run away with one of their neighbours, Michael Cassidy.

Samson had come directly from the military airport, still wearing his overseas uniform. The police were searching for the runaways, but it had taken little effort for Samson to track the pair and wrest his half-sister away from her lover. On that journey home, he had discovered she was a stranger to him.

He switched on the headlights, alert for wandering kangaroos. The narrow bridge at the bottom of the steep gully rushed towards him, as he shifted into a lower gear. The shallow river seemed harmless, yet long ago, a torrential flood had stranded the Kidman family for weeks. His stepfather sometimes spoke about the river's transformation.

Safely across the bridge, his mind drifted to the dream river. He could lose himself forever in its wild majesty and freedom. But then his vehicle hit a pothole and he was jerked back into the present. As the LandCruiser roared up the hill into the sharp, sweeping bend a dark shadow bounded across the road. Samson narrowly avoided the collision, fighting for control as the LandCruiser drifted sideways in the gravel. The sleeping passenger slid across the bench seat and pushed against him. He brought the vehicle to an abrupt halt. The engine stalled. The lights failed.

He sat in the darkness, listening to her breathing. She hadn't cried out during the Sydney transfer, despite Sigrid's rough handling. Nor had she stirred during the journey. Her warm body pressed against his. Delilah was attractive, and God said she was to be his bride—

He shook his head. This woman was dangerous. He shoved her sideways and adjusted her seatbelt.

It had been hours since Nelson had messaged "all clear". Samson prayed for sufficient time to prepare before Delilah's enemies arrived.

Restarting the engine, Samson drove with more caution. When he arrived at the final gate, he paused to greet the two kelpies he had raised from pups. They ran ahead to the house, barking and chasing each other.

The LandCruiser stopped near the kitchen door.

Samson went inside to turn on the lights. He could hear the television in the lounge room, but he didn't go there.

When he returned to the kitchen with Delilah in his arms, his sister was waiting with her hands on her hips.

"Who's this?" Kim demanded. "You go away, leaving me to look after Mum and Dad. Not a word about when you're coming back, and then you arrive with *her*."

Samson frowned, declining to answer. Kim's eyes were bright, and she was twitchy. He elbowed her aside and walked towards the door that led to the servant quarters. The last housekeeper had quit years ago, after one of Old Jack's drunken rages. He dumped the sleeper on top of the housekeeper's bed.

"Why are you putting her here?" Kim asked. "If you're bringing home a whore, at least be man enough to put her in your bed."

She pulled back when Samson approached her. "Be careful what you say about my fiancée."

"Your fiancée?" She laughed. "You're a bigger fool than I thought. You haven't gone further than town for the past three years, then one trip away ends like this. What kind of promises did you make? Just wait until Dad hears—" As she turned to leave, Samson grabbed her arm. Kim looked at his clenched fingers, and her face went pale.

"Leave your father out of it!" Samson released her, going to retrieve Delilah's bags. When he returned, Kim was still there. "If you're going to stay," he said, "you can help me get her into bed."

"What's wrong with you?" Kim complained. "You growled at me, and then you hurt my arm."

"I'm sorry. It's been a long day."

He considered the two bags. The one Delilah had guarded was secured with a sturdy lock. He laid the other one on the double bed and threw back the lid. Three wigs sat on top. He hesitated when he saw what lay beneath them.

Kim shrieked and leapt forward. Her hands grabbed two bundles of cash. She waved the money in his face. "What kind of trouble are you in?"

CHAPTER 8
(Sunday 6th August)

Time to Choose Sides

*Philippians 3:18 - I have told you often, even with tears,
that many live as enemies of Christ.*

Early the next morning, Butch entered the kitchen to see his uncle disappearing through the opposite door. He waited to hear whether Uncle Sam had gone outside, but the silence unmasked a different sound: his mother Kim's spiked heels on the floorboards in the hall. Butch leapt into the walk-in pantry, closing the door behind him. What was her rush? He peered through the crack.

The rapid staccato ceased. "Samson," Kim shouted.

Uncle Sam came back into the room.

Butch's red-faced mother confronted her half-brother, glaring at the keys in his hand. "Where are you going?"

"It's Sunday morning." Uncle Sam raised his Bible. "I'm going to church."

She frowned. "Who's watching Mum while you're gone?"

"Nikki's sitting with her until your father gets back from his ride."

"Dad's gone for a ride? What's he doing up this early?"

Good question, Butch thought, but more importantly, what are *you* up to? His mother wore a short skirt and heels, and extra makeup.

Uncle Sam raised an eyebrow. "Were you going somewhere?"

"Is it a crime to dress up?" she huffed. "I thought your *guest* might be awake..."

Uncle Sam glanced towards the other door. "No, and don't go into her room while I'm gone. If she wakes, call me."

"I don't have any phone credit."

Uncle Sam shook his head. He pointed to the wall-mounted phone. "Use the landline. My number's on the noticeboard." After glancing at his watch, he left.

Kim followed him out. Butch pushed the pantry door open.

"What time will you be back?" she asked.

"The same time as usual. Why?"

"Are you bringing lunch back with you?"

There was a pause, followed by his uncle's deep sigh. "Don't I always bring lunch home on Sundays?"

The outer door creaked, then a closing car door broke the silence. Butch waited. The house door slammed. The teenager ducked back into the pantry. He wriggled until he had a clear view of his mother, who stood at the large kitchen window. Uncle Sam's LandCruiser roared into life, and the farm dogs barked. Butch grinned. The dogs enjoyed a good race.

When the noise faded, his mother surveyed the kitchen. Butch smirked. She didn't suspect his hiding place. A sly smile appeared on her face as she moved towards the hallway. Was she going to search Uncle Sam's room? His uncle wasn't stupid. He wouldn't leave cash lying around. Maybe she was going to try breaking into the safe again?

Instead of moving towards the study, Kim shut the door leading to the hallway and hurried to the servant wing. With her hand on the doorknob, she glanced over her shoulder. Butch groaned. He'd heard his uncle's warning. After the trouble last time, his uncle had been reluctant to let them stay. His mother slipped through the door, closing it behind her.

Butch stepped from the pantry. He prepared to follow her, but the door reopened. Kim balked when she saw him.

"Whacha doin' in there?" he demanded. "Uncle Sam said that room's outta bounds."

"He asked me to open the window," she said.

Butch nodded, even though he knew she lied. She threw a glance towards the wall-mounted telephone. One of her hands slipped into her skirt pocket, where she kept her stash. His eyes narrowed. That pocket had been empty for days.

"I'm gonna check the chickens," he said, heading towards the outer door. Once outside, Butch bobbed out of sight. There was a listening place where he would hear if his mother used the phone. She didn't delay.

"Hi, it's me. Sam's back so meet me at the back gate." There was a pause. "Bring me the good stuff. I have cash."

Butch waited.

"Of course, I remember I owe you..." she continued. "Yes, I know I promised that's how I'd pay. But after this, you can pay *me* if you want— Don't say I'm ungrateful. I only agreed because I didn't have any cash." Kim sounded as if she was crying. "Two hundred dollars..."

Where did she get that amount? The dealer must have asked the same question.

"I told you," she said. "Sam's back."

Butch was considering his options when the outer door opened. He squeezed in between the water tanks which sat close to the wall. It was a tight fit. He'd grown since he had last hidden there. Kim didn't check to see if anyone was watching. She went straight to the quad-bike shed.

The dogs rushed over, but stayed inside the compound when she left. They stood at the fence, barking as she disappeared from view. Butch was wondering why they didn't follow her when a harsh voice interrupted his thoughts.

"There goes your Ma," said his grandfather.

Butch jumped in alarm, banging his head on the pipe that connected the tanks. "Ow!" He staggered from concealment.

"Give me some warnin' next time, crazy ol' man."

"Show some respect."

'Old Jack' Kidman swiped his grandson across the back of the legs with his walking stick. "You should be more careful. Takes a sneak t'catch a sneak." Then his grandfather doubled over as a hacking cough shook his bony frame.

Butch went to close the gate, and when he returned, he was careful to stay out of reach. "Watcha doin' up so early?"

"Same thing as your Ma." Old Jack chuckled. "Sam's gone to church, and she's securing her supply for the week."

"Ya kept that ol' still?" Butch asked. "How come Uncle Sam never finds it?"

"We have an unspoken agreement, Samson and I." Old Jack lowered his voice and crept closer. "I don't drink where he can see me, and he stays."

"What if he knew yer mates come over while he's away?"

"I've got my own questions," Old Jack snapped, "about that woman he's hidden in the house. I heard him telling Grandma. He said he'd brought home the woman God wants him to marry. Your Ma tattled on him too. She said Samson's touchy about where he met this woman. Your Ma thinks he paid her to be with him and he's kidnapped her."

"Uncle Sam never do nothin' like that," Butch huffed.

Old Jack whacked him with the walking stick again. "Use your brains. You've been with your Ma all your life. You know the world's a twisted place. Samson acts like a saint, but his halo's slipped. He's a man, and not gettin' any younger. If he wants to pay a woman to keep his bed warm, I won't criticise him. I'm thankful he's stayed here as long as he has."

Butch rubbed his legs. "One day, ol' man, I'm gonna break that stick. Then I'll tell Uncle Sam— Ow!"

"I'm still more than a match for you, Butch Cassidy Kidman," Old Jack laughed. "I know what you're thinking. Before you try to get back at me, I'll offer you a deal."

"What kinda deal?"

"Your Ma's making trouble again. She found my home stash and is using it as leverage. I'd let her think she's won, but yesterday she stole a couple of bottles. If Sam finds them—"

"You want me to move yer stash?" Butch suggested. "Where?"

Old Jack grinned. "The hayloft in the tractor shed."

"Howz I gonna get up there?"

"Try the ladder you're already using."

"What's to stop me drinkin' it all, or sellin' it to me mates?"

His grandfather stopped smiling. A bony hand gripped Butch's shoulder. "You care about your sister."

Butch snarled, and his grandfather stepped back. "Don't think I'd do anything to hurt her. A phone call to Welfare's all I'd need. Your Ma would blame Samson."

Butch carried bottles while his grandfather kept watch. He was coming back from hiding the final load when he heard the quad bike in the distance. The engine was revving too high. The red quad bike zigzagged down the hill. Butch began to run. Kim wasn't slowing for the closed gate.

BANG! The vehicle bucked, as the reinforced bull bar Uncle Sam had fitted absorbed most of the impact. His mother was thrown forward, and then pulled back by the harness, towards the moulded seat that was another safety feature. Kim swore, pulling on the restraining straps, before she reversed. If she had unbuckled the straps, the engine would have died, saving them all from further trouble. She glared at the gate.

The dogs barked while Butch wrestled the buckled gate open. Broken glass from the headlights littered the ground.

Vroo-ooo-mmmMMM. Kim waved and pushed through. Her momentum thrust the full weight of the gate into him and he fell. She didn't look back. The dogs gave chase.

Butch dragged himself upright, watching in horror as Kim turned the vehicle sharply sideways to avoid her father who was marching towards her. She must have unfastened the harness, because the engine cut out. Deprived of momentum, the bike began to tilt as she leapt off. After tumbling across the ground Kim came to rest against her father's feet.

The driverless quad bike kept going, and overturned into the ditch. The back wheels spun in the air. Old Jack's walking stick tapped the ground impatiently. Kim seemed unhurt. Butch limped towards them. Behind him, the dogs barked while Old Jack cursed her stupidity.

"I'm sorry, Daddy," Kim whined.

"You could have died!" Old Jack shouted, flailing the air with his stick. Kim cowered before him, but the blow never landed. He dropped his arm. "You knocked over your son. What kind of mother are you? Go to your room! And don't come out until you understand what you've done."

She scrambled to her feet and staggered past Butch. "I'm sorry," she whispered. He didn't respond. One look at her glazed eyes was enough.

Butch faced his grandfather, who was pale and clutching his chest. He pushed Butch away.

"Don't worry about me," Old Jack said. "I've got pills for this. You try to straighten that gate. There's nothing we can do about the quad bike. Samson will winch it out when he gets back. If I thought it would do any good, I'd tell you to pray for a miracle."

The teenager stared at the quad bike. He turned to his grandfather, his mouth open, but Old Jack interrupted him. "You're not too hurt, are you? We Kidmans are tough."

Butch shook his head. This was not the time to talk about his injuries. He didn't need to pray. It should be easy to convince Uncle Sam his troublemaking nephew was to blame.

CHAPTER 9
(Sunday 6th August)

Time to Hide

ಹೊ ✿ ೮೩

Psalm 44:24 WEB Why do You hide Your face,
and forget our affliction and our oppression?

ಹೊ ✿ ೮೩

When Samson arrived home from church, Butch was swinging on the open gate. The boy stared at the car that followed him into the compound.

"That's the new doc!" Butch cried. "Did Ol' Jack call you?"

Samson's smile faded. "No."

At church, his friend and pastor, Caleb, had introduced him to the new GP, Dr Tim Chappell. Their family doctor had unexpectedly retired while Samson was away. The young doctor had explained Kim's refusal to allow him to visit Grace, and offered to follow him home today.

His LandCruiser jerked to a halt, and Samson ran into the house. He went to Delilah's bedroom. She still slept. He shook his head and hurried to his mother's room. The bed was empty.

He stood in the hallway and listened. Behind him, Butch was bringing Tim Chappell inside. Ahead, he could hear Nikki's voice. He searched for her, peering in each open doorway until he came to his stepfather's room. Jack lay on the bed, fully dressed with his eyes closed. Nikki was reading aloud from a storybook. Beside her sat his frail mother, Grace. He gasped at the unfamiliar light of recognition as she raised her eyes.

"Jack, here's Samson," Grace said, patting his stepfather's hand.

Butch arrived with the doctor, and Samson drew him aside. "Where's your mother?"

Butch pointed to Kim's closed door. Samson knocked before entering. Kim was asleep. He called her name.

"It won't do any good," his nephew muttered from the doorway. "She's sleeping off whatever she's taken. I've checked – her heart rate and breathing are normal."

"Why didn't you call me?"

"About Ma?" Butch shrugged.

"About your grandfather?"

"Ol' Jack said no." The boy shook his head and went towards the kitchen.

"Keep Nikki occupied," Samson said.

Butch hesitated. "Come on, Nikki," he called. "Let's play hide'n'seek. You go to the tower end of the hall 'n' count fifty, then come find me."

Nikki appeared in the hallway. "Inside or out?"

"Both," Butch said. "Not many places for me to hide here. I won't go outside the fence."

"One, two, three..."

Samson spoke briefly to Tim, before retrieving the food he'd purchased for lunch. He had heard Butch slam the outer door, but there was no sign of him outside. Returning to the kitchen, Samson wrapped the bagged chickens in tea towels to keep them warm. The salads he shoved into the almost empty refrigerator. Tomorrow, he would have to go shopping.

⇝ ☯ ℳ

Butch grinned. Slamming the door should convince everyone he was outside. He tiptoed across the kitchen. Quietly, he opened and closed doors before entering the forbidden bedroom. The curtains shut out the light.

He thought he heard his sister shouting: "Fifty! Coming, ready or not!" He waited for the kitchen door to slam.

50

Nikki was searching outside.

First, Butch looked under the bed. Nothing there, and the old dresser drawers were also empty. The large mirror gave a clear view of the room. There was only one place left. The hinges on the ancient wardrobe creaked, and Butch stood motionless, but the sleeping woman didn't stir.

Butch searched the hanging clothes, before unzipping the first of two suitcases. His hands worked while he watched the mirror. She mustn't catch him.

His mouth dropped open when he pulled out the money. Why would Uncle Sam leave this here? Butch tugged at the sturdy lock on the other bag. If this fortune lay unsecured, what treasure did she hide here? Had his mother asked the same question?

಄ ✿ ಃ

Samson waited in the kitchen for the doctor to give his report.

"He's asleep," Tim began. "Butch told me Jack was shouting and waving his walking stick, before grabbing his chest. Your stepfather refused help, telling Butch he had medicine to take." Tim held up his phone. "I've reviewed his medical records. The tablets beside the bed match what I would have administered. He seems to be stable now. I've phoned for the ambulance, but they're delayed. There's been an accident near your turn-off. Some city driver going too fast for the corner."

Samson frowned. They were too high in the hills for tourists. He shook his head to stop this train of thought. "How's my mother coping with this?"

"Surprisingly well," Tim replied. "She doesn't understand the seriousness of Jack's condition. But it won't do any harm for her to sit with him while we wait. She's reminiscing about the early years of their marriage. I'll check her later."

Samson sank onto a kitchen chair.

Tim frowned. "Where's your sister?"

"Sleeping off whatever drugs she managed to get her hands on," Samson muttered. "It's not the first time." He rose to his feet again. "There's another patient I want you to see."

₨ ⚘ ₳

Butch knew Nikki must be close. "Butch Cassidy Kidman, where are you?" A door slammed. "Uncle Sam, have you seen Butch?"

"He went outside."

Was that voice in the hall? Butch leapt into the wardrobe, leaving the door ajar. He held his breath, listening as Nikki's feet stomped away.

The bedroom light flashed on. Uncle Sam entered, followed by the doctor, who was the same height. The visitor had the shoulder-length sun-bleached hair of a surfer. Neither adult looked towards the wardrobe. His unsmiling uncle leaned on the dresser. The doctor examined the sleeping woman. Butch exhaled slowly. If he was careful, he might learn something useful.

"You said she's been like this since yesterday?" Tim asked. "Do you know what she took?"

Butch leaned forward to catch the answer. Uncle Sam had his eyes averted. "I had help in Sydney. They said the pills were new – Black Bishops they called them. The side-effects are unknown."

"Why didn't you take her to hospital?"

"It's complicated. Some men were looking for her, and I couldn't risk the hospital."

"Why were they looking for her?" Tim asked.

Butch could feel the locked bag pressing against him. He fought the panic as the silence lengthened. Would Uncle Sam retrieve it?

"I don't know," his uncle confessed. "I only know her name. She calls herself Delilah; sometimes Jezebel. Her real name is Ruth Foster."

The doctor stared at Uncle Sam. "You're not well. What happened to you?"

Uncle Sam fumbled with the top buttons on his checked shirt. The doctor leaned closer and peered at his uncle's exposed neck. "Take off the shirt," Tim commanded.

Butch's jaw dropped open. The bruises and scratches on Uncle Sam's shirtless back were distinct. The doctor asked Uncle Sam to turn around. Now the purple marks on his neck and chest were impossible for Butch to ignore. The doctor poked and prodded, then studied the reluctant patient's eyes. Tim said something that Butch couldn't hear, and Sam shook his head.

"I've had concussion before, and I survived. I have to stay here."

"How did this happen?"

"I tried to stop her taking more pills. She went crazy. I thought she was going to kill me."

"Are you responsible for her bruises?"

Samson shook his head. "She already had those when I met her. I know you've talked to Caleb, and he's told you my story. If I had retaliated, she wouldn't be alive."

"So how did you get away?"

"You probably won't believe me..."

"Try me. I'm a good listener."

"I prayed. I asked God to deliver me. Then a Scripture came into my head: 'you wrestle not against flesh and blood but against spiritual powers and authority'..."

The doctor waited. Butch pushed the wardrobe door open a little more.

"I was desperate – blacking out. I pleaded the blood of Jesus and commanded the spirits to leave me alone. Delilah screamed, and after she collapsed, I pushed her away. She's been like this ever since."

Both men looked at the sleeping woman as a heavy silence filled the room. The doctor handed Uncle Sam his shirt. "You invited me to lunch," Tim said, picking up his medical bag. "Caleb said I should get to know you." Tim shook his head. "I've never met anyone who lives out 'love your enemy' like this."

Butch didn't hear anything else. The room darkened, and he fell out of the wardrobe. His eyes locked on the terrible woman while his heart pounded. He leapt up, rushed around the bed, and pushed behind the heavy curtains. The window was already open at the bottom. With a shove, he had it up and was halfway out before he remembered the weight in his hand. He swore as he tumbled to the ground with the locked case.

Frantically, he looked for a hiding place. Would that shadowy space behind the nearest water tank be large enough to hide it? He shoved the case ahead of him until it was stuck.

Before he could get back out, his sister arrived. "I can see you, Butch!"

He felt Nikki's hands pulling at him, trying to "help". This made it much harder to wriggle out. He straightened and looked at his sister. She seemed more like eight years old than twelve. She bounced with delight, and he grinned with relief. Careful not to look back, he let her fuss over the cobwebs caught on his clothes. Then she shrieked at the huge spider crawling on his arm. He laughed as he flicked it off. She wouldn't visit his hiding place now.

Time to Reconnect

𝔅 ☼ ℭ

*Proverbs 18:24 - A man with companions may be ruined,
but there is a friend who sticks closer than a brother.*

𝔅 ☼ ℭ

Samson sent Butch and Nikki to wash their hands. He left the doctor seated at the kitchen table while he checked on his mother, asleep in her chair. He adjusted her knee rug and kissed her forehead.

Thank You, Lord, that Mum knew me today. That's so rare, and I'm grateful. You know what set Old Jack off this time. He doesn't look good. Please extend him Your mercy. Forgive me for holding on to the old resentment. He's had a hard life. Losing Jack Junior broke something inside him. Watching Kim make a mess of her life hasn't helped. She said she was better...

I have to check on her. Thanks for listening. Help me to remember You have everything under control. I can't do this without You.

Kim lay on top of the bedcovers. Samson crossed to the window, throwing open the curtains. He jiggled the catch before pushing up the sash to let in fresh air. Afternoon shadows crept across the clearing. He stuck his head out the window and breathed deeply. His eyes stopped at a flash of red in the middle distance.

Turning too fast, he hit his head on the wooden window frame.

The pain awoke other emotions. He strode to the bed. "Kim!" As he leaned closer, his feet kicked something under the bed. *Clink, clink!* A cold sweat chilled him. He reached down and brought out two empty bottles. One sniff told him Kim had found Old Jack's stash.

Samson stormed into the kitchen. Her children were already seated at the table. A look of alarm appeared on the new doctor's face. Samson shook his head. He walked to the counter, dumping the bottles in the empty sink. He shuddered as they banged together. He kept his eyes on his chair, and took his place, no longer hungry.

An uncomfortable silence greeted him, broken only by a hurried munching. Butch had decided not to wait. Nikki touched her brother's arm, and Butch lowered his fork.

Samson tried to talk and choked on the words. He tried again. "T-Tim – could you say the blessing?"

The guest blinked and then reached across to take his hand. Nikki and Butch joined hands to complete the circle. Nikki's eyes sparkled with anticipation, but Butch frowned.

"Thank You, Lord, for this day, and for the food before us. We are grateful You have promised to take care of us and ask that You watch over each of us as we share this meal. Watch over those in this house who are unable to join us at the table. We entrust them into Your hands. These things we ask in Jesus' name, amen."

Samson pushed food around his plate, forcing himself to slow down. He had wolfed down the first portion without tasting anything. When the dogs began to bark, he went to the window.

"It's too early for the ambulance," Tim said.

A greater fear swallowed Samson's disappointment. His childhood friend Kurt Jensen was opening the gate. Samson glanced at Tim and then looked towards Delilah's bedroom. He ran his fingers through his hair and grimaced.

Butch rushed to the window. "What's *he* doing 'ere?" The teenager snatched up the bottles.

"I don't know," Samson said. "Maybe he's heard about Old Jack."

Butch swore and ran from the room with the evidence. Samson lowered his head, taking a deep breath. Kurt knocked at the door and then entered. His blue police uniform and his stern expression were a clear warning.

"I saw the Cruiser, and knew you were back," Kurt began, then hesitated when he saw Nikki and Tim seated at the table.

"We were having lunch," Samson said. "Have you eaten? There's plenty. You know what Sunday's are like around here..."

Kurt smiled. "Thanks. I won't say no. I don't know when I'll get another chance to eat." He chose the empty chair beside Tim. "You're the new doctor?" Kurt reached out to shake Tim's hand. "I'm Kurt Jensen. When the call came for the ambulance, they said the doc was here. If Samson needs a character reference I've known him for years."

"Good to meet you, Kurt. I'm Tim Chappell."

"How's Old Jack?"

"He's stable, but I'll be more comfortable when I get him to hospital. Have you been to the accident scene?"

The policeman looked at Nikki. The girl's eyes locked on her lunch. Kurt accepted a plate of food before asking, "Where's Kim?"

Samson struggled to answer. "Sh-she's—"

"Kim's asleep," Tim interjected. "The morning's excitement is catching up with everyone." Samson stumbled and grabbed the back of a chair, reinforcing the doctor's assessment. "Samson, sit *down!*"

"Is Uncle Sam sick too?" Nikki asked. Her warm hand rested on Samson's arm.

He forced a smile. "I'm okay. Why don't you go and find Butch. Get him to take you for a walk before it gets too cold."

"You're getting rid of me," Nikki said, her blue eyes flashing. "Mum's in trouble again, and you don't want me to know. I may be little, but I'm *not* stupid."

Samson shook his head. "This time, I'm the one in trouble."

She frowned at him, tilting her head to one side. Then Nikki patted his hand. "Don't worry, Uncle Sam," she said. "Mum said you never do anything wrong, so it can't be too bad. And God sent you this policeman who knows you're always good." She skipped from the room.

Samson busied himself at the counter. "I'll put the kettle on."

"What was that about?" Tim asked Kurt. Samson watched the exchange.

"Kim and I have history," Kurt replied between mouthfuls of food. "We were close once. A few years ago, during my time in Newcastle, we reconnected – professionally. Nikki and her brother Butch know me as the enemy..."

"And you're not here about Kim?" Tim asked.

Kurt raised an eyebrow and waved his fork. "I'll accept that Kim's *sleeping* if that's what you're asking. I'm curious about why you came straight here after church. You're not here because of Old Jack's condition. You were on your way when the operator phoned."

The kettle boiled. Samson brought three cups of plunger coffee to the table. Good coffee was his only luxury. He returned with milk and sugar, before sitting on his chair. He shoved aside his lunch and wrapped his hands around his mug. His head dropped forward.

"Samson?" Kurt asked. "What happened to you?"

Samson looked directly at his friend. He'd forgotten about his missing hair. Kurt held his gaze, reaching into his pocket for his phone. He brought up a photo on the screen and laid the device on the table. Samson tried to focus on the phone. Kurt flicked through several images before removing his hand. "Who are these men?"

Samson studied the images. He frowned. "I've never seen them before."

"Then how do you explain them asking around town for directions to *Mountain Rise*? This isn't Kidman business. They were looking for the Davidson family. You've been the only Davidson here since your mother married Old Jack."

Samson stared at the images again before Kurt retrieved his phone.

"They were on their way here in a hurry. I already know who they are and who they work for. Enforcers from a major Sydney cartel don't come here for a Sunday drive. It's lucky for you they crashed their car. They'll live, but their silence worries me. You have to tell me what you know. I won't be able to keep this quiet."

"I don't know anything about them," Samson said. Kurt looked at him, and then the policeman reached into his pocket. He brought out a plastic bag and laid it carefully on the table. Tim and Samson leaned forward to look at the photograph it protected.

"But you can't deny this is you," Kurt said. "Who's the woman? *You* obviously know *her*."

"Where did you get this?" Samson asked, picking up the bag and staring at the photo of Delilah kissing him.

Kurt retrieved it from him. "This is evidence. One of the men had it in his pocket."

A Trying Time

Ꮽ ☼ ☾

2 Corinthians 12:10b WEB
For when I am weak, then am I strong.

Ꮽ ☼ ☾

"Her name's Delilah," Samson said.

Kurt's eyes widened. "What kind of fool do you think I am?"

"Come with me." Samson led the way to her bedroom. Despite Tim's warning, the policeman tried to wake her.

Samson opened the wardrobe. He frowned at the solitary suitcase before he retrieved her wallet from the outer pocket. Flipping it open to her ID, Samson handed the evidence to Kurt.

"Delilah Jones, with a Melbourne address," Kurt muttered. "Obviously an alias. Did she give you any other names?"

Samson nodded. He slipped his hand into the suitcase, making sure he kept the lid down. He found what he was looking for. He pulled out a book and zipped the suitcase closed again. Kurt opened the book. The volume was hollow. Inside were identification documents in multiple names. Kurt took photos, using his phone, and then replaced them in the book.

He returned it to Samson, then held out his hand for the suitcase.

"Unzip it and show me what you didn't want me to see."

After a brief hesitation, Samson obeyed. Kurt searched the suitcase. He set the money aside. His hand lingered on familiar items that betrayed this woman's trade. When he finished, he put everything back into the suitcase. He seemed puzzled. Kurt turned towards Samson. "Even you have to know what kind of woman this is. Why have you given your heart to a prostitute?"

৪০ ✿ ୦୫

In her dream, Delilah lay on the forest floor. The rain had ceased, and a breeze wafted over her. She shivered. *Ugghh!* She pushed herself upright, brushing the rotting leaves from her body.

She scanned the clearing. It was the same location as before. How many times had she tried to leave here?

Something had woken her. She listened carefully. The wind carried a whispered voice.

What kind of woman are you?

She jumped to her feet. "Who's there?"

A different voice took up the refrain. "What kind of woman?"

"Who wants to know?" Her heart pounded as she held her breath.

"Ha, ha, ha." The sinister voice mocked her.

"I'm not here for your amusement." She ran towards the familiar path. The disembodied laughter chased her. Finally, this nightmare had changed. The well-trodden path opened before her, almost as if the forest was retreating.

Instead of reaching out to entangle her, the trees held themselves back.

She stretched out her hand to touch the branch beside her. *Swish. Snap.*

With a jerk, it flashed out of her away. Delilah stared at the muddy place where the tree had stood a moment before. She heard a noise behind her and turned. The vision of the walking trees was back, but in reverse. They were running away.

Delilah dropped to her knees as hysterical laughter burst from her throat. She rolled on the ground as the laughter gave way to tears. The violent sobbing continued until her breathing came in ragged gasps.

ꙮ ✲ ꙮ

Samson and the other men stood transfixed as the sleeper began to writhe upon the bed. The room filled with hideous cackling. Delilah sat up and turned wild eyes towards them. "You want to know who I am?" she shrieked. Slowly her arm raised and her finger pointed towards Samson. "They call me the Destroyer. Nothing can save you from me."

As soon as Delilah started screeching, something unseen knocked Samson off his feet. He was no longer dealing with a physical enemy. The battleground had moved into the supernatural realm. Samson writhed on the floor, clutching his throat. Vile thoughts flooded his mind. As darkness pressed upon him, that horrible laughter intensified.

Jesus! Help me.

Remember who you are and whom you serve.

Tim and Kurt leapt to his aid, but Samson was already on his knees.

"You have no authority!" That was his voice?

The woman jerked, and the laughter ceased.

He gasped for air. "Jesus is Sovereign here. Get out." As the darkness pressed in, he cried, "Le-ea-ve. Her. A-lone!"

☉

Chop! Thud! Clatter.

Thump!

Samson opened his eyes. He sat outside on a tree stump. He swivelled his torso towards the noise. His nephew, Butch was a few metres away, wielding an axe. The red-faced teenager swore. Samson watched the axe strike, shattering the small log. Butch seized the shards and tossed them onto a disorganised stack that hadn't been there earlier. One of the pieces smacked the wall of the nearby chicken coop, scattering the chickens.

"Careful!" Samson cried, leaping to his feet. The ground moved, and hands grabbed him. Tim pushed him back onto the stump.

"It's you who should be careful," Tim said.

Butch stomped towards his uncle. "Don't!" his nephew panted, poking Samson's chest. "Don't you *ever*. Do. That. Again!"

Tim turned his head away. Was he trying to stifle a laugh?

"Don't do what?" Samson asked in confusion.

"You was in some kinda trance," Butch muttered. "You kep' whisperin' crazy God stuff. I've seed Ma outta it enuff to know..."

"Ah!" Samson sighed.

"Don't you 'ahhh' me!" Butch spluttered. "The amb'lance took Ol' Jack away, an' if the doc hadn't bin 'ere, that cop would of sent you too."

Samson turned to Tim with a silent question. Tim shook his head. Butch's eyes widened, his face even redder. The teenager's hands balled into fists. Samson began to silently pray. The boy was growing more like Old Jack every day.

"What's so special about *her*," Butch snarled. "Why's *she* more important than family?"

Samson swallowed his reply. He looked towards the homestead, then back to his nephew. "I have my own question."

"What?"

"When did you go into Delilah's room and steal her suitcase?"

"I didn't *steal* it!"

Samson waited.

"I didn't mean to take it," Butch muttered. "It's your fault! You shoulda knowed Ma would be desperate for cash. You didn't leave Ma enough an' she—" Butch closed his mouth and looked away.

"What did she do?"

"Not saying nuthin'," the boy muttered.

"I already know enough," Samson said. "Kim found Old Jack's stash. And she's still meeting regularly with her dealer. He's kept her supplied, and I don't want to ask how she's been paying. She went to meet him while I was at church."

"Ya know this because?"

"More than one 'friendly neighbour' came to tell me what's been happening while I was away."

Samson faced the ditch where the red quad bike was impossible to ignore. "And don't tell me *you* put that in the ditch. I know Old Jack taught you to drive. If you were responsible, there'd be more bruises. You got those when she rammed you with the gate."

A Shocking Moment

ಜ ✿ ಲ

Luke 18:27 WEB
Things which are impossible with men are possible with God.

ಜ ✿ ಲ

Twenty-four hours later, Delilah awoke in an unfamiliar room. From the bed, she could see an old-fashioned washbasin through an open door. She was desperate to relieve herself, and as she leapt up, some kind of padding dropped to the floor. She kicked it under the bed, recognising its purpose. If that tiny room contained a toilet, she wouldn't need the disgusting thing anymore. *Yes!*

As she returned to the bedroom, a breeze shifted the curtains. Her bare feet made no sound on the polished wooden floor as she crossed to the window.

A dog barked. "Git away, Red," a male voice muttered. "Can't go nowhere without you followin'."

With her back to the wall, Delilah peeked between the curtain and the window frame. The window was half-open. She frowned. There was no sound of city traffic. Nothing she saw made any sense: a curved metal wall and an open space – patchy grass mixed with gravel.

Crunch. Crunch. Crunch.

Delilah pulled back against the wall. The curtains fluttered as someone opened the window wider. The intruder was cautious. When a young man's head and shoulders pushed through the curtains, Delilah was ready. She grabbed him and hauled him into the room.

"Ow! Ooff! Uh-nngg."

Quickly, she pinned him face down on the floor, with the curtain cord knotted around his neck. "Don't move."

She applied pressure.

The youth stopped struggling. Delilah knelt on his back and twisted his head. He was younger than she expected, his eyes wide with fear. She increased pressure to the ligature. When he was almost unconscious, Delilah loosened her hold. His body flopped onto the floor.

With practised skill, she dragged him to the end of the bed. He was too heavy to lift, so she secured him to the leg of the wrought iron frame, using both curtain cords. When his eyes fluttered open, she was lying on the bed, leaning over the edge. She brushed her fingertips across his forehead.

"Time for a friendly conversation."

He flinched at her touch. The sudden movement educated him about the silk-stocking ligature twisted around his neck. She had secured it to the bed frame. His eyes bulged, and he wriggled until he could breathe again. Without any encouragement, he began to babble.

"I didn't mean to take it! I didn't want Ma to steal it! – I seed her sneakin' out of yer room – an' she – she had two hundred bucks. I knowed Uncle Sam – keeped his cash – locked in the safe, so Ma don't pinch it—"

"Uncle Sam doesn't know you're here?" she asked. "How about a little deal? I won't tell him I caught you climbing in my window, and you promise to help me. What's your name?"

"Butch – Butch Cassidy Kidman."

"Well, Butch Cassidy Kidman, you can call me Delilah." She loosened the fabric around his throat before caressing his shoulders. She untied his hands, and he rubbed his wrists. He swallowed as he tried to wriggle out of her grasp. "How old are you?"

"F-fif-fifteen."

"Almost a man," she said and rested her hand on his chest.

He threw his upper body away from her. "Keep those hands to yerself! I seed what you did to Uncle Sam."

Delilah threw her head back and laughed.

"Shh!" Butch scrambled to his feet. "If my sister finds me 'ere, the deal's off. She can't keep secrets, and Uncle Sam said no more trouble if we wanna stay."

"Uncle Sam's away?" Delilah reclined on the bed.

"I didn' say that."

"No, but you wouldn't be climbing in the window if he, or your mother, was here."

He looked from the door to the window, then at his restless feet. "There's just me and Nikki, and Grandma. Grandma goes walkabout, so I've left Nikki watchin' her." Butch looked directly at Delilah. "But Uncle Sam be back soon. He wanna be here when yer— umm – when you wake..."

Delilah uncurled from the bed. "There's no need to tell him I'm awake. Take yourself back out the window."

He threw himself out the window. A few moments later, the curtains burst inward. The suitcase containing her future flew across the room. Delilah ran to the window and ripped the curtains open.

Forested hills covered the horizon. The dramatic unveiling dropped Delilah to her knees. She clutched the window sill. From this low position, she examined her surroundings. She took in the huge water tanks, the open space between the outbuildings. And the gated barrier that separated this homestead from the terrible bush beyond.

There were no cars in the compound. Her eyes traced the gravel driveway. It curved through the gate then disappeared. A red dog leapt up at the window and panted at her, before dropping from view. When the animal appeared again, it was further away. Delilah followed the dog with her eyes. She caught a glimpse of the boy escaping over the fence towards the hills.

Delilah yanked the curtains closed. She fought the unexpected tears and berated her weakness. Crawling forward, she pulled her suitcase onto her lap. The stitching around the zipper had burst, making the lock redundant. Delilah wrapped her arms around the bag and rocked herself to sleep.

CHAPTER 13
(Monday 7th August)
Time to Prepare

ཀྵ ☼ ༄

James 4:14a WEB
You don't know what your life will be like tomorrow.

ཀྵ ☼ ༄

That afternoon, Butch had grocery bags to carry. He dumped the final load on the kitchen table. He'd never seen so much food outside the supermarket. Uncle Sam asked Kim to unpack the groceries, then went outside again. Butch heard an engine roar into life and ran to the window. Uncle Sam's LandCruiser was leaving.

Kim grabbed Butch by the shoulders and shoved her son towards the groceries. "Put everything away." She flung the pantry door open. "Do it right, this time."

Kim turned to the counter to make herself plunger coffee. She added four sugars, stirred briskly then dropped the spoon in the sink. As she sipped the hot beverage, Kim leaned against the kitchen table.

"Waste of time," Butch muttered, peering at the labels on the almost empty shelves. He grabbed one of the large calico sacks, comparing the writing to a shelf label. It had the same number of letters. His mother did not comment. He returned for another load. "Why does it matter?"

"Someone has to keep up the traditions," Kim laughed. "You've heard your grandfather talking about the old days."

Her talkative mood surprised him. "What was it like in the 'old days'?"

"I'm not old enough to know," she reminded him. "Dad said the house was always full of people."

"What people?"

"There were the stockmen, ringers and farm hands, as well

71

as the household staff. The housekeeper spent all day organising meals. She didn't have time to supervise the housemaids when she sent them to the pantry."

"I'm not a housemaid," Butch complained.

Kim leaned forward and sniggered. "Just as well. You're hopeless. Why did you put the flour there? That goes on the opposite shelf."

Kim didn't even look to see if he moved it, already focused on continuing her story. "Mum came as the new housekeeper after Dad's first wife died, leaving him four-year-old Jack Junior to raise. She was only here six months when Dad married her. She was a widow, and brought Samson with her."

"I'd rather be helping Uncle Sam." Butch glanced out the window at the lights disappearing into the hills. "It's not fair he's drivin' round in the dark. If someone told me that was Ol' Jack's job, I coulda checked the boundary fences."

"You're a town boy," she snapped. "You'll never be a farmer. Don't give me that look! We're not staying here. As soon as Samson gives me the money, we'll be gone."

"He's never gonna give ya mon-ney!"

His mother glared at the forbidden door. "If he's got enough money for his *fiancée*, he can find some for us."

"Why can't we stay 'ere? Uncle Sam—" Butch wasn't quick enough. Kim swatted him with her hand. "Oww!"

"I don't know why you listen to him. He's not a Kidman. When your grandfather dies, *Mountain Rise* is mine."

"What about your brother, Freddie?" Butch asked. He shoved the bags and boxes on any shelf.

"He ran off and abandoned us," Kim snarled.

"That's not what I heard."

"Well, you *heard* wrong!" This time he ducked. She sighed impatiently. "Haven't you finished yet?"

Butch switched off the pantry light and slammed the door.

He glared at his mother. "Why did Uncle Sam buy so much stuff? Is he preparing for a siege?"

"That's what I asked," Kim muttered. "Samson said a big storm's coming and the bridges might flood. That could isolate *Mountain Rise* for a week or more."

"Did that ever 'appen when you lived 'ere?" Butch shuddered. "It gets dark early. It's only three-thirty but the sun's disappeared behind them trees."

"Town boy missing his streetlights?" Kim reached out and messed with his hair. "When did you get so big? You're almost as tall as your father."

Butch stopped breathing. She never talked about—

He glanced at her. "Why do you hate it here?" Butch didn't think she heard him. He was walking away when she spoke.

"Did you know the Cassidy family used to live over that hill?" Kim pointed into the darkness. "And the Jensen's property is over there. Our three families have owned the mountain since first settlement."

He swallowed, not trusting his voice.

"Dad bought the Cassidy land and let the trees reclaim it," she continued. "Jensen's place is for sale now, but the bank won't let your grandfather buy it. The overdraft's too large."

Unanswered questions stuck in his throat.

His mother was crying. "There's a cemetery, up in those hills, where the three properties meet. I haven't been there since..." She turned her back on the window and dropped onto a chair. Kim stared at her hands. "You ask why we can't stay here? I have nightmares just thinking about that place. All those old headstones marking off the generations for three families. One crazy thing ruined everything. Your dad's not buried up there, but Jack Junior lies beside his mother. He's there with all the other Jacks – I don't know what happened to Johnny Jensen." She sighed and wiped her tears.

"*Mountain Rise* hasn't always been like this," she said, returning to the window. Kim leaned forward. "There are more trees now. See how their shadows stretch towards the homestead. It feels like they're coming for me."

The silence lengthened, and then she straightened her shoulders. Kim looked at her empty coffee mug, and a familiar smile appeared. "Make yourself useful and find Old Jack's new hiding place. I need something stronger."

Butch was about to answer when he heard a small noise across the room. That end of the kitchen was in shadow. The room suddenly felt crowded. He bolted for the door. "I gotta feed Ol' Jack's horse!"

"You're lucky *Mountain Rise* doesn't keeps house cows anymore," Kim called after him. "Winter milking is no fun."

Butch snatched a large torch from the shelf and rushed outside. He wasn't planning a quick return. The door banged. At full gallop, Butch vaulted the fence, the gathering gloom heavy about his shoulders.

He glanced towards the hills, then kicked at a clump of grass. Something moved at his feet. "Arrgh!" Rabbits scattered in every direction. If the dogs hadn't gone with Uncle Sam, he might have tempted them out for a run. The dogs loved the chase but were hopeless for anything else. He hesitated. Why had Uncle Sam taken the useless animals with him?

The teenager marched to the stable, pausing to look around before he went in. Butch was closer to the trees now. But they were just trees. He was a Cassidy *and* a Kidman. No matter what his mother said, he belonged here.

Ca-aww! Caw! Caw! He whirled around. A dark low-flying shadow glided towards him. Butch rushed for the doorway, and the old horse snorted. *Idiot! Town boy!*

Chapter 14
(Monday 7th August)

A Timely Meeting

෪ ☼ ഗ

Matthew 12:37b WEB - By your words you will be condemned.

෪ ☼ ഗ

Delilah had awoken when the dogs barked. She was peeping through the curtains when a small truck went past her window. It stopped near the water tanks. The bearded man she had met at Sydney airport stepped from the vehicle. Butch appeared beside him. The pair unloaded grocery bags from the tray.

Delilah's fingers curled in anticipation when Samson easily shouldered a large sack.

Certain her *fiancé* would visit her soon she carried the returned suitcase to the wardrobe. Her remaining bag was already there. The treasured case settled in the corner. Delilah hoisted the other bag onto the bed. What had the boy's mother taken? It was clear someone had rifled through her possessions. She stood with her hands on her hips. Only a few hundred dollars were missing.

She saw her reflection in the dresser mirror and hurried to the small washroom to tidy herself. When she returned, she undid the top buttons on the man's shirt she was wearing. Delilah smoothed her hands down the crumpled white fabric that concealed her figure.

She reclined on the bed.

Long minutes passed. Why was he taking so long?

Those dogs barked again, followed by the sound of crunching gravel and the quiet roar of an engine. Delilah rushed to the window, careful in her concealment. The truck was idling before the gate. Two excited red dogs danced around Samson as he opened the gate. He leaned in the truck window, and the vehicle rolled forward. He didn't check its progress, focused on the gate. The dogs leapt onto the tray. The moment the truck was clear, he secured the gate. Without a backward glance, Samson trotted alongside the accelerating vehicle. He snatched open the door, climbed in and closed the door again in a smooth movement.

"How did he do that?" she asked, and then she gasped. *He's leaving?*

No! Her bare feet stomped on the floorboards.

Sharp pain refocused her attention – her acrylic nails digging into her palms. "Ahhh!" She ripped off the white shirt, scattering buttons across the room.

The bundled fabric hit the back of the wardrobe. She snatched the airport disguise from the hangers and dumped it beside his shirt. After dressing in her own clothes, Delilah applied her make-up. The only thing she lacked was a pair of heels. She wriggled her toes, shrugging at the discomfort. The chilled floor would keep her alert.

The wooden door was heavy, but it opened without a sound. She peered around the edge. A pair of black-lined eyes stared at her. She leapt back, but immediately recognised her error. A carved wooden hallstand sat outside her room, a sentinel beside another door. She poked out her tongue at the narrow mirror's reflection. Delilah opened this second door a few centimetres.

She looked into a large kitchen, partially illuminated. A voice broke the silence—

Delilah could not make out the words. She pushed the door shut. With her back against the door, she counted to thirty.

Apparently, no one had noticed her.

She turned to explore the narrow hall. At the further end, she spied another promising door. Delilah padded quietly in that direction. She glanced into open doorways as she passed them. More bedrooms, sparsely furnished.

What was it about their emptiness that unsettled her?

The room she had awoken in was preferable to the other bedrooms. It had a colourful quilt and matching curtains. Perhaps the previous occupant had been someone special. Is that why Samson had put her there? Delilah shook her head.

No. He had dumped her there because nobody visited this wing.

She hesitated at the end of the hall. The door pushed inward. Delilah entered an icy bathroom. High above the free-standing basin, a narrow bar heater hung on the wall. The claw-foot bath was small, with no shower.

Behind the door, a wall-mounted porcelain cistern loomed above the toilet bowl. Delilah blinked away a childhood memory as she tested the chain. *Whoosh.*

She listened for a reaction, but there was only silence from within the house. She retraced her steps. Beside the hallstand, she frowned at her reflection as she reached for the kitchen door.

Cautiously, she opened the door. The people in the kitchen were still there.

"Why do you hate it here?" That was Butch.

Delilah couldn't hear the woman's answer.

The opening widened until she could slip through. She crept towards them, keeping to the shadows.

The pair looked out the window. The spotlights above the sink were the room's only illumination. The teenager was taller than the slender woman beside him. Delilah came closer, making a quick assessment. This woman cared about her appearance – her strawberry-blonde hair was fashionably styled. She also had excellent taste in shoes.

They remained oblivious to her presence. Suddenly, Butch spun. Delilah became a statue. He looked across to the door she had left ajar, but he failed to notice her. Silently, she rejoiced at his hasty exit. The mother leaned towards the window as if she followed his departing figure.

"About time he left," Delilah said, appearing beside the woman who must be Samson's sister.

"Eek!"

Delilah covered the sister's mouth with one hand. "Shh!" Her other hand scooped a knife from the counter. The spotlight glinted on the blade as it gyrated in the narrowing space between them. "Did Sammy-boy tell you I like to hurt people?"

The victim trembled, her eyes fixed on the knife. Delilah chuckled. There was a fruit bowl on the bench. She skewered an apple and sat at the table. Kim's eyes didn't leave the knife. After slicing the apple into segments, Delilah stabbed the blade into the wooden table.

"What's your name?" Delilah asked.

The woman flinched and finally focused on her attacker. "K-Kim – Kim-ber-ly K-Kid-m-man."

"Now that we've established who's in charge, Kim-ber-ley," Delilah sneered, "make me a strong black coffee. Then we'll talk about why you took *my* money."

"I didn't think you'd notice," the woman sobbed, fumbling with the coffee plunger. "I only took four notes."

"What did you do with my money?"

Hope awakened in Kimberley's eyes. "I gave it to my dealer." She dipped her hand into her pocket. "Here."

Delilah pointed to the table. Kimberley dropped a small plastic bag there. The four pills were sky-blue. Each bore a familiar black stamp.

"How many of these did you buy?"

"F-five – I've only taken one. I have to be careful. Samson thinks I'm clean. I'm trying to convince him to bankroll my new rental."

"You gave your dealer two hundred dollars for *five* pills?" Delilah's voice rose sharply.

"Not any pills. They're Black Bishops," Kimberley whispered. "The blue ones are better than the yellow ones I'm used to. I only took one of these, and I don't remember getting home. I take them to forget, and I slept all afternoon."

Delilah tapped the plastic bag. "Does your dealer have a name?"

Kimberley moved her hungry eyes to Delilah's face. "A-Aiden. Why?"

"Aiden cheated you."

Kimberley leapt to her feet. "He said this was the good stuff. It cost extra."

Delilah laughed. "In Sydney, they sell for ten dollars each."

"We're not in Sydney."

"No, but even if he gets them at market price, he's making a killing with you. And I haven't even started to value the *extras* he's conned you into giving him."

Kimberley ran from the room.

Delilah remained at the table, her hand resting on the plastic bag. "I wonder how many customers he has?"

She sipped her coffee, watching the clock. Kimberley didn't return. At four-thirty, Delilah pocketed the plastic bag. She deposited the coffee cup and the remnants of the apple on the bench and returned to her room. The knife remained upright in the table.

A Past Alliance

ಠ ☼ ಡ

Ephesians 2:19 WEB - You are no longer strangers and foreigners.

ಠ ☼ ಡ

Samson scanned the horizon as he drove, with his heart open to the Creator of the heavens. Sunset had passed, yet there was no sign of the promised storm. The faintest glimmer over the treetops heralded the moon. Soon the sky above the forested mountain would shine with silver. Tomorrow night, the moon would be full. This early in the evening, shadows shrouded everything.

The headlights bounced on the corrugated road. It was seldom travelled, and Samson had allocated no time to fix the potholes. Finally, the boundary fence came into view. He stopped the LandCruiser twenty metres from the gate, extinguishing the headlights. The door clicked open, but the deactivated cabin light did not disrupt the darkness. At his whistle, the dogs scrambled down from the tray. With a gesture, he sent them out to investigate. Their presence faded into the night. Well trained, they ran silently.

Samson leaned against the LandCruiser. He slowed his breathing. That rustling – leaves dancing on the breeze. That bellow – an early calf. There – the answering calls from the scattered herd sheltering in the scrub. Twittering birds secure in their nests. The undergrowth astir with unseen creatures: both hunters and hunted. The gentle pad of approaching paws.

One of the dogs nudged him with its wet nose. Both animals settled at his feet. He pulled on his night-vision goggles before reaching behind the seat for his rifle. The concealed case was already open, the ammunition loaded. He collected a box of bullets.

The dogs went ahead. Keeping to the grassy verge, Samson studied the distinctive quad-bike tyre tracks. Kim came here yesterday. Here she parked and dismounted – who else wore heels in the bush? The spiked indentations disappeared at the cattle grid.

The farm gate was secure, its padlocked chain intact. On the other side, the dust continued to disclose the tale. Kim's heel marks reappeared, heavy where she had leapt from the gate. Another person, a man – fancy tread and larger feet – met her here. The two sets of footprints converged.

Samson unlocked the gate and slipped through. The interwoven tracks went in that direction and returned. Kim and her dealer had made no effort to conceal their activity. He closed his eyes and prayed. His sister was old enough to make her own mistakes.

The dogs materialised beside him and then trotted ahead. This road meandered towards the abandoned Cassidy place, *Valley View*. In the opposite direction, it became the rear entrance for the Jensen homestead, *Forest Heights*.

When the dogs turned their heads towards him, he joined them. The vehicle had returned the way it came, past *Valley View*. He followed the path in his mind, the winding curves down the mountain. A narrow bridge and finally a junction with the main road. The vehicle could have gone left to Meredith Crossing or right to Brumby's Run. He scanned the night sky to assess the time, shaking his head. Investigating which direction Kim's visitor had gone would take too long.

The dogs concluded their wider search. Samson led the dogs back through the gate. Dismissed, they went snuffling into the darkness. After refastening the lock and chain, he retrieved a large bag from the LandCruiser. Following the fence, he pushed through the untamed scrub that was once a firebreak. When he could no longer distinguish the fence, he marched ten metres in from the boundary. There he selected a hollow tree stump and began his work.

It took Samson fifteen minutes to install his equipment. How easily he remembered what to do...

He rechecked his connections, concealing the wires leading from the fence. It was essential to hide the location of the energiser and batteries. He secured distinctive warning signs to the gate, then walked back along the boundary. He removed any foliage that might short-circuit his setup.

Samson attached the clamps to the battery terminals. At the gate, he tested the current. Next, he checked the foot-activated switch. Finally, he stood listening for the familiar *tick-tick-tick*.

With his rifle strapped over his shoulder, Samson gathered the tools into his bag. His movements were slower as he retraced his steps. The headache and lethargy were winning.

One of the dogs appeared at his feet, facing towards *Forest Heights*. A flicker of light came over the rise. Samson ripped off the night goggles, dumping them into his bag before dropping it into the tray. He and the dogs were hidden before the vehicle came over the rise. He crouched low with the rifle held ready.

> Lord, Thank You for Your constant presence. Please guide my decisions. Keep my hands from doing evil and my mind from fear. Make me an instrument of Your peace, and an agent for Your justice.

A distinctive vehicle braked suddenly and spun towards the locked gate. Powerful headlights pointed at his LandCruiser. Samson squinted. He counted to twenty. The engine stopped. Another twenty count before the door opened. A single occupant stepped forward, standing in clear view with his hands outstretched.

"Samson! It's Kurt Jensen. Don't shoot me!"

Samson rose. At his movement, the dogs trotted towards the gate. He whistled, and they dropped where they stood. "What are you doing here?"

"The same as you," the policeman replied. "Checking your security."

Samson walked closer, remaining in the shadows.

"You've gone commando," Kurt continued. "Does Old Jack know you've still got that gear? I thought he smashed all the guns after Jack Junior died."

"He knows I need the rifle to keep the feral pigs at bay. I keep it locked in one of the old stockmen's huts."

Kurt pointed to the gate. "These warning signs are new. Anything else I should know about?"

"I plan to close the road past the Cassidy place and block rear access to your father's property. I held off because I wanted to give your family fair warning."

"Don't blow up Cassidy Bridge."

Samson smiled.

"Don't tell me you haven't thought of it," Kurt said. "In the months before you joined the army, all you talked about was explosives. I had nightmares about you blowing yourself up, and taking me with you."

"I promise not to blow anything up without your permission," Samson said. "You don't have to worry. That hot-blooded eighteen-year-old is long gone."

"Your assurance isn't enough. Not when I'm facing an ex-combat engineer holding a rifle."

Samson made no response.

"I'm not the enemy," Kurt said. "You can trust me."

"It's not a matter of trust," Samson replied. "People change. You've been stationed at Meredith Crossing for nine months and kept your distance. Yesterday was the first time you've spoken to me in years."

"That cuts both ways. I thought you were avoiding me."

"This isn't a social call," Samson reminded him. "You're here as the district's senior police officer. What happened to your dream of becoming an influential city lawyer?"

"The same thing that happened to your army career," Kurt grunted. "Michael Cassidy and his grand plans. After Jack Junior and my brother died, priorities changed. You were overseas on deployment. I didn't think you'd come back. I never expected you to take on *Mountain Rise*."

"My mother needed me. Old Jack had trouble dealing with his son's death, and then Kim went missing. Everyone knew she'd run off with Michael, and Old Jack sent me to get her back."

"So that's why Kim wasn't with Michael when the police tracked him down. I always wondered how she got away." Kurt took a step closer.

"Don't touch the gate!"

Kurt stopped abruptly. "You've electrified the gate as well as the fence?"

"It's not lethal, but you'd learn not to make that mistake again."

"How dangerous are you?" Kurt asked. "I've heard the rumours. How many people have you killed?"

Samson stepped closer. "I didn't keep count. In Iraq and Afghanistan, I did what was necessary. It was either them or the people I was defending."

It was a half-truth. He refused to do the maths, but if he allowed his mind to wander the battlefield, he remembered each one with great clarity.

"How does that sit with your religion?"

"Combat changed me, but it didn't diminish my faith," Samson said wearily. "Go and talk to Caleb. I've told him everything. *He* asked his questions sixteen years ago."

"I'll do that. My sister's boy works at the hardware store. You caused a stir when you went shopping today. People remembered your military training, and tongues are wagging."

"Is that why you told me not to blow up the bridge?" Samson laughed. "Is it a crime to go shopping now?"

"With your shopping list, it might be."

"I want people to talk. I need the men who are hunting Delilah to think twice before they trespass on Kidman land. I'm not planning a killing spree. I'm only defending my family."

"She's not family," Kurt reminded him.

Samson turned towards his vehicle. "I have to get back. I've been away too long." The dogs leapt onto the tray.

"Let me help."

Samson rested his head on the door.

"Come on, Samson," Kurt persisted. "Deactivate the gate and let me through. I have my key. If you don't, then I'll be wondering what else you're hiding, and I'll have to get a warrant. One look at your military record and the bomb squad will be out here."

"Kim was right about you," Samson muttered. "You don't know when to back off." He stepped away from the LandCruiser, snagging the night-vision goggles with his hand. The dogs jumped down and remained on guard.

"Wait for me to give a signal before you open the gate." Samson stalked along the fence line without waiting for a reply. He didn't look down, as he activated the hidden switch.

Click-click-click.

He kept walking for twenty metres before he pretended to reach into the undergrowth. He could not risk anyone else knowing how to deactivate the circuit. "Safe!"

Kurt approached the gate. The police vehicle drove through and then Kurt re-secured the chain. "Clear!"

Samson repeated his pretence. As he tapped the switch again, he called out, "Your dad still visits the cemetery? Tell KJ not to come the back way for a while."

"I already have," Kurt confessed. "I confiscated his key to make sure. From his reaction, I think Dad and Old Jack have their distillery hidden nearby. I'm yet to decide what to do about that."

"I wouldn't come looking," Samson suggested as he returned to his vehicle. "Leave the two old men with their shared grief."

"I haven't been up here since Johnny's funeral. From the road, it looks as if the trees have reclaimed the mountain."

"Let's go." Samson reached into his bag and retrieved a pair of portable two-way radios. "You can ask your questions along the way." He tossed one to Kurt and switched on the other one. "I have a few stops to make before we get to the homestead."

"I can't believe you kept these," Kurt remarked, striding towards his vehicle.

Three times, Samson stopped to activate the electric barriers he had installed earlier. Until today, the only electrified fences were on the front of the property to protect the pasture.

Now he had established multiple barriers in each direction. All he had to do was secure the locks and step on the hidden switches. He could feel Kurt's eyes studying him as he came back to the LandCruiser.

"That's the last stop for tonight, Kurt. Go on to the homestead and put the kettle on. I have to stow my gear and check that everything is secure for the night.

A Time of Revelation

ॐ ☼ ೞ

Isaiah 41:10b WEB - Don't be dismayed, for I am your God.

ॐ ☼ ೞ

Butch stepped from the darkened stable. Two sets of headlights descended towards the homestead. One vehicle turned towards the old stockmen's huts at the edge of the home paddock. That would be Uncle Sam.

When Butch was younger, he had made a thwarted attempt to break in through the barred windows. His curiosity about his secretive uncle brought only disappointment. A few hours later came a summons to explain his actions.

Back then, he didn't understand there was no hiding anything from Uncle Sam. His uncle was a mind reader. There was no lying to him either. His grandfather warned Butch to pay close attention. His mother told him not to make his uncle angry. Butch shivered. That day he had seen something dangerous in his uncle's eyes. Something that silenced Old Jack, and made his mother tremble. Butch shook his head. His mother seemed to have forgotten, but he never would.

He kept his promise not to go near the hut, and his uncle never mentioned it again.

Butch shook off the memories and ran. The second vehicle continued towards the house, but the chicken coop blocked the boy's view.

When he reached the house, there was no sign of the visitor. His torch flashed over the familiar police vehicle before he burst into the kitchen.

Senior Sergeant Kurt Jensen stood inside the room. The officer turned towards Butch, his hand reaching for the gun at his belt.

"Hey! It's me!" Butch screamed. "Don't shoot me! Whatcha doin' in our house?"

Kurt pointed to the kitchen table. "Was that knife there when you went out?"

Butch stared at the embedded blade. He rushed into the hallway. "Nikki! Ma! Where are ya?"

Nikki stuck her head out from the lounge room. He could hear the television. "Shh! You're frightening Grandma—" The girl's eyes widened, and she disappeared back into the lounge room. Butch glanced over his shoulder. The policeman stood in the hallway behind him.

The door to his mother's room swung open, and she appeared. She looked as if she'd been crying. Butch walked over and studied her eyes. She blinked and pushed him aside.

"What's going on?" Kim asked. "What's he doing here?"

"Samson invited me," Kurt said. "Do you know why there's a knife stuck in the kitchen table?"

"Is she still there?" Kim asked, peering past the policeman's shoulder.

Colour drained from Butch's face. "Did that woman 'urt you?" He checked her for injuries.

Kim hit him. "Stupid boy. I can take care of myself. I gave her what she wanted, and she left me alone."

Butch narrowed his eyes.

"What did she want?" the policeman asked.

Kim wouldn't look at him. "Information – and – and a cup of coffee."

Kurt nodded. "What kind of information?"

"Nothing important. If she isn't in the kitchen, I'll put the kettle on." Kim pushed past them. "Did you say Samson's coming? We've been waiting for him to cook dinner."

Butch narrowed his eyes. His mother's hand had gone towards her pocket while grief flashed across her face. Then she put on that false smile.

"What does your mother keep in that pocket?" the officer asked, making no attempt to follow her to the kitchen.

Butch scowled, shaking his head. "Not tellin' you nuthin'."

"What's your problem?"

Butch shoved the policeman. "Gran told me what ya did to Ma when she was a kid."

"What are you talking about?" Kurt brushed away the angry teenager's hand.

"Gran said yer visited Ma's bedroom."

"That wasn't me."

"Liar," Butch cried. "Gran said it was the boy nex' door. One of her brother's friends."

"Not. Me." The voice was quiet, his eyes slits.

Butch took a step backwards.

"But if I'd suspected that was happening, I'd have done something about it. Samson wasn't the only brother living here, and I wasn't the only neighbour."

"If it weren't you, who?"

The policeman hesitated. "Your grandmother's talking about Michael Cassidy."

Butch backed into the wall. "No... Ma said—" His chest hurt. "She said..." He choked on the words. "You're lying."

"Why would I do that?"

"Ma said police killed me farva." His legs wouldn't hold him. Butch slid to the floor. "I thought you *killed 'im.* I thought you killed me farva 'cos he took her away from you..." He held his head in his hands. "I thought the police cover it up."

Kurt shook his head. "He didn't die with the others in the shootout. I don't know what happened. I wasn't there. I didn't join the police force until after Michael went to jail. All I know is he didn't last long in prison."

"How do I know yer not lyin'?"

"Ask your uncle. He came back to deal with the fallout."

"What?"

"There's a lot of unanswered questions about what happened," Kurt said. "Your mother was never mentioned in the reports. It's as if someone erased—"

The policeman turned towards the kitchen.

Butch lifted his head. "Huh?"

Kim had spoken, and Uncle Sam answered her, but their words were indistinct.

Bang! That must be the door to the other wing opening so hard it hit the wall.

Butch jumped and scrambled to his feet. The policeman was already running towards the kitchen. Butch chased him. "Hey!"

His mother was standing near the kitchen window, crying. Kurt didn't pause. The officer went directly to that other woman's bedroom. Butch was a few steps behind. Kurt came to an abrupt halt inside the room.

The teenager almost collided with him, and lurched sideways towards the dresser. His hands scrambled for something to hold him upright. His fingers knocked a small plastic-wrapped object onto the floor. He bobbed down and snagged it, his eyes riveted on the sleeping woman. Uncle Sam was shaking her unresponsive body.

His uncle turned towards Kurt. Then those piercing eyes caught sight of his nephew. Butch's hand trembled as he folded his fist over the object. He knew without looking what the plastic contained. He kept his eyes fixed on the sleeper, hoping desperately his uncle wouldn't know.

Without a word, Uncle Sam pushed past them, returning to the kitchen. They followed.

Kim stood near the window.

"Is she still there? What did she say?"

"Did you know that Kurt and I searched the house on Sunday afternoon when you were asleep?" Uncle Sam demanded. "You must have been lying on top of your drugs."

"Wh-what are you talking about?" Kim demanded indignantly. "Search again. I've nothing to hide." She held her arms out from her body.

Kurt smiled. He looked at Uncle Sam and took a step forward. Uncle Sam shook his head. *The policeman obeyed him!* Butch couldn't hide his surprise.

Uncle Sam didn't take his eyes from Kim's face. "Butch, put what you found on the table."

"What?" Butch cried. His mother stumbled forward. The teenager looked at the policeman, then back to his uncle. He glanced towards the exit. His uncle was beside him before he could move.

That quiet voice whispered in his ear. "Trust me."

The teenager's hand stretched forward, and he opened his fist. The plastic bag fell onto the table. Butch stared at the two blue pills, holding his breath.

Kim's face turned red. "That greedy – umm – woman took two. I told her one was enough."

She pulled out a chair and slumped onto the seat as everyone stared at her.

Butch waited. He flinched when a voice called out from the hallway. "Grandma's asleep. Can I change channels, I want to watch..." Twelve-year-old Nikki stood on the kitchen threshold.

She bolted from the scene.

"I'll go and talk to her," Uncle Sam said. "While I'm gone, Kim can heat the frying pan. There's meat in the fridge. Butch, wash your hands. It's time you learned to cook."

Samson left to find Nikki. Kurt circled the table, and the plastic bag disappeared into his pocket. Kim watched him and recoiled when he took hold of her arm.

"Let go of me," she snarled as he pulled her upright. He pushed her towards the stove.

"I wouldn't make your brother any angrier," the policeman said. "Even a saint has limitations. You know what he's capable of."

Kim dropped the frying pan. She retrieved it, banged it onto the counter, and wrenched open the fridge. Her angry movements continued until the meat in the pan began to sizzle.

"What are you doing about *that* woman?" Kim asked, arms folded across her chest. She glared towards Kurt. "She's more trouble than me."

"That all depends on whether she stays."

"Why don't you take her away?" Kim snapped. "She's no good for Samson."

"That's for me to decide," Uncle Sam said from the doorway. He took charge of the meal preparations, keeping Butch busy.

His nephew kept watch, but his uncle's face was unreadable.

ॐ ☼ ೞ

She was dreaming again.

Pushing her way through the trees, Delilah stumbled into a clearing. In the centre was a structure surrounded by a tall stone wall. She could see the corrugated roof of a hut inside the wall. She ran along the narrow path towards a high wooden gate. Unable to see any latch, she shoved at the gate. Behind her, she could hear the trees stirring.

The shadows lengthened, although the sun remained overhead. Delilah abandoned the gate, seeking another way inside the wall. When she stepped from the path, darkness fell, thick like molasses. She shook her fist towards the sky, cursing this unpredictable dream.

Groping her way forward, Delilah found the wall again. With one hand on the stone barrier, she circled the structure. The noises from the approaching trees intensified. Something touched her arm. With a cry, she threw herself forward, landing on her knees. Immediately, the darkness retreated.

With her arm shielding her eyes from a blinding light, Delilah looked up. She was kneeling on the path in front of a gate. Was this her starting point, or another entrance? The densely packed trees were only a few metres away. Long slender branches reached towards her, but the trees seemed stuck in place.

With a sob, Delilah crawled towards the gate. "Please let me in," she wept, pressing her hand against the barrier. The gate groaned as it began to open. She scrambled to her feet. The faintest whisper came from inside the gate.

Ruth.

"Don't call me that!" Delilah took a step backwards. "I won't answer to that name."

The gate swung shut with a loud snap. Delilah fell forward. The hut, the gate and the surrounding wall vanished. She spun around to face the advancing trees, and darkness enveloped her.

CHAPTER 17
(Monday 7th August)

Time to Remember

ജ ✿ ൫

*Philippians 2:3 - Humbly consider others
as more important than yourselves.*

ജ ✿ ൫

Samson and Kurt ran to Delilah's bedroom when the screaming started. She was in the grip of another terrible dream. Unable to wake her, Samson wrapped his arms around her writhing body. He prayed softly as he rocked her. This response was automatic. His mother was no stranger to night terrors.

Immediately, her screaming stopped, replaced by heart-wrenching sobs. Delilah's hands snagged the front of his shirt as she pressed her face against his chest. He looked over her head to his childhood friend.

Kurt frowned back at him. "She needs to go to hospital."

"No. There's nothing a doctor could do."

"She might die."

"If those Sydney men find her, can you guarantee her safety?"

"What about the drugs she's taken?" Kurt pulled the small bag from his pocket.

"What about them?" Samson asked. "They're the same kind I saw her take in Sydney. Someone told me they're new."

"Someone? Tell me what you know."

Samson hesitated, carefully releasing the woman from his arms. He led Kurt into the hallway. "Are you asking as my friend, or as a policeman?"

"I can't believe you asked me that."

97

"I'm sorry." Samson edged towards the bathroom end of the hall – his sister and her children were in the kitchen. "We need to be clear where we stand. I don't want to draw you deeper into this trouble."

"It's too late to warn me. I've kept your girlfriend's presence from my superiors. They're asking questions about yesterday's accident, and they're not happy I don't have answers."

Samson shook his head. "My information isn't going to give you any satisfaction."

"Try me."

"I needed help to get Delilah out of Sydney. Have you heard of Piper Maxwell?"

"No."

"What about *Maximum Security*?"

Kurt shook his head.

"*Operation Phoenix*?"

This time the policeman's nostrils flared, and his eyes narrowed. His lips became a thin line.

"I'll take that as a yes," Samson said. "I met three operatives. They wanted Delilah gone from Sydney. They said her presence interfered with their undercover operation. They told me to forget I'd seen them. I've tried to research them on the internet, but gotten nowhere."

"I'd stop trying," Kurt said. "Don't draw any more attention to yourself. I've only heard whispers. The last person who made official enquiries about *Operation Phoenix* retired suddenly. Their disbanded team ended up in dead-end jobs. The rest of us got the message."

The door from the kitchen opened. "Uncle Sam!" Butch poked his head into the hallway. "Granma's awake. You need to get out 'ere."

With long strides, Samson went towards the kitchen. His mother stood beside the table, a confused smile on her face.

"Why didn't someone tell me we had visitors?" Grace asked, turning to Samson. "Where's Jack?"

"Jack's away, Grace." Samson steered his mother towards the table. "You sit here. Kim will get your dinner out of the oven."

Grace Kidman turned towards Nikki. "Thank you, dear."

"She's not Kim," the real Kim muttered. "She's your granddaughter, Nikki." With a bang, she put the warm plate in front of her mother. Kim glared at her half-brother. "How long are you going to ignore the facts, Samson? She's lost in the past. Put her in a home, and she'll forget you exist."

The older woman jumped up. Samson guided her back to her seat.

"I don't want to go anywhere," Grace whimpered. "Jack Kidman said I could stay. *Mountain Rise* is my home because I took care of his boy, Jack Junior. My youngest children were born here."

She glanced around, her frail hands flapping as her voice rose. "What have you done with Freddie? And where's Jack Junior? I don't know who you are, but my Samson's in the army. I'll phone him, and – and..."

"This is Samson," Kim said.

Grace turned her eyes to Samson.

A vague smile appeared on her face and she began to eat. The words continued between mouthfuls. "You're a Davidson. You look like my first husband. Davy died overseas." Tears rolled down her cheeks. "He was in the army too." She patted his hand as he knelt beside her. "I always told him to be careful. Davy promised me he would be. Not killed in a battle, they said, but in a car accident while he was on leave..."

Grace's voice faded. Samson caught her before she fell forward into her dinner. She was asleep. He gathered his mother into his arms and carried her to her bedroom like a sleeping child.

A Strategic Moment

ॐ ✿ ॐ

Isaiah 41:10 - I will uphold you with My righteous hand.

ॐ ✿ ॐ

"I didn't think that policeman would ever leave," Delilah said from the doorway.

Kimberley sat at the kitchen table, a fresh mug of coffee before her. She leapt up. "Samson said you were asleep."

"We'll leave him with that impression. You and I need to come to an arrangement."

"Why would I want to?"

"Because I have something you need." Delilah brought two wads of notes from behind her back and slapped them on the table.

Kim's hand darted forward, then she hesitated, sinking onto her chair. "What do you want?"

Delilah walked to the refrigerator and opened the door. She considered the neat stacks of labelled containers. After making her selection, she reheated the slab of lasagne in the microwave. Her stomach grumbled at the delay.

Kim pressed the cancel button before the counter reached zero. "You don't want Samson to hear the ping. He's a light sleeper. I've learned to avoid anything that brings him running to the kitchen. He should lock Mum in her room, but he thinks he knows best."

"It's not even nine o'clock."

"He likes everyone in bed early."

Delilah chewed thoughtfully. "Your brother likes to control everything. He's ex-military?"

"He should've stayed in the army." Kim wrinkled her nose. "He's worse since you got here. He's booby-trapped all the gates! I'm a prisoner in my home."

"Why doesn't he want you to leave?" Delilah asked, finishing her meal. After dumping the food container in the sink, she flicked the switch on the kettle.

"You tell me," Kim retorted. "He said something about preparing for unwelcome visitors."

Delilah leaned her back against the counter. "Where does he keep his guns?"

Kim stared at her. "There are no guns in this house. Not since Jack Jun—" She stopped suddenly. "I've said enough."

"Jack Junior's dead?"

"Who told you?" Kim looked frightened. "What did Samson say?"

"Sammy-boy didn't say anything. Your reluctance said enough. Did Jack shoot himself?"

"No!" Kim hissed. "The police shot him."

"Is that why that policeman's hanging around?"

"Kurt Jensen's always hanging around." Kim leaned closer. "His brother Johnny died too, so he'd rather no-one talked about the bank robbery. There used to be three families here on the mountain. The Cassidys are gone. The Jensens are still here, but not for much longer. Their farm is for sale. My dad bought out the Cassidys. Samson says the bank won't extend the overdraft to buy any more land. Especially as my father intends to let the trees take it back."

Delilah shuddered, looking towards the moonlit hills. "Why would anyone want more trees?" She doubled the strength of her coffee. "Tell me more about Sammy-boy and his tame policeman."

"Kurt and Samson were older than the rest of us. They were so sure everything they did was right. The only thing we had in common was a desire to leave this mountain. Kurt left to become a hot-shot lawyer. My father wouldn't pay for Samson to go to university, so he joined the army. We were glad to see them gone."

Delilah joined Kim at the table. "Before we talk about the money, fill me in on everyone living here..."

€3 ☯ ℛ3

Samson climbed the narrow stairs to the tower. The first Kidmans built this architectural eccentricity. Footprints in the dust reminded him to find a new hiding place for the key. He didn't begrudge Kim's children their curiosity, but he didn't want his mother risking the stairs.

Memories from earlier days seemed more potent here. The square tower had been a favourite hideout for Kimmy. She used to have sleepovers with her teenage friends up here in the summer months. The space would comfortably sleep half a dozen teenage girls and all the accumulated gear they thought essential for a party. He smiled, remembering his complaints about having to carry everything up and down the stairs.

He glanced up at the pitched tower roof, twice his adult height, even if he stood on the perimeter railing. He recalled the adrenalin rush that came from shimmying up the thick posts to that higher roof. The railings had never been a deterrent, with gaps in the vertical posts that were wide enough for his size 13 work boots. He resisted the temptation to hoist himself up and out onto the homestead roof. The view of the surrounding landscape and the unending sky was breathtaking.

He recalled how he and his friends had used the tower as a launching point for greater adventures. He leaned out and looked upwards to the tower roof. There was sufficient light to see that the hooks once used to secure zip-lines from the tower to anchor points below were still there. He pondered the hooks for a moment, a plan to use them to make the homestead secure from the air awakening within him. He added metal cable to his wish list, already calculating how much he would need to crisscross the open space around the homestead.

Samson scanned the horizon before turning towards the road. There was still no sign of the promised storm. The moonlight made the surrounding terrain easy to see.

Kurt had left ten minutes ago. The police vehicle's lights wound their way towards the road far below. Did Kurt know anyone travelling from *Mountain Rise* was visible from the tower? He drove at speed, familiar with the twists and turns.

Samson prayed his childhood friend would exercise more care outside the perimeter fence that marked where the untamed bush began. Careful management minimised the kangaroo population inside the electrified boundary. But the animals were prolific in their native habitat and a constant hazard on the roads at night.

When Kurt's lights disappeared around the final bend, Samson stepped to the painted rail, extracting a device from his pocket. After he pressed the button, he held his breath. In the distance, an orange light flashed: once, twice, three times. He waited for the system to relay the message to the other solar-powered sentinels.

Samson smiled wearily. There were three rows of electric fences between the homestead and the bridge that led to the main road. It had been a simple task to add the extra connections to energise the gates. He had increased the electrical current as an extra deterrent. When the final signal replied, he pushed the control into his pocket.

He allowed a brief inventory of his aches and pains. He needed the stronger pain medication locked in the study. Samson descended the stairs. He had to check the rest of the house before he tried to sleep.

Moonlight streamed through the bathroom window. The nightlight midway along the hallway was off. Outside Old Jack's empty bedroom, he prayed for his stepfather's safe return. In the adjoining bedroom, his mother snored.

Lord, please help her sleep through, tonight.

No light shone beneath his niece or nephew's bedroom doors.

His sister's open door banished any concern about Butch's early retirement. Kim's bedside lamp was on. A glance revealed her absence. He looked towards the light outlining the closed kitchen door.

With a sigh, Samson approached the kitchen. He hesitated. A woman's voice broke the silence. His heart leapt at his sister's sharp reply. Should he leave the two women to their scheming, or confront them?

A click behind him announced another problem. He edged along the hallway to his nephew's door.

Butch stuck his head out. The teenager jumped. "What-cha lurkin' for?"

Samson nodded towards the kitchen. Butch tried to step past. He gently pushed the teenager back into his room. "Only one of us needs to keep watch. Tomorrow's a school day—"

"No school. Ma said we're not gonna be 'ere long enough–"

"With your grandfather ill, Kim's changed her mind."

"We're stayin'?"

"I promised your mother I'd find somewhere in town when your grandfather gets out of hospital. Which means you and Nikki have to go to school." Butch opened his mouth.

Samson silenced him with a stern look. "You've already missed too much. I've phoned the Brumby's Run school. They said your mother's in trouble because she didn't tell your last school you were leaving."

"We moved three—" Butch shut his mouth, before retreating. Samson frowned at the closed door. The more he learned about Kim's itinerant lifestyle, the greater his concern.

A Temporary Truce

৪৩ ✿ ৪৩

Ephesians 3:12
We have boldness and confidence through our faith in Him.

৪৩ ✿ ৪৩

Moving silently to the kitchen door, Samson wrenched it open. His sister refused to meet his eye, but Delilah watched him over the rim of her mug.

He closed the door behind him and moved past Kim towards the kettle. Satisfied the water was hot enough, he reached for the bag of coffee beans still on the bench.

"You're out of coffee beans," Delilah said.

His shoulders tensed. There was another bag in the pantry, but he left it there. Beside the kettle sat the bottle of instant coffee powder. His stepfather preferred this blend. Samson unscrewed the lid, dumped coffee into his mug, splashed hot water over the granules and stirred.

The taste activated Samson's darker memories: combat rations and foreign campaigns. His stomach rebelled, but he drank it. He slammed his eyes shut, gritting his teeth.

> Not now, Lord. Not battlefield flashbacks on top of everything else. Can't You see I'm out of my depth with this woman? I need help if I'm to match her cunning.

Neither woman said anything when he joined them at the table. He sat with both hands wrapped around his half-empty coffee mug as if it was a shield. Samson waited until his heart rhythm settled. "Don't let me interrupt your discussion."

His sister watched him beneath mascara-thickened lashes. She was wearing even more make-up than his guest.

Delilah met his gaze with boldness and a hint of mischief. "Your sister says you're keeping her prisoner."

Kim gasped. Then he heard the faintest noise behind him. Butch must be listening at the door. Good. If the boy's grandmother stirred, Butch would be there to intercept her. Samson leaned back in his seat and smiled. "If Kim wants to go somewhere, she only has to ask."

"You said!" Kim spluttered, spilling coffee on the table. She snagged a tea towel to clean up the spill. "You told me you'd rigged the gates and I couldn't go anywhere!"

"I'm more interested in keeping unwelcome visitors out." Samson kept his eyes on Delilah.

"What unwelcome visitors?" Kim asked, slapping him with the damp towel. "You can't keep me from seeing my friends."

His smile faded. "These visitors aren't interested in becoming *friends*." Samson removed the towel from his sister's hands and tossed it into the sink. "But that's something I need to clarify with our guest."

Confusion replaced Kim's indignation.

Delilah folded her hands in front of her. "I'm not expecting visitors."

"That's a pretty lie," Samson said. "The evidence says otherwise."

The corners of her mouth twitched.

"What evidence," Kim demanded. "Where did you get evidence?"

Samson retrieved a folded photocopy from his shirt pocket. "Some strangers appeared in town asking questions." He took time to smooth out the creases. "They had this photo."

Kim snatched it from his hand. After ten seconds, his sister threw it on the table in front of the other woman.

Delilah spun the paper around using a manicured nail. She dropped her eyes to the photo, before flipping it back to him. "What makes you think these men were looking for me?"

Samson left the photograph on the table, beside the bundles of money. His sister stole glances at the digital image of Samson and Delilah embracing. Kim nibbled on her bottom lip.

"Kurt Jensen let me see the police report," Samson said. "I'm convinced they're the same men from the airport. He said they have organised-crime connections. Kurt approved my increased security."

Delilah's smile didn't waver, but she began to draw on the wooden tabletop with one finger. The hair on the back of his neck rose. Samson dropped his eyes to the money. His left fist released the mug. He had to loosen his muscles before he could grasp a wrapped bundle. "Are they looking for this?"

"That money's mine," Delilah said.

Samson rested the end of his bundle on the table at arm's length.

"I earned it," she added.

Kim gasped, her eyes bright. "Are you a drug runner?"

"No." Delilah picked up the remaining cash. "This came from a babysitting job."

"What type of babysitting pays this kind of money?" Kim grabbed Samson's bundle, flicking through the fifty-dollar notes. "There must be twenty thousand dollars here."

"A very expensive baby," Samson said. "Thank you for confirming your involvement in that Melbourne woman's kidnapping."

"Don't let him con you," Kim cautioned. "He doesn't know anything."

Delilah smiled at Kim. "I don't care if he knows." She drained the coffee mug and licked her lips. A frown appeared for a moment, replaced by a nasty smile. "It was a one-off job. A simple pickup. We expected a few hours of entertainment while we waited for someone to collect the victim. She turned out to be more trouble than I expected." Delilah pushed the mug aside. "My deadbeat accomplice betrayed me, and my employer wasn't grateful."

Samson took a quiet breath. "Your employer wasn't grateful because you lost the kidnap victim."

Delilah narrowed her eyes. Her nails tapped on the table. "What makes you think I lost anything? Maybe I killed her, and made off with the ransom."

Samson shook his head. "If you did, the men at the airport wouldn't want you alive."

"You think you have all the answers," Delilah sneered. "You tell me what happened."

"The kidnapping failed. The victim escaped. You grabbed whatever money you could find and ran."

"I only took what he owed me. You could say I cashed out my insurance policy. This money's rightfully mine."

"And the person who owned it?"

"He has no use for it now." Delilah laughed. "If you play with sharks, expect to get eaten."

Kim shuddered. The bundle of cash dropped from her hand. Her wooden chair scraped on the floor. "I'm going to bed."

Samson caught his sister's arm. Kim frowned at him.

"You'd better stay," Delilah said. "Your brother's afraid to be alone with me."

"Yes, stay, Kim," Samson agreed. "There shouldn't be any secrets between you and your new ally."

Kim sat glaring at Delilah. "I haven't agreed to anything." She dropped her eyes to her coffee mug and took a hasty sip.

"Tell me about the men at the airport," Samson said.

"They're not interested in the money. I only have to stay ahead of them until they lose my trail."

"If they're not after the money, why are they chasing you?" Kim's curiosity earned an approving glance from Delilah.

"I gave up my employer, in return for a ticket out of Melbourne. Naturally, they wanted to take advantage of my situation." She raised her chin and shimmied with her shoulders. "I'm a valuable asset."

Samson ignored her assertion. "You're certain no-one is coming after the money?"

"I made phone calls before I boarded my plane," Delilah said with a dismissive wave. "Only three people knew about this money, and the other two didn't survive."

Samson steepled his fingers. "Does the name *Operation Phoenix* mean anything to you?"

Delilah blinked in surprise, her smile relaxing. "No."

"*Maximum Security*?"

A quick intake of breath and a slight narrowing of her nostrils gave her away. "No." He held her gaze. Her lips parted in a wider smile. Delilah shrugged. "I don't see what you hope to achieve with these random questions."

He tapped his fingers on his empty mug. "I thought meeting *Maximum Security* agents at my Sydney hotel was a lucky break, but now I'm not so sure."

Delilah didn't blink.

"Who or what is *Maximum Security*?" Kim asked.

"Delilah thinks they're responsible for ruining her kidnapping."

Delilah hissed. "How do you know that?"

"An educated guess. The men in Sydney almost caught us. *Maximum Security* agents helped us escape."

The colour drained from Delilah's face. Samson continued, "I'm confident I can manage the men who followed you from the airport. But *Maximum Security* is a different problem. Perhaps they helped us on our way so they knew where to find you later."

It was Delilah's turn to leap to her feet. Her eyes flew to the external door, then over Kim's head to the darkened hills. Her trembling fingers folded on her chest. She recovered quickly, turning back to him with contempt. "All I need from you is some supplies. Then I'll be gone."

"If *Maximum Security* can lift a kidnap victim out of your hands, how far do you think you can get when they come after you?"

"Do you have any better ideas?" she demanded.

"I'm still working to make the perimeter secure. But the homestead is the safest place if these people get too close. If you promise to listen to my advice, I'll do everything I can to protect you."

Delilah's eyes narrowed. "Why do you care what happens to me?"

"I told you. I've promised God."

Delilah stamped her foot in frustration. "You're only going to get hurt."

"This is a test of my obedience," Samson murmured. "What you do is between you and God. I only ask you to remember my sister has responsibilities. Don't let her do anything to put her children at risk."

Kim snorted. "Any promise this woman makes is worthless."

Delilah glared at Kim until his sister lowered her eyes. "I'm going to teach you a lesson. Wait here."

Delilah strode towards her bedroom.

Samson's head was hot and heavy. His heart pounded in his chest.

Be still and know that I am God.

Like a refreshing stream, the whispered words washed his fears away. Samson relaxed. His sister's darting eyes betrayed her panic. She gathered the coffee mugs, dumping them in the sink. She swore, removing a smashed one to the bin. When she finished fussing at the sink, Kim turned her back to the window.

Delilah returned carrying the locked suitcase. The zip had broken. Bundles of cash protruded through the burst stitches. Kim sat heavily on the closest chair. Delilah stuck her hand through the tear. She pulled out another two bundles of cash, adding them to the two already on the table.

"This pile should be enough to guarantee your loyalty, Kim," Delilah said, leaning close. "And set us up in luxury for a few weeks." She took hold of the younger woman's chin and squeezed. "But I don't want to hear any more criticism from you." Taking a step back, Delilah smiled. "Do I make myself clear?"

Kim nodded.

Delilah faced Samson, shoving the suitcase into his arms. "Keep this as my security. I won't do anything to put the kids at risk. If I break my promise to you, the money is yours."

"And if Samson fails you?" Kim whispered.

"Don't you know your brother? He's a man of promise," Delilah declared. "You're not going to fail me, are you, Sammy-boy? We both know I'll kill you if you do."

"I accept your promise." Samson extended his hand and Delilah shook it.

Before he could retreat, she laughed in his face. "This is going to be a lot of fun."

Samson nudged her aside. He pulled the hallway door open. The listening teenager tumbled into the room. "Get up, Butch. Look after this suitcase. Tomorrow you can hide it. Don't tell your mother where."

Butch retreated along the hallway with the suitcase.

Samson faced the two women. He smiled before he stepped into the hallway and closed the door behind him.

Troubled Hours

ॐ ☼ ॐ

Philippians 3:19 - A mind focused on earthly things glorifies in shame.

ॐ ☼ ॐ

"It's been a week without trouble," Delilah said. "I want to go to town. Will you drive me, or do I take your truck?"

Samson glanced up from his breakfast. "You're not driving the Cruiser. I can take you after lunch."

Kim walked into the room. "If you're taking Delilah to town, I want to go too. I've had enough of being stuck here."

"Someone has to stay with Mum," Samson said. "Your father won't be home for a few more days, and then you can have your freedom."

"Why can't Butch and Nikki stay home from school?" Kim whined. "One day isn't going to matter."

"If you're so determined to go to town, phone one of the ladies on the list I gave you. Mrs J said the Ladies Fellowship offered to sit with Mum. They're waiting for an invitation."

"I don't want to invite them. Visiting Mum isn't all they want. I'd have to put up with their endless questions. When are you going to get a job, Kim? What are you doing with your life? Then they'd move on to talking about some nice young man, and how my children need a father. Of course, they won't forget to tell me they're praying for me. I get enough of that from you." She flounced from the room.

"Where's the list?" Delilah asked.

Samson sighed. He pointed towards the wall-mounted phone. Delilah strode to the noticeboard. Her manicured nails ran down the list. Snatching his plate, Samson dumped his remaining breakfast in the chicken scraps bin. He left the room, but not fast enough.

"Hello, Mrs Jensen..." Ten minutes later, Delilah shouted in the hallway. "All sorted! Mrs J will be here at noon."

Samson stepped from the bathroom.

Kim burst from her room. She threw her hands in the air. "You let *her* make the call?" Then her door slammed.

Butch and Nikki appeared, dressed in their uniforms.

"What's up wiv Ma?" Butch asked, following Samson.

"Mum's not a morning person," Nikki said, pushing past them both. "Nobody can do nothin' to please her this early."

Butch corrected her. "Nobody can do *anything*."

Nikki poked out her tongue. "I can say *nothin'* if I want to. Why do I have to talk proper when you say whatever ya want." She stepped into the kitchen. She stopped when she saw Delilah standing at the bench. The smell of hot toast wafted across the room.

"You should speak proper-*ly*," Delilah said. "You don't want anyone thinking you're uneducated. That will make you an easy target; a tragedy for such a pretty little thing."

"Nobody ask you," Butch grumbled.

Samson frowned. Delilah placed four slices of toast onto a plate and walked to the table. She grinned at him as she spread a piece with butter and jam. "Sammy-boy, I'm only trying to be helpful."

Butch grabbed one of the other slices. "Don't need yer help." The teenager ducked as Delilah took a swipe at him. Samson caught Delilah's raised hand. Butch stepped out of the way, as she dropped her toast. Her other hand reached towards Samson. He released her quickly, withdrawing a safe distance.

Samson headed for the exit. "I've got things to do. Butch and Nikki, be ready in fifteen minutes. I'll drive you to the bus." He glared at Delilah. "If you want me to drive you to town, keep your hands to yourself."

"Aye, aye, Captain," Delilah snickered.

❧ ☼ ☙

Samson leaned against his LandCruiser. The sun was setting. Delilah and Kim should have returned an hour ago. He could see his nephew and niece through the windows of the internet café across the road. At least he didn't have to worry about them walking up the mountain alone. The school bus had dropped Butch and Nikki in Meredith Crossing. Butch waved. Samson shook his head before shifting his attention to the Police Station next door. Uniformed officers came and went, acknowledging Samson's presence.

An unfamiliar vehicle drove past, the driver hidden behind tinted windows. The SUV slowed to a crawl before turning left at the next corner. It entered the car park beside the single-storey red brick motel. Two large men in dark suits stepped from the vehicle to disappear through the entrance.

While Samson considered his options, the phone in his pocket vibrated. He stared at the unfamiliar number. "Hello?"

Delilah's voice replied. "Sammy-boy, don't wait for us. We've made plans and will be home later."

"What plans?"

"Kimberley's friend found me a car. We're taking him out to dinner."

"I've just watched some of your Sydney friends arrive."

"Don't worry about me. I can take care of myself."

"Where are you?"

Delilah laughed. "Guess."

Through the phone, he heard a chorus of "Hello, Samson". Glasses clinked, loud music in the background. There were only two places in Meredith Crossing where Delilah could be. Either the Bottom Pub two blocks away or over there at the motel, otherwise known as the Top Pub.

"Don't go looking for trouble," Samson muttered. She ended the call. He stared at his phone before climbing the

Police Station steps, two at a time. After leaving a message for Kurt, he collected the teenagers and headed home.

⚛

It was midnight when Samson's phone rang again. This time, it was Kurt confirming that Delilah and Kim had left Meredith Crossing.

"A patrol car is following to remind them not to take a wrong turn. There's been enough trouble tonight."

"What kind of trouble?"

"A few skirmishes over who would buy Delilah the next drink. Then the Sydney mobsters tried to *persuade* her to leave with them. Her damsel-in-distress performance had the Top Pub in an uproar. The brawl spilled into the car park. The strangers jumped in their SUV and roared out of town. A posse chased them, hurling bottles and rocks."

"Delilah didn't decide to stay in town?"

"There were offers. Delilah told everyone she mustn't *disappoint* her fiancé. You wanted her in her *lonely* bed before sunrise."

Samson groaned.

"It gets worse," Kurt continued. "Did you know she promotes herself as a relationship therapist?"

"You don't have to sound so amused," Samson complained.

Kurt ignored him. "She spoke about her plans to overcome your *religious prohibitions*. She's determined to break you."

Samson headed for the kitchen.

"The Top Pub odds are three to one you won't last until the weekend," Kurt said.

"Thanks for keeping an eye on Delilah. I'll release the gates, and make sure nobody else makes it through."

Season for Change

ℰ ✺ ℬ

Ecclesiastes 3:1
There is a season for everything.

ℰ ✺ ℬ

Ten days later, Samson drove down the hill as the sun dropped below the treetops. He frowned to see at least a dozen vehicles in the homestead compound. What mischief had his houseguest prepared for him this time? The gate was open. His dogs tore across the open pasture, and he wound down the window as they raced along beside him. Samson parked outside the fence, as the only space remaining inside would block access when it was time for the visitors to leave. He identified each vehicle as he walked past them to the house.

Kurt's parents were here, and Mrs Mac, a Kidman relative. There were other neighbours, all friends of his stepfather. He increased his pace. The new doctor had parked beside Kurt's patrol car. He passed those larger vehicles, and was relieved to find Delilah's Hyundai Getz hidden behind them, closer to the house. He ran his hand along the dented panel. Delilah had connected with a guidepost on her way home two evenings ago. Her driving was like everything else: fast, and reckless.

As he opened the kitchen door, warmth and delicious aromas hit Samson.

He recognised familiar voices. Mrs J – Kurt's mother – and Mrs Mac were loading platters from a mountain of food.

"What's going on?" Samson asked.

"There you are," Mrs Mac said, wiping her hands on her apron and coming to greet him. "I'm glad you're not late for your father's birthday dinner. It's good that he didn't have to spend his birthday in hospital."

He choked back the protest about Old Jack not being his father. Mrs Mac was a short plump woman who hugged everyone, whether they welcomed it or not.

He disentangled himself. "What party? We can't afford—"

Mrs Mac laughed. "The girls said that would be your first response. You don't have to worry. They've paid for everything."

"They didn't say anything about a party."

"It was a last-minute decision," Mrs J said.

"Your mother's had a good day," Mrs Mac continued. "She remembered it was your father's ninetieth birthday. She thought she'd already organised a party. Your sister phoned, asking for our help."

Another neighbour was entering from the adjacent dining room.

"Of course we're delighted to help," this woman added. She seized a platter and disappeared again.

"The girls told us you'd walk in at five-thirty," Kurt's mother said. "You're right on time."

"You must be very proud of your girls," Mrs Mac added.

"My girls?"

"Your sister and your fiancée," Mrs Mac said. "It must be such a relief that Delilah has taken Kimberley under her wing. One less problem for you to worry about."

"You must be grateful Delilah's business is doing well," Mrs J added.

"Now, Samson, don't frown like that." Mrs Mac patted his shoulder. "Everyone knows how conservative you are. The counselling and physical therapy Delilah offers isn't everyone's cup of tea. But she's done wonders for quite a few locals. People are even coming from outside the district for appointments."

"You know more than me." Kurt had assured him that Delilah was walking the right side of the law. Samson prayed everything stayed that way.

"Go and change," Mrs J said, heading towards the dining room with her platter. "We've set up a buffet. That room's been under-utilised for too long. It's time the families on this mountain made some happier memories."

He straightened his shoulders in acknowledgement of the shadow behind her eyes. She nodded, smiling her approval before going on her way.

Ten minutes later, Samson entered the dining room, having quickly showered and changed into his Sunday best. There were twenty-five guests seated around the large table.

His stepfather, Old Jack, sat at the head, watching him. Samson's mother, Grace, was on Jack's left, a bright smile on her face. Her eyes sparkled, her hands fluttering with excitement. Jack reached for the glass in front of him, raising the golden liquid in salute. He took a small gulp, watching Samson over the rim, before setting the glass down.

"Your mother insisted we start with a toast," Old Jack said.

Another message lay hidden in his words. Samson nodded. Grace would not remember their table had been dry for fifteen years.

Samson sat between Grace and Delilah. Across the table, his grinning sister had a wine glass in her hand. Was it his imagination, or did Kim poke her tongue out at him?

Before he could clear his mind of awakened memories, his mother placed her hand on his arm. He turned to her.

"There you are," His mother's soft voice sang. "We couldn't start without you, Samson. I know how much you like to say grace."

The joy of her recognition was more intoxicating than any wine. Samson glanced around the table. As if he had given a signal, everyone reached for their neighbour's hand. A tremor ripped through him as Delilah's hand closed over his own. Afterwards, he couldn't remember what he said. He kept his head bowed long after the "Amen".

Noisy conversation wafted over him. The diners served themselves. He thought of other meals from long ago, when the house had filled with laughter. His mother once delighted in playing hostess for similar celebrations. A tear ran down his cheek.

"Aren't you hungry?" Delilah whispered, her breath grazing his cheek. He opened his eyes. She captured the tear with her finger. She smiled, kissing her fingertip, before lightly touching that finger to his lips. His breath caught. She leaned back, pressing her hand on his shoulder. "Stay. I'm here to serve you."

He could find no words to answer her.

Lord, I'm in trouble.

૪ ✿ ৪

Dinner was a great success. His mother's presence of mind lasted until she burst into tears over dessert. After that, the party came to a swift conclusion. Kim and Delilah ascended to the tower with bottles of wine and their cigarettes. The older women cleared the dining room. Old Jack and his friends went outside. Samson, Tim Chappell the doctor, and Kurt washed dishes.

With those tasks accomplished, the kitchen emptied. The guests went out to their cars. The doctor visited Grace, and Kurt went up to the tower. Samson remained to put away the final dishes.

It was only eight o'clock, but Samson was beyond weary. He busied himself preparing coffee. He glanced out the kitchen window. Old Jack was bidding the guests farewell. His stepfather was drunk, more talkative than Samson had seen him in years. Yet there had been no sign of his bitterness.

Old Jack came inside. "Thank you," he said, resting his hand on Samson's shoulder.

Samson smiled at his stepfather, who nodded before heading towards his room. Samson could hear movement on the stairs. He brought his coffee to the table, and took out his phone. The new cameras covered the road between the gates. He confirmed the departing guests had passed the first checkpoint. Then he pressed that activation switch.

First Kim and then Kurt appeared along the hallway. He couldn't hear what they said. Kim went into her room, closing the door. Kurt continued to the kitchen.

"Coffee?" Samson asked.

"You stay there," Kurt said. "I can get my own. Where's Delilah?"

Samson jumped to his feet. "She wasn't with you? She didn't come through here. I've already double-checked all the exits. Without my key there's no other way out. Her car's still here."

Kurt followed Samson into the hallway. There were lights under four doors. Was she with Butch, Kim, Grace or Old Jack? Samson signalled for Kurt to approach the teenager's door, and was at his mother's door, talking with the doctor, when Kurt moved towards Kim's room.

Kim's sharp rebuke sent the policeman across the hall towards Old Jack's room.

Before Kurt could knock, the door sprang open, and Delilah stopped in surprise. For an instant, something that looked like guilt appeared on her face, but then she reinstated her confident smile.

"I couldn't let my future father-in-law go to bed without a birthday kiss," she laughed. Kurt edged back to allow her to pass. She turned towards Samson, and laughed at the expression he was unable to hide. Samson turned on his heel, returning to the kitchen.

She chased after him. "Don't you walk away from me, Sammy-boy."

Samson went to the kitchen window and stared into the night. He tried to gather his rebellious thoughts to formulate a prayer.

Her angry reflection appeared in the glass. She stood close behind him, her hands on her hips. He could also see Tim and Kurt standing together near the table.

With a groan, he turned to face her. "I expected better of you, Ruth."

A flash of something unreadable appeared in her eyes. Delilah punched Samson. He staggered, before straightening to face her. From past experience, the excruciating pain told him she had broken his nose.

"Never call me that," she hissed. "This is all. Your. Fault. Why won't you retaliate?" She looked at the other men and stepped to the side.

Tim and Kurt dragged Samson to a chair. Tim opened his medical bag, while Kurt shoved a tea-towel into Samson's hand and pressed it to his bloody face.

Delilah shook her head. "Maybe there's another way? Your tame policeman can arrest me."

The angry policeman took a step towards Delilah. "He won't press charges. You don't know the story? Samson in the Bible was betrayed by Delilah again and again. His love for her destroyed him."

Samson closed his eyes.

"There's more to it than that," Tim said. "Caleb and I have tried to make him see reason. His full name is Samson Hosea Davidson. Hosea was a prophet. To illustrate God's forgiveness, God asked Hosea to marry a prostitute."

Samson held his breath. The heavy darkness pressed in. Delilah's heels walked away.

"I'm *not* a prostitute," Delilah said. "And I don't want God's forgiveness. I gave up on God a long time ago. I'm done with Samson. I'm leaving in the morning."

His heart threatened to explode.

A door slammed. He struggled to open his eyes.

The door reopened. She returned, hissing in his face.

"Nothing happened between me and the old man. He told me I was trash and he wanted nothing to do with me."

Samson stared into her eyes.

"I'm wasting my time here!" She waved her hands in the air, turning to Kurt.

"Kim said her father despised Samson, but she was wrong. Jack said Samson's forgiveness and loyalty had changed him." She shoved the policeman in the chest.

Kurt frowned, holding his ground.

"I don't want to change," she screamed as she fled to her room.

With a sigh, Samson surrendered to the darkness.

Moments of Regret

ဆာ ✿ ಎ

*1 Chronicles 29:11 - Yours is the kingdom, LORD,
and you are exalted as head above all.*

ဆာ ✿ ಎ

Delilah was ready when Samson entered the kitchen the next morning. His face was badly bruised, one of his eyes swollen shut and the dressing over his nose bloodied. Kimberley rose to her feet, her mouth open, her eyes wide. Nikki began to fuss over Samson, but Butch was the first one to ask, "What happened to you?"

Her laughter silenced them. "I happened to him. Now hurry with your breakfast. Sammy-boy can't drive, so I'm taking you to school." She turned to Kimberley. "If you want to come, you'd better hurry."

Samson offered no resistance. Had he realised her suitcase was already in the boot and she wasn't coming back? Fifteen minutes later, he deactivated the security gates. Her blue car roared down the mountain to freedom.

ဆာ ✿ ಎ

(Tuesday 29th August)

It was three hours before sunrise on Delilah's fourth night at the Top Pub. Dim lights illuminated the motel car park. Apart from the streetlights, and a few illuminated signs, the rest of the town lay in darkness. Her room gave her a good view of the Police Station. Did she still think Samson's tame policeman might be useful? Delilah shrugged.

Her escape to freedom had been an illusion. Butch wouldn't tell his mother where he'd hidden the money, and Delilah refused to contact Samson. She would show that man she could survive without his help.

The fugitive dropped the curtain and threw herself across the motel bed. She rolled over, unable to settle. After resuming her pacing, she returned to the gap in the curtains.

Movement caught her attention. In the distance, a solitary pair of headlights wound its way up from the bridge. That road meandered through the countryside all the way to Newcastle. It crossed the river several times, passing through rural communities. Eventually, it arrived at the big regional city.

Delilah had driven that way with Kimberley yesterday. Had she only imagined a constant police presence wherever she went? The menacing men who approached her at lunchtime were no phantoms. They had marched across the city restaurant towards her table. At the last moment, one of them answered his phone.

After their hasty retreat, a stranger approached. "Go back to Meredith Crossing."

A most unsatisfactory outcome.

Her mind drifted to the homestead high on the mountain. Samson had done nothing to prevent her from leaving. Would he come for her when the marriage licence was ready?

She was about to turn from the window when a car without lights entered the car park. Doors opened and closed with care. The crunch of gravel sent a chill up her spine. She reached for her phone. In seconds, she had the display unlocked and the call register open. Help was only a click away.

Pop. Pop. Pop.

One after another, the car park lights extinguished. A fiery missile arched across the darkness to smash through the motel's main entrance. A second missile followed. With a roar, the motel reception became an inferno. In the light of the fire, two men turned in her direction. She dropped the curtain. She was already in the kitchenette with the rear exit open, when a loud knocking came at her front door. "Fire! Fire!"

Delilah was outside before she took her next breath. Did the arsonists know her room accessed this unlit courtyard? She looked at the gate leading to the street. She must hide.

The courtyard was long and narrow. A row of trees concealed the retaining wall running parallel to the building. She crept towards the shrubbery. Already, she could see a bright orange glow on the other side of the building.

The leafy trees embraced her. She stuffed her fist into her mouth. With her back against the earthen wall, Delilah sent a message to the number Kurt had given her after offering to help her move somewhere else.

Top Pub on fire. Help

ಹ ☼ ೮

(Friday 1st September)

The light faded. Delilah glanced out the front window to where she had parked her blue Hyundai Getz on the main business street, in front of her hired rooms. She could see the Police Station from here, and it was a calculated risk that her enemies would not return during daylight hours. The previous tenant had been a naturopath, whose services included therapeutic massage. That had been an unexpected advantage. She was making enough money without offering any "extras".

During the day there was a steady stream of passing traffic. But as the afternoon chill crept in from the hills, the locals headed home. A variety of professional services populated the main street. Her neighbours included a hairdresser, a tax agent, a firm of lawyers and a real estate agent. On the other side of the road were the post office, a laundromat, a chemist shop and the local doctor's surgery.

She was waiting for Kimberley to return from the chemist. Samson's sister emerged, but walked away in the opposite direction. Tempted to follow her, Delilah noticed another person watching. Tim Chappell stood on the footpath outside the surgery for a few minutes, before shuffling to his car. It was obvious to everyone except Samson's sister that the quiet doctor admired her.

Kimberley returned ten minutes later, her face flushed.

Delilah took the parcel from her. "You were a long time at the chemist."

Kimberley's eyes darted to the window. "I met a friend. He's invited us to dinner."

"I've already told you, I don't want to stay in town after dark." She put the parcel on the reception desk, straightening the bookings ledger.

"You need to find yourself another place in town," Kimberley advised her. She flopped onto one of the waiting room sofas. "It's been four days since the fire. We could have a nice dinner, and see what other opportunities arise."

"You can stay if you want." Delilah put on her coat and collected her keys. "Just make sure you phone Samson and tell him."

Kimberley grimaced. "Why should I? I'm working, and my kids are going to school. I won't be spending *his* money."

"How much have you given him for food this week? Your kids have expenses, and you're not paying anything to help him. They're your kids. There's more to being a mother than making them go to school."

"You don't have kids, so what makes you the expert?"

Delilah frowned, pulling Kimberley to her feet. "I don't have kids because I'm *careful.*"

"Well, I'm careful too," Kimberley said, shaking free. "That's why there are only two kids. Aiden helped me last time, and I won't make that mistake again."

Delilah's eyes narrowed. "Did Aiden invite you to dinner?"

"He's only looking out for *my* interests."

"How?"

"He said we'd make better money if we set up in Brumby's Run. More customers, more opportunities. We wouldn't have to worry about Kurt poking his nose in where it isn't wanted."

"There'd be no opportunities if Kurt and your brother weren't protecting me."

"Ha!" Kimberley snorted. "Aiden said he can provide us with protection."

"How much would that cost?"

"You'd more than cover the fee by adding some extras."

"What does Aiden suggest you do with your children while we're providing the 'extras'? You can't leave them with Samson. If you do, you'll lose your government money."

"Sometimes I wish I didn't have them," Kimberley snapped, following her out the door. "If someone offered me enough money, I'd sell them."

A car stopped. Kimberley ran to Aiden and threw her arms around him.

Delilah secured the door. She watched the exchange, careful to keep her expression neutral. She had only met Aiden three times, but she despised his kind. Aiden's arm snaked around Kimberley's waist. Another man stepped from the car. He smiled at Delilah.

"She doesn't want to come," Kimberley whined.

"Perhaps another time," Delilah said, walking towards her car. She had her key in her hand, ready to defend herself.

Aiden laughed and shoved Kimberley towards the other man. "Looks like we have to share." Taken by surprise, Kimberley missed the opportunity to protest. Delilah turned, but the younger woman lifted her chin defiantly. "You go home to Samson. My friends and I are going to have fun."

Both men laughed as they bundled Kimberley towards the car. When she was in the back seat, the stranger climbed in beside her.

Delilah stood on the footpath until the car disappeared from view. They were heading out of town.

She got into her car and gripped the steering wheel. "Why do you care?"

Kimberley was right about one thing: they both needed to get away from this place.

Reschedule the Week

ಬ ☼ ಛ

*Genesis 28:15b WEB - For I will not leave you,
until I have done that which I have spoken of to you.*

ಬ ☼ ಛ

"Tomorrow," Delilah whispered in the dark, "I will find a way to talk to Butch alone. When he tells me where he hid my suitcase, I'll leave."

For the umpteenth time, Delilah thumped her pillows. She lay in her bedroom at *Mountain Rise*, listening to the rain pounding on the roof. Her phone told her it was two-thirty – Monday morning. She tossed her phone onto the floor.

All the arguments for remaining were overruled by the one reason she must leave. Samson expected her to marry him on Wednesday.

This thought fuelled a compelling mix of anticipation and dread. Samson said God wanted them to marry. That only mattered if God was real. She shook her fist at the ceiling in defiance. An imaginary God could do nothing to prevent her departure.

Outside, the storm intensified. Flashes of lightning chased the shadows across her ceiling. Rolling thunder shook the homestead. Delilah pulled the covers over her head.

ಬ ☼ ಛ

The phone rang. Samson pushed himself upright, throwing off sleep easily. "What time is it?" he asked, reaching for the bedside lamp. He flicked the switch, but nothing happened. The power must be out.

"Four am." Kurt's voice was difficult to hear.

"That's heavy rain in the background."

"It's been raining all night. Don't tell me you've slept through the storm. Hang on." Samson listened as the policeman issued distant orders. He filled the interval with prayer. Kurt's voice became loud again. "It's crazy here. The SES has been busy since midnight. There's an all-rivers flood watch. The roads to Newcastle are already closed. *Mountain Rise* will be completely isolated by mid-morning."

"I'm prepared," Samson said. "You haven't phoned to give me a weather bulletin."

"A convoy of four vehicles roared through Meredith Crossing around ten pm. They didn't slow for the speed limit and ran Mrs Mac off the road on her way home from the prayer meeting. They headed your way. I now know they split up. Two went the longer way, via Cassidy Road, while the other two came at you directly."

Samson silently counted to five, a practise learned on the battlefield. Overreacting to the first sign of trouble ruined too many missions. "They haven't reached the homestead."

Kurt snorted. "They didn't bring a tank. I had a crew drive by. There's a mangled four-wheel-drive blocking Kidman Road. They tried to ram the first gate. The key is still in the ignition, but the shock fried the electronics. Whatever you had rigged to that gate no longer has power, but there's enough damage done."

"What makes you say that?"

"Someone turned up at Newcastle hospital claiming his friends survived a lightning strike. Three men are being treated for electrical burns. Another has heart problems. The driver absconded before police arrived. The vehicle description matches the one that ran Mrs Mac off the road. The men aren't talking, but even if the missing driver managed to round up reinforcements, there's no getting through."

"And the others?"

"There were a few scattered sightings. Then, an hour ago, two vehicles crashed through the flood barricade the SES were setting up this side of Brumby's Run. One made it across the bridge just before a wall of water came surging through. That vehicle destroyed the barricade on the other side and headed east. The other vehicle went into the river. A rescue attempt saved four men. The river gave up the fifth man's body five kilometres further down."

Samson pushed thoughts about the dead man's family behind the barriers in his mind.

"This death will bring trouble," Kurt said.

"The storm has given me some time."

"Not enough. If I were seeking revenge, I'd send someone in by helicopter while *Mountain Rise* is cut off by the floods."

"I've already made plans," Samson said.

"You can't protect the whole mountain."

"I don't have to. I only have to ensure that it's not safe for a helicopter to come near the homestead."

‚☼È

(Wednesday 6th September)

Samson paused at the door. The rain had stopped, but the wind was still howling.

"Where are you going?" Kim demanded.

"I left you a note. I'm going down to the bridge to see how high the water has risen."

"I'm coming too. I want to see for myself. Perhaps the river's low enough for you to take me into Meredith Crossing."

Samson pulled the door open, stepping into the blustery morning. More storms were forecast. He surveyed the scene. Broken branches littered the homestead compound. A charred streak ran down one corner of the chicken coop, testimony to Monday's lightning strike.

Kim struggled to stand. "I've changed my mind!" She slammed the door.

"A perfect day to get married," he muttered.

The roaring wind snatched away his words. Except the wedding celebrant was on the wrong side of the flooded river. Perhaps that would appease Delilah?

When Kim had told Delilah about the flood on Monday, the angry woman walked out into the storm and raged at the sky. Samson had stayed inside and watched. When she lay exhausted on the ground, he carried her inside. Since then, Delilah had refused to speak to him, hiding in her room.

He had plenty of work to distract him from her anger. Samson detoured via the shed where the emergency generator belched oily fumes. He checked the fuel tank. There was more than enough to guarantee the homestead power. Kurt predicted another two days before the regular electricity supply resumed. As he battled against the gale to reach his LandCruiser, Samson reviewed the local map in his mind. Access from the east was still impossible. There were other circuitous routes for anyone with enough determination.

When he started the LandCruiser, the radio burst into life. The newsreader was updating the road closure information. Samson listened to the end. He reached out to silence the broadcast as the next story began. A private jet was missing. As he pondered why anyone would risk a small plane in such a violent storm, something large flew towards the LandCruiser. Samson ducked. The impact sounded like an explosion. When he looked up, a massive branch was resting on the bonnet. A jagged crack had appeared in the laminated windscreen. He turned off the engine with shaking hands.

He made it safely back to the house, but he couldn't stop thinking about the missing jet. The newsreader said the plane had been flying from Melbourne to Sydney. It had come down in the mountains. He began to pray for the missing pilot and his passengers. Then he remembered Kurt had said the next intruders would come by air.

80 ✿ 03

When Delilah emerged from her room, Samson was outside in the courtyard. The sky was clearing and the gale force winds had eased. Kimberley complained about the isolation, in what must be a familiar refrain. "How long are we going to be trapped here..."

Old Jack snapped. "Be thankful you have a home. If that lightning hit the tower, this old weatherboard house would have burned to the ground."

Kimberley scoffed. "The house was never in danger. Samson sleeps under the tower."

"What difference does that make?" Butch demanded.

"He's always claiming God is protecting him."

Ha! Delilah glared out the window. If God is protecting Samson, why is He keeping me here? Doesn't God know I'm the greater threat?

Samson walked past without looking. Delilah leaned forward to watch him. He wrestled branches onto a trailer attached to some kind of mini-tractor. A thick rope secured the awkward load before he climbed onto the tractor. The machine roared like a motorbike, disappearing from view.

Delilah grumbled about boredom. She collected her coat, heading for the tower. As she surveyed the compound, her eyes landed on the lightning-damaged chicken coop. She leaned on the waist-high railing and frowned.

For a moment, the wind dropped. The tractor motor was silent.

Chop! Chop! Chop!

Samson was using an axe to cut the branches into smaller pieces. He attacked the timber like a knight wielding a battle sword. When he had finished demolishing the branch, he slammed the axe into a stubby wooden block. He stacked the smaller pieces in an open shed.

She leaned on the railing, pleased with the timber's efficient destruction. If only she could conjure Samson into her dreams! Delilah faced the wooded hills. She wanted to shout her defiance.

Instead, she made herself comfortable and studied him. Three times, he went in search of more wood. The afternoon sun was warm. When he stripped off his shirt, a new emotion awakened.

A gust of wind roared through the tower, knocking her off her feet. She picked herself up.

"Thank You," she laughed. The wind snatched her words away. She imagined them whirling towards the trees, making the whole forest tremble.

CHAPTER 24
(Friday 8th September)

Day of Mercy

ಹಿ ✿ ಆ

Jude 1:21 WEB - Keep yourselves in the love of God,
looking for the mercy of our Lord Jesus Christ to eternal life.

ಹಿ ✿ ಆ

Samson usually slept with his door open. Delilah visited him late on Wednesday evening. Alerted by a small noise, he sprang to his feet with the light on before she reached his bed. One glance at the negligee she wore inspired him to snatch his clothes and flee the house.

After that, he only visited the homestead for meals. The storm damage provided plenty of work to keep him physically active. He pushed himself to the limits of his strength. But this did nothing to stop the direction of his thoughts.

On Friday morning, he awoke in the stockmen's hut, stiff and sore. Every muscle ached. He threw himself into the LandCruiser and headed down the hill to look at the river.

He stopped the engine above the high-water mark, shaking his head in wonder.

He stood on the bank, in awe of the river wild with power. He picked up a small branch and hurled it into the roaring torrent. The stick swirled and danced before disappearing downstream. He did this again and again until his shoulders lacked the strength to continue.

Dropping to his knees beside the river, Samson prayed until there was nothing left to say. He listened for God's voice. All he could hear was the flood. The river's song was inside him now, loud and ferocious, tearing at his soul.

"I surrender all. All to Jesus, I surrender. I surrender all..."

Someone sang his mother's favourite hymn. He looked around, before realising the words came from his own mouth.

He'd gone mad!

Surrender.

Samson bowed his head.

Look to the river.

He went cautiously to the water's edge. The flood was only two hundred meters wide at this point. Movement on the further riverbank caught his attention.

A large man stood on the other side. He wore a military uniform and held a rifle. Parked in the middle of the road further up the hill, a dark van waited. A second uniformed man stood beside it – younger, less certain. This man's rifle hung over his shoulder.

The first man shouted. The river snatched away his words. The man held up his phone. Samson brought his own phone from his pocket, wondering what good this would do. He almost dropped the phone when it began to chirp.

"Who is this?" Samson demanded.

"Piper Maxwell."

Samson staggered, dropping his phone. His eyes flew to the second man further up the hill, whose weapon was now aimed towards him. All Samson's plans had led to this moment, and proven inadequate. He refused to run. Wave after wave of grief stripped him of the last resistance. With him gone, there would be no-one to protect Delilah. She would never be his wife. He prepared for death.

The roar of the river's song filled him again. "I surrender."

The moment stretched. He looked across the river. The closest man continued to talk into his phone. Samson's phone lay in the mud at his feet. The display was dark.

The other man paced and argued with someone unknown. The call ended, and Piper looked at Samson again. His anger and frustration were obvious.

The muddy phone chirped again.

Samson retrieved it. "Why am I still alive?"

"I didn't come to kill you. I came to get the woman you're protecting."

"I'll die before I give her to you."

"That won't be necessary." There was a long pause. "How do you know Evie Romano?"

Samson frowned. "I read about her kidnapping."

"The woman you're protecting was responsible."

Samson waited.

"I have a message for you," Piper Maxwell continued. "Evie said she forgives her attacker. Jezebel is free from any retribution."

"Why would Evie Romano forgive the woman who kidnapped her?"

Piper Maxwell shook his head. "Evie said God had already done everything necessary to bring Jezebel to account. The river that stands between us is apparently a sign from God."

"You're not the only one trying to capture my fiancée. Can Evie make them stop?"

"Evie's asked me to buy the Sydney contract."

"Thank you," Samson replied. "God will richly reward you for your mercy."

"Don't thank me," Piper snapped. "I don't want God's reward. I'm angry. You talk about mercy, but I'm hungry for justice. I'd rather be a weapon for vengeance than deliver messages of forgiveness."

"You'll get your opportunity to be His weapon, but first you have to accept His forgiveness."

"I get enough of that argument from Evie," Piper snarled. "You're not what I expected."

"What did you expect?"

"I've seen your military records."

"Then you know my weaknesses. We're having this

conversation because God arranged it. He has a purpose for your life."

"I could snuff out *your* life in a second. What could your God do to stop me?"

Before Samson answered, the second man appeared beside Piper, with his phone in his hand. Piper shoved him away.

"Evie again?" Samson asked.

Piper swore and disconnected the call. The angry man turned his back on Samson and the river. He stormed the hill, with his companion scrambling to keep up. Samson waited until the van had turned and disappeared from view. He fell on his knees beside the river, singing a song of praise.

80 ✿ C03

A few hours later, Samson received a phone call from Kurt.

"Why didn't you tell me you met Piper Maxwell?" Kurt asked.

"I wasn't sure you'd believe me. How do you know?"

"He came here on an 'unofficial visit'."

Samson frowned. "What did he want?"

"Piper asked about Delilah. He didn't have any information about her new identity. He said there'd be no more trouble from Sydney. Someone purchased that contract and cancelled it."

"What else did Piper say?"

"He said Delilah will destroy you. I told him you're a survivor. He asked if I believed God was watching out for you. He didn't wait for my answer."

"What did you make of him?" Samson asked.

"I wouldn't want to be on the wrong side of him," Kurt confessed. "He acts as if he has authority and power to do whatever he wants. Expect him to show no mercy to anyone who stands against him."

Samson remembered the scene by the river.

He closed his eyes and said the first thing that came to his mind. "Kidman Road's still underwater. Is your road open?"

"That's the other reason I'm calling. Dad's been asking a similar question. Mum's getting restless in the homestead. I've been to inspect Cassidy Bridge. It should be useable in a few hours. But there are your roadblocks to clear first. I didn't want to organise a work team without your permission."

"I'll make a start straight away."

Fifteen minutes later, Samson loaded his LandCruiser. He had filled as many fuel containers as he could carry. He stowed them beside the chainsaws. He waited for Butch to join him. The boy seemed thankful for an excuse to leave the house. Samson looked at his equipment, remembering a supply of leather work gloves in the shed. As he strode across the compound, Delilah came outside. She wore work clothes from his wardrobe. She must have borrowed Kim's old boots. She sauntered toward him. "You're going to clear trees from the road? I'm coming too."

He opened his mouth to protest, and she wrapped her arms around him. "The sooner the road is open," she laughed, nestling her head on his shoulder, "the sooner you can have your wedding." *You return to your old life, and I'm free to leave.*

"I'm ready," Butch shouted.

Delilah released Samson. He stumbled towards the shed, grabbing a pair of his mother's gardening gloves. He shook out the spiders, before snatching the other work gloves. He strode back to the LandCruiser. Delilah waited on the bench seat. She slid across, pressing closer when he climbed in. He drove from the compound, the heat from her body an uncomfortable distraction. Butch closed the homestead gate. The dogs barked, jumping on top of his load.

When he came to the next gate, Samson climbed out to deactivate the power. He opened the gate. The LandCruiser rolled forward across the cattle grid. Delilah grinned at him from the driver's seat, continuing a few metres before stopping. After he closed the gate, she made room for him. "I told you I could drive your LandCruiser. When we're married, what's yours is mine."

"And what's yours is his," Butch reminded her. "Better take yer money an' run."

Delilah slapped Butch on the thigh. "I'll get my money later."

ೞ ✿ ೞ

Samson wiped the dusty sweat from his eyes. Three vehicles came to a halt on the other side of the fallen tree he was working on. He acknowledged familiar faces, then stopped in surprise. "Caleb, what are you doing here?"

His friend usually preferred office clothes, but today he wore jeans and a workshirt.

"Kurt said you needed help getting the road open," Caleb replied. "But I can see you managed most of the work on your own. This is the last blockage."

"The help is welcome," Samson replied. "There are still trees across the road towards the Jensen property. I'll leave this one to your group, and go in that direction."

He signalled to Butch to load his gear into the LandCruiser. Delilah talked with Caleb, away from the others.

"If yer go now, you can ditch Delilah," Butch suggested.

Delilah hurried to join him as he strode to his LandCruiser.

"Whatcha talkin' to 'im for?" Butch asked her as they drove.

"Wedding plans," she replied.

Samson missed a gear and stalled. Delilah laughed until she cried.

A Time to Forgive

ജ ✪ ൙

2 Corinthians 12:10a WEB
I take pleasure in weaknesses,
in injuries, in necessities, in persecutions,
and in distresses, for Christ's sake.

ജ ✪ ൙

With the extra help, Samson had the road open by mid-afternoon. The other vehicles left without Caleb. His friend kept throwing Samson troubled glances but made no attempt to talk to him. Everyone stacked wood. Delilah remained closer to Samson than his shadow.

A vehicle approached from the Cassidy direction. Delilah danced across to Caleb. Kurt's police vehicle stopped beside them. Kurt handed Caleb a folder as a female constable climbed from the passenger side. The constable passed a shopping bag to Delilah.

Samson busied himself, packing his gear into the LandCruiser. The dogs yapped, alerting him to Delilah's approach. She dumped the bag behind the seat.

"Okay, Sammy-boy," Delilah announced, pulling him into the middle of the road, "time to get married."

Samson frowned, surveying the group. Caleb and Kurt weren't smiling. He wiped his dirty hands on his jeans. This was not how he imagined his wedding day. Delilah had managed to keep herself tidy, but he was a mess.

"Yer gettin' married 'ere?" Butch cried, demanding Samson's phone. "Mum'll never believe me without photos."

Delilah insisted on the barest essentials, with the mandatory questions covered speedily. Samson surprised her by producing wedding rings from the glove box of his LandCruiser. Kurt and the constable witnessed their signatures on the licence. Caleb declared them husband and wife. Delilah concluded the ceremony with a brief kiss.

In command, Delilah dismissed everyone. Kurt would deliver Butch to *Mountain Rise*, before taking Caleb back to town. The dogs were going too. Samson stood in the road, watching the police vehicle disappear from view. Only then did he remember Butch had his phone.

Delilah demanded the LandCruiser key. Samson settled in the passenger seat. He gritted his teeth, as she executed an impatient three-point turn. She roared past the *Mountain Rise* gate and didn't slow until they came to *Valley View*. When she spun the steering wheel and braked, Samson braced himself for a collision. She laughed, coming to a grinding halt centimetres from the gate.

After he unlocked the barrier, she drove towards the abandoned Cassidy homestead.

"What are we doing here?" he asked.

"I saw a clearing from the road." She retrieved the shopping bag and led the way along a narrow track. The wild cattle had kept it clear.

She flinched when a tree branch brushed against her. Her speed increased, her sharp nails digging into his arm. The trees crowded in. A fallen forest giant blocked their way. Only when he lifted her over the massive trunk did he see the open space. She stepped into the centre and spun slowly, surveying the towering trees. His heart raced as he watched her.

The familiar bush sounds seemed amplified. Hidden animals scurried from their presence. A bird flew overhead, and then he noticed the sound of nearby water. This was the clearing he had visited in his dreams. He looked for the pathway leading to the water. It was gone.

Delilah sat on the ground, inviting him to join her. He made himself comfortable. From the shopping bag, she brought out a bottle of champagne and some plastic cups.

"I-I don't—"

She put her hand to his lips. "My wedding, my rules."

 ❖

The lengthening shadows made Delilah impatient to be gone. She opened the champagne. The foaming bubbles cascaded into the plastic cups. She only needed him to avert his eyes for a moment. As if he understood her wish, he asked if he could pray. His eyes closed. Her hands worked swiftly. She didn't pay attention to his words.

With a satisfied smile, she waited until he said, "Amen", before pressing a cup into his hand. "Drink."

He took a sip. He leaned back on his elbow and gazed into her eyes. "I don't know anything about you."

"I know all I need to know about you. Drink your champagne."

She thought about his statement as she drained her cup. She topped up his drink and poured herself another one. Something unlocked inside her. She shared her story in graphic detail, holding nothing back. He was a devoted audience.

His eyes moistened when she told him that her mother had sold both her children when Delilah was ten. She didn't realise she was crying until he brushed away her tears.

She relived her experience. She felt again the cruelty. Those men had punished her for helping her little sister escape. Afterwards, they left her alone in the bush in a rough hut. Bleeding and frightened as a storm raged. It was a relief to confess how the long hours of terror had broken her spirit.

She even told him about the nightmares that still tormented her. He listened, responding with different emotions as her story unfolded.

She talked about her progression from a helpless victim to a mistress of torture. Finally, she concluded with the promise that he would regret he had ever known her.

⁝☼⁞

"Goodbye, Sammy-boy."

His eyelids fluttered. He roused himself from his drugged stupor long enough to focus on her face.

She frowned. Had she misjudged the dosage? She tarried. He might say something useful for banishing her nightmare.

"I forgive you."

Delilah screamed and fled.

⁝☼⁞

(Very early, Saturday 9th September)

The hard ground lay beneath Samson. The moon shone through a gap in the tree canopy. His body shivered uncontrollably. Fragments of memory teased him as he struggled to his knees.

He looked at the gold band on his left hand, and his body convulsed. He was violently ill, then fumbled for his clothes. He dressed quickly.

He searched his pockets. She had taken his keys. He still had his wallet and watch. It was two forty-five am. Samson stumbled towards the path that led back to the Cassidy homestead. He didn't have the strength to climb over the fallen tree, venturing into the scrub instead. The tree branches blocked out the moonlight. As the darkness enveloped him, he

148

remembered Delilah's story. Tears flowed down his cheeks. He dropped to his knees to pray for her.

ಐ ☼ ಣ

Samson rubbed life into his aching limbs. A hint of colour announced the breaking dawn. The vibrant oranges and purples faded to grey, as hidden birds welcomed the day. The gathering clouds promised another storm. A cold wind rustled the leaves in the nearby trees.

At first, he couldn't identify the huddled shapes that surrounded him. They resembled mythical creatures, lined up in military formation. When he realised his error, Samson leapt to his feet in horror. The marshalled watchers were headstones and graveside monuments. Earlier generations of Kidmans, Cassidys and Jensens placed them there. He had wandered into the old cemetery at the top of the mountain.

This neglected corner seemed familiar. He looked down at the tiny grave. Here lay his mother's last child, born too early. He let the memories awaken. Jack Junior dead after the failed bank robbery, Kim missing. Grace mourning her dead baby and on the verge of losing her mind. Old Jack descending into drunken oblivion. Freddie too young to understand.

It fell to Samson, the outsider, to deal with the unfolding family emergency.

His first task, to bury the unnamed child.

Samson traced the inscription he had gouged into the small concrete slab: "Psalm 54:7 For He has delivered me from all my troubles".

As he poured out his petition to God, new troubles layered over the older ones. He had no answers. Still, he clung to the promised hope for deliverance. The sun was high when he ran out of things to say.

149

Into the silence, came the distinct clip-clop of approaching horses. Samson stirred.

Old Jack and Kurt's father, KJ, were at the gate before they saw him.

"What are you doing here?" Old Jack shouted, climbing down from his horse. "Your Cruiser was outside the compound this morning, but Delilah's car was gone. We thought you went with her."

Samson stumbled. His stepfather caught him. "Why didn't you phone for help?"

"Butch took my phone."

Kurt's father relayed news of Samson's fate to the homestead. Samson was too heavy to manoeuvre onto a horse, but Kurt soon arrived with his police vehicle.

Tim was already waiting to provide medical care when they reached *Mountain Rise*, and Caleb came half an hour later. In the privacy of his room under the tower, Samson gave his three friends a sparse account of what had befallen him. He assured them he would survive. Then he asked them not to mention his trouble again.

Time to Travel

ಹಿ ✿ ಚಿ

*Proverbs 12:25 - Anxiety weighs down a heart,
but a kind word brings joy.*

ಹಿ ✿ ಚಿ

The past three weeks had not brought Delilah the satisfaction she desired. The nightmares, instead of diminishing in power, intensified. In her dreams, she returned to the clearing again and again. Samson always lay unconscious and unresponsive on the ground. She tried different drug combinations, but the side effects made her situation worse.

She must have reactivated hidden memories. That was the only logical explanation. Why else would she have imagined she saw one of her childhood tormentors yesterday?

Her cash reserves had dwindled, despite her success in the city. Running away to Newcastle without her second suitcase had been an unforgiveable mistake. This regret tortured her as she drove towards Brumby's Run.

If her everyday suitcase hadn't already been in the boot of her car, she might have left with nothing. *Idiot! Why didn't you go into the house and make the boy tell you where he had hidden that money?*

She glanced in the mirror. Her makeup concealed purple shadows under her eyes. It was three days since she'd slept.

It took too long to find the house where Kimberley's drug dealer lived. It was past noon when she arrived. Weariness made her careless. Aiden grinned when she asked for Kimberley's new address, ushering her inside. She was not surprised by the payment he expected for the information. Afterwards, she could not look at her reflection in the mirror.

"Kim doesn't need your help anymore," Aiden said as she left. "She's made new friends."

Delilah puzzled over his words. What would evoke that look of fear and uncertainty beneath Aiden's bravado?

She drove past the address he'd given her, parking around the corner. Immediately opposite Kimberley's rental house and backing onto the river sat a dilapidated cottage with a weathered "For Sale" sign on the lawn. After a stroll around the neighbourhood, she went to the riverside playground. She ignored evidence of the recent flood, keeping to the high ground that backed onto the row of houses. Each one had a convenient rear gate.

The garden of the abandoned cottage was overgrown, and the back gate hung from its hinges. After checking for witnesses, Delilah disappeared among the overgrown fruit trees.

Within seconds, she stood at the unlocked back door. A broken pane of glass warned her someone else had come this way. She knocked and waited. Nobody responded. Delilah stepped inside, closing the door behind her.

The cottage was sparsely furnished. She moved systematically through the building. In one of the front rooms, a faded armchair sat before the window. A pile of drink cans and takeaway food containers lay beside the chair.

At first glance, the overhanging shrubbery in the front yard obscured the house across the road. Only when she dropped into the armchair did she have the perfect view. Someone else had been watching Kimberley's house. Delilah sat in the gloomy room and waited.

There was a large car in Kimberley's driveway. It was a city vehicle, impractical and expensive. After waiting an hour,

Delilah leaned forward as two men came out of the house. She was too far away to make out their features. After they left in the car, she scrambled for the back door.

Ten minutes later, Delilah marched to the side door of Kimberley's house and knocked loudly. Kimberley opened the door, her eyes wide with surprise. Delilah pushed her way inside.

"What are you doing here?" Kimberley demanded.

"Just passing," Delilah said. "A mutual friend gave me your address."

"It's not a good time. I've got company."

Delilah raised an eyebrow, walking across the small kitchen. She went through into a cosy lounge room. An attractive man lounged on one of the sofas. He smiled at her entrance. Her heart almost stopped.

She blinked. Her first impression was wrong – he bore a passing likeness to an old enemy, but he was too young.

Kimberley pushed past her, dropping onto the young man's lap. His arms wrapped around Samson's sister.

"I see you kept my furniture," Delilah said, sitting on the opposite sofa.

"You didn't want it," Kimberley muttered. "You left without saying goodbye."

"Aren't you going to introduce me to your visitor?" the man asked.

"Matteus, this is Delilah."

"Ah!" Matteus said, his smile intensifying.

Delilah guarded her expression. He was twenty-something, handsome and self-assured. His tailored suit and shoes were expensive.

He spoke again. "Are you staying?"

"Why are you asking her that?" Samson's sister whined.

He kissed Kimberley. "You've so much to learn."

His words had a threatening undertone. Before either woman could respond, a vehicle stopped in the driveway. His companions had returned.

"Excellent," Matteus said, shoving Kimberley aside. "Now my cousin Cosima and my brother Quin can meet Delilah."

After he left the room, Kimberley landed heavily on the sofa beside Delilah. "You've ruined everything. Matteus was taking me away with him tomorrow."

"I'm not here to stop you."

"But now he wants you to come too."

"I haven't agreed to anything," Delilah reminded her.

"Ah, but you will," another voice said.

Delilah's stomach cramped. She adjusted her position on the sofa as the three men chose their seats. A younger man joined Matteus on the opposite sofa. The family resemblance was obvious. This must be his brother Quin.

The third man settled gracefully into the armchair closest to the window. Cosima had aged well. He still exuded confidence in a sensuous way. He wore heavy gold rings on the fingers of both hands. Two shopping bags lay on the floor at his feet. From the first one, he brought out packets of sandwiches, which he distributed.

"The two of you will have to share," he said. Kimberley accepted the offered food. She opened the plastic case and pressed a white bread ham and cheese sandwich into Delilah's hand.

Delilah took a bite.

"Have we met?" Cosima asked.

Delilah shrugged.

"You wouldn't forget her," Kimberley muttered, and then choked on her sandwich.

Suddenly, Quin was beside them, patting Kimberley on the back. "Drink this," he said, bringing an open can of bourbon and cola to the choking woman's lips. Delilah continued eating her sandwich, pausing only to accept a similar can. Quin nodded his approval.

With the crisis over, Kimberley drained her can. She tossed the remaining sandwich onto the coffee table.

"Finished?" Cosima asked. Kimberley nodded. "We have some business to discuss with your friend. Take Quin to your room."

Kimberley opened her mouth to protest, her eyes pleading with Matteus to disagree. Matteus leaned forward and tossed a small plastic bag onto the table. "Here's a little sweetener."

The bag slid on the polished wooden surface, landing at Delilah's feet. She picked it up, recognising the black stamp on the coloured pills. She feigned disinterest, but her hunger awoke.

Samson's sister snatched the bag from her, anger replacing her dismay. She leapt to her feet. The younger brother welcomed her into his arms. Quin winked at Delilah as he led Kimberley away.

"Fifteen minutes," Cosima called after them. "The girl will be home from school soon. She doesn't need to know how her mother spent her afternoon."

Delilah finished the last sandwich and brushed the crumbs from her hands. She sipped her drink and endured Cosima's scrutiny in silence. Years of practice assured her that her face did not betray her inner turmoil. At the mention of the child, Delilah understood what was happening in this household.

Delilah had known many innocent children who had shared the same fate. For some, death had been the preferred option. Bleak despair flooded her mind. Why had Delilah fought so hard to survive?

For such a time as this.

She put down the can before her shaking hand betrayed her. That voice came from her dreams!

A glance at the two men assured her they had heard nothing. What did that voice mean? What could she do? She was alone, and these men represented a powerful organisation.

"I know where I've seen you," Cosima announced.

It took all of Delilah's strength to sit still.

"You were in Newcastle yesterday."

A small defiance burst into flame. He didn't know who she was! Her smile was genuine this time. "I have a small business there."

CHAPTER 27
(Thursday 28th September)

An Afternoon Adventure

ℰ☼ℬ

*Isaiah 26:3 - A mind that is steadfast will find perfect peace,
because they trust in You.*

ℰ☼ℬ

Delilah hid her growing unrest.

"What are you doing here?" Cosima asked.

"I came to visit Kimberley."

The two men exchanged glances.

"She wasn't pleased to see you," Matteus said.

"That's nothing new," Delilah laughed, "but I'm bored. I came with an offer."

"You're too late," Matteus said. "The Removalist is coming in the morning."

"The Removalist?" She waved her hand at the cheap furniture. "This old rubbish isn't worth moving."

"It's important," Cosima said, "to ensure everyone knows she has moved."

"Ah! A trail of breadcrumbs," Delilah said. "For the woodcutter to follow. Have you met her brother? All muscle, but too good for my liking. Sammy-boy will come looking for her, but will Kimberley be where the trail ends? I'd like to see his reaction when he realises what you've done."

"Don't talk about my brother," Kimberley snapped, re-entering the room. Her tear-stained face was pale. Quin appeared behind her. When he placed his hand on her shoulder, she flinched. Matteus drew her onto his lap. Kimberley snuggled into his embrace.

The younger man showed no remorse. After an approving nod from his cousin Cosima, he sat beside Delilah. One arm reached around her shoulders. The other hand rested on her thigh as he leaned closer. "Perhaps your friend Delilah will appreciate me?"

Ignoring his hands, Delilah found a pressure point on his neck. Quin cried out in pain, and she smiled, ready to defend herself. His eyes flashed, and his right hand pulled back to retaliate.

"Quin," Cosima said. "Remember your manners."

When Quin sank back on the sofa, Delilah patted his hand. "I'd ask you to visit me in Newcastle, but I don't think you can afford me."

Quin folded his arms across his chest, like a moody teenager.

"Forgive the impetuous boy," Cosima said. "He's recently turned twenty-one, and yet to learn to wait for an invitation."

"But you encouraged him," Delilah said, "because you wanted to know how I'd respond. Let me guess: you have an attractive offer for me, something to bring me under your protection? Kimberley will tell you I can look after myself."

Before anyone responded, a small figure passed the window. The kitchen door creaked. Kimberley shuffled sideways onto the sofa and Quin unfolded his arms.

Twelve-year-old Nikki called out, "Mum, I'm home. Is that Uncle Cosi's car in the driveway?"

Nikki ran into the room. She seemed tiny in her school uniform. Her twin plaits swung as she came. "Uncle Cosi!" she cried, rushing to embrace him. He pulled her onto his lap, producing a pink parcel wrapped with a big bow. "You brought me a present!" She kissed the man on both cheeks.

Her hands ripped at the paper, as her eyes took in the other adults in the room. When she saw Delilah, Nikki sprang to her feet with the parcel clutched to her chest. "What's she doing here?"

"Don't you have a kiss for your aunt?" Delilah chuckled, pleased that her presence had gotten the child off that man's knee.

"You're – you're not my *aunt!*" Nikki spluttered. She whirled to the others. "She's *not!*" Nikki's face reddened. "My grandfather says you're a—"

Cosima placed his hand over Nikki's mouth. "Young ladies do not use that language," he said sternly, before smiling to soften his words. "Open your present, and then go to your room to try it on."

Nikki nodded, refocusing on the parcel.

Delilah was not surprised when the little girl revealed a beautiful party dress. The garment was frilly and pink. The skirt had layers of tulle. With a glad cry, Nikki threw her arms around Cosima's neck. The child rewarded him with kisses before running from the room.

Memories of another parcel brought a tear to Delilah's eye. Another dress, another little girl, affectionate kisses given to a similar man. On that occasion, there had been two little girls. Her three-year-old sister's dress had been pink, while Delilah's dress had been purple. She had thought that dress the most beautiful one she had ever seen. Her happiness lasted until the next day. Then the new grandfather became The Removalist who took them away. By nightfall, their mother was gone.

Delilah dug her fingernails into her hands. That was the last time she saw her beloved little sister.

"You do have a heart," Quin declared. "You're crying."

"I am not," Delilah snapped, brushing away the errant tears. "I don't care if the despicable child hates me."

"Of course she hates you," Kimberley cried. "You stole my brother's heart and left him for dead."

"He gave his heart willingly." Delilah examined her nails as if they were talons. She fixed her glare on Quin who edged further away. When she returned her attention to Kimberley, her words were harsh and cold. "I made my intentions clear. You knew I would hurt him."

Running feet announced Nikki's return, wearing her dress.

"We'll talk about this later," Cosima said.

The child danced around the room. "I love it!" She settled on Cosima's knee. Nikki poked her tongue out at Delilah.

"Tomorrow, I'm taking you on a picnic," Cosima said.

Nikki frowned. "But tomorrow's a school day. Uncle Sam said we mustn't miss any school."

"One day won't hurt you," Kimberley said.

"What about Butch?" Nikki asked. "Is he coming on the picnic?"

"Of course," Cosima said. "But where is your brother?"

Nikki pouted, staring out the window.

"Where is he?" Kimberley demanded, rising to her feet.

"I don't know," Nikki conceded. "He said he had things to do."

Delilah marvelled that the others didn't recognise Nikki's deception.

"He'll be home when he's hungry," Matteus said. "One rebellious teenager isn't going to ruin our plans."

૎☯૓

Half an hour later, Delilah made her escape. She could not avoid giving Cosima her phone number. Quin walked her to her car.

"My cousin likes you," Quin said. The young man tried to steal a kiss as she unlocked the car. She efficiently dropped him to his knees in the car park. He scrambled to his feet, wincing in pain, but there was danger in his eyes. "How much—"

"Think of the highest price you've ever paid, as long as it's in the thousands, and then double it." She smiled wearily. "But not today."

Her heart raced as she turned her back on him. She left the doors unlocked, refusing to reveal her fear. She started the engine, but while she buckled her seatbelt, he pulled the door open. He dropped a handful of money into her lap.

Before she could respond, he kissed her hard and then withdrew, slamming the door. Delilah stomped on the accelerator, roaring from the car park. His laughter still haunted her when Brumby's Run was ten kilometres behind her.

Checking the mirror again, she sighed. Nobody followed her. She took the connector to the main road, driving for another fifteen minutes. When she pulled over to the verge, her hands shook as she counted the money. Quin had thrown ten crisp hundred-dollar notes at her. Her first instinct was to return to Brumby's Run to buy something from Aiden. An intense hunger burned in her veins.

Then she remembered the pretty child, seated on the knee of that evil man. Delilah barely escaped the car before nausea overwhelmed her. Her body still trembled when she returned.

Using her phone, she searched for local accommodation and made a booking. She opened the glove box, located the gold wedding band and slipped it on. Driving forward, she came to a side road that arrived back to Brumby's Run by a circuitous route.

Her first stop was the local department store. She purchased two suitcases and the necessary supplies to fill them. Her next stop was the supermarket, for grocery items.

Delilah went to the public toilet block in the deserted picnic ground. She removed her working-girl disguise – bright wig, short skirt and outrageous heels. She replaced them with a t-shirt, jeans and sneakers. Discarding the wig, she changed her makeup, transforming herself into a country wife.

By four-thirty, she was ready. Delilah slipped into the rear garden of the neglected cottage. As she expected, Butch was in the front room, seated in the armchair.

He jumped when Delilah appeared beside him. "Don't move," she whispered, a hunting knife held to his throat. "I'm not going to hurt you, but I can't have you giving me away. If those men in your mother's house find out I came back, I'm dead. Do you promise to keep quiet?"

He nodded.

She lowered the knife. "What are you doing here?"

"Watchin'," he muttered. "I don't trust 'em."

"What have they done to you?"

He leapt to his feet, and she pressed him back into the chair. He wouldn't look at her. "I take care of meself!"

"Do you know why these men are here?" she asked. If he already suspected, there was no need to reveal her secret.

"Ma's gonna work for them," Butch grumbled. "Matteus made her promises, but he don't want us kids. He's convinced Ma that Cosima's adopting us."

"You don't believe him?"

"It make me sick to see that man cuddlin' Nikki."

Delilah leaned closer. "If you don't get your sister out of there tonight, it will be too late."

Butch stared at her. His mouth opened and closed. The teenager grabbed Delilah's arm. "Whatcha gonna do?"

His wild desperation reactivated her stomach cramps. She shook herself free. "*I'm* not going to do anything. *I'm* not here. If those men find out otherwise, I'll come back and kill you both. Make sure you pass that on to your sister."

Three Day Drama

ॐ ☼ ॐ

*1 Chronicles 29:11 - Yours, LORD, is the greatness, the power,
the glory, the victory, and the majesty!*

ॐ ☼ ॐ

Samson leapt to his feet, his phone in his hand. It was five am.

"I'm on my way to get you," Kurt's voice shouted from the phone. "Butch and Nikki are missing."

Kurt didn't wait for a reply.

These days, Samson slept fully dressed. He pulled his boots on before knocking on his stepfather's door. The nightlight shone in the hallway behind him. When Old Jack called out, Samson entered.

"What's happened?" his stepfather asked, flicking on the bedside lamp.

"Kurt phoned – Butch and Nikki are missing. He's on his way to collect me."

"What about Kim?"

"He didn't say, but she's been evasive the last few times I've visited. I don't know what kind of trouble she's in. I'm sorry to leave you to watch Mum by yourself."

"Do what you've trained for, boy. Bring them home."

ॐ ☼ ॐ

"What kind of emergency are we heading into?" Samson asked. "I tried phoning Kim while I waited, but she didn't pick up."

Kurt's police vehicle raced down the hill. When they reached the sealed road, Kurt activated the lights and siren. Familiar countryside flashed past to the accompanying wail.

"There was an anonymous phone call," Kurt said. He navigated another winding corner at excessive speed. "The caller said a child abduction ring was about to snatch two children from a Brumby's Run address. It wasn't my watch, so the officer-on-duty dispatched a patrol car. They visited the address at eight pm."

"It was definitely Kim's address?"

"Yes. There were four adults at that address, one woman and three men. The woman's description matched your sister." Kurt slammed his hand against the steering wheel.

They rushed towards an early morning delivery truck on a narrow section of road. At the last minute, the truck found somewhere to pull over. "When they asked to inspect the premises, the woman became hysterical. One of the men said he was her uncle. The other two were her boyfriend and his brother. The uncle said his niece was in the midst of a messy divorce. He assured the officers this was a terrible hoax. Her children were spending the night with their father."

"Did they ask for this fake father's address?"

"It took time to get someone to check," Kurt grunted. "The Newcastle apartment was empty."

"You've just missed the turn to Newcastle," Samson cried, pointing back to the road sign.

"We're not going to Newcastle," Kurt said. "A woman phoned the Meredith Crossing station a couple of hours ago. She said she worked for Piper Maxwell and asked for me by name. She left a Brumby's Run address: a B&B that has self-contained cottages. The message said Kim's kids were waiting for collection. If I wanted to save the children, I'd better get there fast."

"What does this have to do with Piper Maxwell?"

"I called the number Piper Maxwell gave me. He denies any knowledge. When I asked him about the allegations of a child abduction ring operating in this area, he hung up."

"Have you confirmed the children are there?"

"I phoned the B&B. They have a family, a mother and her two children, booked into one of their cottages. The family checked in around six pm. The owner couldn't give a detailed description of the woman. Just another stressed mother in need of a holiday. However, she did say Mrs Davidson paid in cash."

"Mrs *Davidson*?" Samson asked in alarm.

"Mrs *Ruth* Davidson," Kurt said grimly. "She had the right ID to register. Her husband would be joining her in the morning. The owner didn't speak to the children, but the youngest child was screaming. The mother gave a believable explanation: an autistic tantrum. The teenage boy carried the girl into the cottage. That was the last the owner saw of them. The screaming stopped not long after they went inside."

"Drive faster!" Samson cried. He searched the contact list on his phone. Finding the number he wanted, he waited, holding his breath. The message service picked up. He listened to his absent wife's voice but left no message. His whole body began to shake. Why would Delilah take Kim's children?

Nothing made sense.

He closed his eyes and prayed.

ஐ ✿ ෴

Samson unbuckled his seatbelt, ready to leap from the police vehicle as it pulled into the vacant space beside the rented cottage. Dawn was breaking. The owner of the bed and breakfast establishment was uncertain when the car that should be there had left.

Kurt approached the cottage and knocked loudly. "This is the police. Open the door."

He waited, calling twice more. At his instruction, the worried owner used her key. Kurt waved her away before he hurried inside. Samson followed close on his heels.

"This is Senior Sergeant Kurt Jensen from Meredith Crossing," Kurt shouted. He stepped into the main room. A door burst open. Butch stuck out his head.

"Uncle Sam," he cried, ducking back into the bedroom. "Nikki, Nikki, wake up! Uncle Sam's here."

ঙ ☼ ଓ

(Sunday 1st October)

Samson didn't go to church that Sunday. Mid-morning, Kurt arrived at the homestead. Two women from the Child Protection department accompanied him. Tim Chappell had already declared the two young people physically unharmed. But Nikki had not spoken a word since the rescue. The doctor reported his concerns to the child protection caseworkers.

One of the women asked Nikki if there was anything she needed to tell them. The girl held her hand to her throat and dragged it across in a slicing motion. She then turned to the wall. The twelve-year-old refused to acknowledge them again.

In contrast to Nikki's silence, Butch had plenty to say. One of the women scribbled copious notes. The caseworkers exchanged troubled glances.

The note-taking stopped.

"And your mother said nothing?" the caseworker asked.

166

"Nah," Butch declared. "She told us to be nice to Uncle Cosi. Ma said he was payin' for her new life, 'cos he'd adopted us."

Samson's hands balled into fists.

The woman's folder closed with a brisk slap.

"The children will go into alternative care immediately." The authoritative woman turned to Kurt, who leaned against the kitchen bench. "Do you stand by your earlier declaration that the children are not safe with their uncle?"

Samson turned to his friend, half rising to his feet. Then he rested his fists on the table. Carefully, he unfolded his fingers and laid them flat. Butch frowned at him. Samson shook his head.

"I'm sorry, Samson," Kurt said. "I know you have the property well defended, but Butch and Nikki need to go to school. A daily journey to Brumby's Run would place them at risk. Their mother may return. Then there's this kidnapping ring the anonymous caller alluded to."

"Which brings me to our second concern," the woman said. "Mr Davidson, the police report suggests your estranged wife was involved. Do you have anything to say to that allegation?"

Samson stared at the gold band on his hand. "The police can't confirm her involvement."

"But if she renewed contact with you," the woman persisted, "you would welcome her back?"

Nikki dropped from her seat and disappeared under the table. The little girl sobbed. Butch crawled under the table and held her in his arms, crying with her.

"That reaction settles the matter," the woman said, rising to her feet. "We will take both of them with us now."

Samson walked to the window. He lifted his eyes to the mountains. The sun was shining, but the light seemed to fade from his world.

> I thought I was following your plan. Kim's children are going into care because I married that woman. Surely there's another way?

> *Your brother will take them.*

"Freddie!" Samson shouted, spinning around. Everyone stared at him. "They can go to live with their Uncle Freddie. My half-brother lives in Melbourne. That's far enough from here to guarantee their safety from their mother."

Butch dragged Nikki out from under the table, and Samson embraced them.

"It's not that simple," Kurt said. "Freddie will have to go through a stringent assessment."

"That won't be a problem," Samson laughed. "His employer uses *Maximum Security* to screen everyone who works there."

Kurt raised an eyebrow. Samson shrugged. "Freddie's in Melbourne, it made sense to ask him if he knew Piper Maxwell." He refocused on the women. "Freddie said even the wrong association can lead to instant dismissal. Get someone from Child Protection to phone Piper—"

"Who?" the woman demanded.

Kurt leaned forward, jerking his head towards the external door. The women hurried outside to consult with the policeman. The trio returned five minutes later.

"Senior Sergeant Jensen has provided an explanation. That doesn't change today's decision. The children cannot remain here. If – and I'm making no promises – if this Melbourne uncle proves satisfactory, I will contact you. Until then, Nikki will be placed with trauma victim specialists. Butch is heading to a group home."

Fifteen minutes later, the children were gone.

୫୦ ✿ ୯୫

Halfway through rinsing the bleach from her hair, a knock came at Delilah's apartment door. She frowned. There had been no security buzzer to announce an impending visitor. She wrapped a towel around her hair and hurried to open the door. Quin pushed past her, a bottle of champagne in each hand.

"What are you doing here?"

"I've brought you the rest of your money." He laughed, making himself at home on her sofa.

The young man unbuttoned his jacket and produced a wad of cash. She pretended she wasn't interested. Where did this twenty-one year old get that kind of money? As he counted the notes, it became difficult to control her expression. He laid ten thousand dollars on her coffee table. The remaining money went back in his pocket.

She put her hands on her hips. "As you can see, I reserve Sunday mornings for washing my hair and doing my nails."

"I'm in no hurry."

"I don't entertain at home," she said. "You should have made an appointment to see me at my studio."

"But you don't *entertain* at your studio. You provide a different kind of service there, with a trainee. I'm not paying for a trainee."

She narrowed her eyes. Everything about this young man screamed a warning.

"Consider this the second stage of your job interview," Quin continued.

He reached into another pocket and produced a small handgun. With a graceful movement, he rested it on the table beside the money. Then he reached for a bottle and began opening the champagne. "Bring me some glasses."

Her open-plan apartment provided no concealment. Delilah lingered near the kitchen bench. Her fingers crept towards the knife block.

Pop! A cork flew across the room, bouncing in front of her. Delilah gasped and pulled her hand away.

By the time she had selected two wine glasses, Quin stood behind her. He reached around her to pour the champagne. She took hold of a glass, elbowing him to give herself room to move. Quin picked up his drink and guided her towards the sofa.

When she sat beside him, he brought out a small packet of pills. Quin dropped two red pills into her glass. The pills fizzed, colouring her drink a vibrant pink.

"Kim said you have a higher tolerance," Quin said, "but we'll start the afternoon with two."

Delilah downed the contents in a rush.

Quin laughed, refilling her glass with champagne.

"I'm going to dry my hair," Delilah said, carrying her glass towards the bathroom. "What else did Kimberley tell you?"

He followed her. "It's what she didn't tell me that interests me."

The drugs were already having an impact.

New Beginnings

ಬಿ ✿ ೮ಬ

Psalm 145:18 - God is near to all those who call on Him.

ಬಿ ✿ ೮ಬ

Despite the strong sleeping tablets, Delilah remained awake. It was three am, and someone was banging at her door. She groaned in frustration, dragging herself to her feet. The persistent headache intensified. After pulling on a robe, her bare feet padded towards the apartment door.

There was only one person who would be calling at this hour. Quin had sent several provocative messages to her phone since his Sunday visit. Why was she trying to discourage him? A wealthy lover would solve all her problems.

"What now?" she demanded, flinging the door open and turning away.

A large hand grabbed her shoulder. "You should be more careful about opening your door to strangers."

She screamed, raising her hands as she spun around. The grey-haired intruder was powerfully built. Unsurprised at her response, he pinned her arms against her chest. She kicked, screamed, and then bit him. He retaliated by throwing her against the wall.

The room spun.

Delilah collapsed to the floor.

Through a haze, she tried to focus on the man's cruel face. "What are you doing here?"

He frowned. "That's not the response I expected." He hauled her to her feet, but her legs folded beneath her. "You haven't asked who I am."

Her answer escaped. "I already know who you are."

The arm around her tightened, pushing back the fog. Now her mind scrambled for a believable lie.

"How do you know me?" he demanded.

Delilah groaned and held her head.

"Quin said the Removalist was coming."

ဆ ✿ ℃

Pacing the departure lounge, Samson checked his watch. The Tuesday midmorning flight to Melbourne was boarding. The flight attendants ushered people through the tunnel towards the plane. Samson stepped onto the busy concourse, two boarding passes in his hand.

An angry teenager, accompanied by an unsmiling woman, came through the crowd. Samson reached for the boy's cabin bag.

"Where's Nikki?" Butch demanded.

"I've already told you," the woman said. "Your sister is staying in Sydney. When she's settled, we'll arrange a supervised visit."

"I don't wanna go wivout 'er."

"Would you rather go back to the group home?" she snapped, before turning to Samson. "Mr Davidson. It will be a relief to sign him over to your care. But I must warn you, he's tried to run away three times, so you'd better watch him."

"I won't run from Uncle Sam."

The handover formalities were brief.

"What's Uncle Freddie like?" Butch asked as they hurried towards the plane.

"I haven't seen him for ten years. He was a quiet teenager. He preferred computer games and tinkering with electronics to working on the farm."

"Ma never talked about 'im."

"Your mother was angry with Freddie. She took it personally when he left."

The stewards checked their boarding passes. After taking his seat, Butch asked, "Why did 'e leave?"

Samson considered his answer. "Your grandfather sent him to Brumby's Run to work as a motor mechanic when he was seventeen."

"Why's he in Melbourne? There's cars in New South Wales."

"Your grandfather was an angry man. Freddie couldn't do anything right."

Butch stared at Samson for a long time. "Ol' Jack used to get drunk. Did 'e beat Freddie?"

A sad smile was the only reply.

"An' Ma?"

"No, never your mother. Kim was her father's favourite."

They sat near the right wing, with Butch in the window seat. Samson glanced at the silent teenager as the safety presentation began.

After the flight departed, Butch spoke. "What if 'e don't like me?"

"You'll have to make yourself likeable," Samson said. "It's not going to be easy, but you're family."

The teenager nodded, facing the window.

"You have a chance for a fresh start," Samson told him. "The choices you make are going to make a difference. I'll be praying for you."

"Don't pray fer me," Butch muttered. "Pray fer Uncle Freddie. Pray that he like me. An' pray that Nikki comes to Melbourne."

CHAPTER 30
(Thursday 5th October)

Present Trouble

ജ ✿ ౮౩

*Ephesians 2:19b WEB - But you are fellow citizens with the saints,
and of the household of God.*

ജ ✿ ౮౩

Two days later, Samson waited for his return flight to Sydney. He remained uncertain. Would the unhappy truce between his half-brother Freddie and Butch last? He took a final sip of his takeaway coffee and dumped the cup in the bin. When he turned, a tall woman blocked his way. He apologised, attempting to step around her.

She followed him to the departure lounge, settling in the seat beside him. He scanned the crowded space. The woman smiled and leaned closer. Samson decided she was older than she looked. Her face was too perfect, but her eyes held his attention with a fierce intensity. Her stare reminded him of that childhood game where the first person to blink is the loser. It would be safer to let her win.

His chest tightened, and he turned his head away. He remembered another woman who didn't like to lose.

"Jezebel did a number on you," the woman said, grasping his chin and making him face her. "I didn't think you'd be the kind of man who cried in public."

"I'm not crying," Samson muttered, pushing her away, "and her name's not Jezebel. She changed it to Delilah." He brushed the back of his hand across his eyes.

"Delilah, Jezebel, her name's not important."

"Who are you?" Samson asked.

175

The woman presented him with her business card: Jennifer Prescott, *Maximum Security*.

"You work for Piper Maxwell? What does he want?"

"Piper didn't send me," Jenny said. "If that boy you left with your brother does *anything* to upset Evie Romano, *I'm* coming after *you*." She poked his chest.

"You'd better kill me now. Upsetting people is my nephew's main mission."

Jenny laughed, punching him hard on the shoulder. "Evie sent me to tell you God's got everything under control."

"I've never met Evie. Why does she keep intervening on my behalf? I tried asking Freddie about her. He said she's married to his boss, and then he changed the subject."

"Piper thinks Freddie's in love with Evie. Her husband's a jealous man."

"I've seen Romano. I can understand Piper's concern."

"Piper's not worried about your brother. Freddie's too timid to act on his feelings."

Her words did nothing to calm Samson. Had it been a mistake to bring his nephew to Melbourne?

Jenny stood. "They're calling your flight."

When Samson reached for his bag, Jenny seized his arm. "You're still wearing your wedding ring. Don't you think you're taking 'love your enemy' too literally?"

Samson shook himself free.

"Evie says your love will bring Jezebel redemption," Jenny said. "I'm sceptical. Evie's too trusting and innocent. It was a miracle Piper and I found Evie before the kidnappers raped and tortured her. I heard your wife boast about her intentions, and you can't deny she tried to kill you. We both know Jezebel's a disturbed psychopath. She's beyond hope."

Jenny's words echoed in Samson's mind during the flight. He dragged his feet towards the parking lot. He was almost to his LandCruiser when his phone rang.

It was Kurt. "Samson, where are you?"

"I'm at the airport in Sydney. I'll be home in a few hours."

"The Newcastle police found Delilah's apartment."

"Newcastle? I thought she'd have gone further. What did she say?"

"They found her apartment," Kurt replied. "But someone got there first."

Samson froze. A passing car honked its horn as a warning. He closed the distance to his LandCruiser.

"A patrol car responded to an early morning call: a woman screaming in an apartment block. They found signs of a violent struggle. The neighbours described the missing woman..."

"Are you sure it was her?"

"They found her stash of identity papers. As we expected, she'd added her married name to her options. She had a copy of the marriage certificate and a photo of the two of you. I remember Butch taking photos at the wedding, but I didn't know he'd sent them to her."

This revelation robbed Samson of his strength.

Kurt continued, oblivious to the power of his words. "The preliminary report says there are no eyewitnesses. There's also no security camera footage and no digital trail. Whoever took her knew what they were doing."

"What makes you certain someone took her?"

"I have twenty thousand reasons. All of them in Australian dollars, stuffed in the wallet left beside her bed. And her car's in the apartment car park. You have to prepare yourself for a call from the coroner."

"No..."

"As her legal husband, you're her next-of-kin. All her possessions come to you. At least you'll get some benefit from this tragedy."

"No." Samson tried again. "You said she was *missing*. There's not going to be a body…" The world around him began to fade. His spiritual eyes opened upon the familiar river vista.

When Samson awakened from his vision, he was in the car park on his knees. He could still hear the roaring waterfall over the city traffic. His strength returned. He drove home, clinging to the certainty that he would see his wife again. Whenever his faith wavered, he shot fervent prayers for her deliverance heavenward. God had promised – Evie said so…

₧✿₻

A gentle breeze chilled Delilah. The window must be open – but the familiar city sounds were missing. She heard the wind blowing in the trees. A shiver ran through her body.

For a moment, she thought she was back at *Mountain Rise*. Then memories of her city life pushed that assumption away. A strange heaviness held her, still. Another dream. If she opened her eyes, she would see the clearing. The watching trees waited for her to run. "Not this time. I refuse to play."

A nearby rustling tickled her ears. A nervous giggle, the hint of shuffling feet. She was not alone.

"Shh!"

A child's voice whined, "But she's awake."

"No, she's not, Holly," said a third voice, "she's still dreaming."

"Let her sleep. In her dreams, she's free."

This must be a new manifestation of her nightmare, a recycling of an older terror. *Keep your eyes closed.* She tried to conjure up recent memories to affirm her adulthood.

The whispering conversation continued.

"She's not free? I thought she was one of the keepers."

"You saw the Removalist carry her in. All the other keepers come and go as they please."

At the mention of her old enemy's name, hope died. Now she was fully awake, her adult body weakened by pain.

Where had the Removalist taken her? No, that was the wrong question. The precise location didn't matter. In her earlier captivity, there had been many addresses, but the house rules remained the same...

"She's one of us?"

"But she's so *old*," Holly said.

A hush fell over the group. Holly's words pierced Delilah's heart. She sensed the children's despair. The only way to escape had been to outgrow a child's body. When her turn came, Delilah had been grateful to be sold to another organisation.

If she was too old, why was she here?

For such a time as this.

Leave me alone.

You cannot deny your destiny.

In defiance, Delilah sat up, startling the watching girls. They huddled together, edging closer to the open hallway door. She counted nine of them of varying ages. She glared at them. Fear awakened in their eyes. Throwing off the blanket, she attempted to stand. Everything hurt. Delilah dropped back onto the edge of the bed.

"Get me something to drink," she snarled. One of the younger girls rushed towards a small bathroom annexe.

While she waited, Delilah examined her surroundings. She was not in one of the dormitory rooms, crowded with single beds. A king-sized bed filled this room. The only other furniture was a mirrored dressing table. Crammed beside the curtained window, it held an assortment of cosmetics.

The child returned carrying a plastic tumbler filled with water. Delilah snatched it from her hands. The curtains shifted. Again, the wind sang in the trees outside. Striding to the window, Delilah wrenched the curtains open. It was dark. She thrust her head into the open.

Suddenly, young hands were pulling at her, drawing her away from the window.

"Don't try to leave," one of the girls cried. "It's too far to fall."

She allowed them to return her to the bed.

"Even if you survive, you won't get past the guards," another added.

"There's nowhere to go," complained a third. "Outside the garden wall, there's nothing but trees as far as you can see."

"All the doors and windows have alarms," the eldest girl said, "so the guards can sleep."

"It's best to let them sleep..." another told her. A chorus of agreement followed those words.

"What will we call you?" the eldest girl asked.

"But Ivy," Holly said, pointing to the open door, "you *know* he put her name on the door.

The Removalist had changed her name many times, and she had learned to predict his plans for her from his choices. Here was her first clue. Her legs trembled, and she scolded herself for her fear. When she read the sign, she staggered: Mistress Destiny. The girls rushed to help her.

A vision of Samson was the last thing she remembered. He was kneeling in prayer beside his LandCruiser.

Up To Date News

ଧ ✿ ଔ

*1 Chronicles 29:13 WEB - Therefore, our God, we thank You
and praise Your glorious name.*

ଧ ✿ ଔ

Samson slept at the table. The dinner dishes still needed clearing. It was six-fifteen pm. His buzzing phone woke him. "What trouble is Butch in now?"

"He's been suspended," Freddie said.

"What? He's only been at his new school a few days!"

"He decided to show those city kids he wasn't going to be pushed around."

Samson sighed. "Is there any good news?"

"That's why I rang," Freddie replied. "I had to take Butch back to work with me. The Boss's wife needed help. Evie asked if she could borrow him for the afternoon. I wasn't sure it was a good idea, but Butch adores her."

"Are we talking about the same teenager?" Samson asked. Then a darker thought arrived. "What about her husband? What does he think of Butch spending time with his wife?"

"He took Butch into the office at the end of the day. I don't know what he said, but Butch was quieter afterwards. Evie has a plan. Her nephew Marco goes to a private school in the city. She's arranged for Butch to enrol at *St Jerome's.* Evie thinks Marco's good influence will make a difference."

"Can we afford a private school?"

"Don't worry about that," Freddie said. "Evie says I'm eligible for an employee scholarship for school fees."

Samson remembered Jennifer Prescott's warning. "Evie sounds like a good friend."

"You'd like her. She talks about God more than you do..."

ಹ ☼ ಚ

"Destiny," she reminded herself. "Your name is Destiny."

It seemed difficult to throw off the old name. Delilah-Destiny sat at the mirror, covering the fading bruises with makeup.

The girls had asked her to explain how she came here. When she refused to speak, they told her what they had seen and heard. Each one of them then related their tale. Against her will, a sisterhood of shared experience bound her to them.

Nothing she said or did could dissuade those girls from offering her comfort she didn't need. Most unsettling were their unexpected outbursts of joy. These girls seemed to view every new situation as a game.

Delilah-Destiny frowned at her reflection. She had an evening meeting with her captors. When told the news, the girls hustled her to her bedroom. A new dress lay across her bed. She examined the black sheath dress. Meanwhile, the girls took turns tottering around her room in a pair of killer stilettos. They fell over themselves giggling.

"You won't be laughing when I lock you in your rooms," she warned them. "You have to be in bed by six-thirty."

"We're happy to be locked in," ten-year-old Azalea said.

"But we're sorry for you," Holly added.

"Finding a dress means you're *chosen*," Ivy said.

"I've already told you I can take care of myself," Delilah-Destiny snapped. Her sharp words only drew the girls to her, with softly whispered words and clinging arms.

When the time came for her to lock the doors, Ivy took her aside, whispering a warning. "Please be careful. If the chosen one does something wrong, the rest of us will suffer."

Ivy's words pierced Destiny's hard heart.

CHAPTER 32
(Thursday 12th October)

An Uncertain Future

ಸಿ ✻ ಲ

ಸಿ ✻ ಲ

With a frown, Destiny studied her reflection. The new dress clung to her every curve. It was perfect for her plan.

So why had Ivy's warning unsettled her?

Even the housekeeper seemed nervous today.

Mrs Smith warned Destiny to be ready for the Young Master's summons around seven pm.

It was important to conceal what she knew about this privileged position. Becoming the Young Master was a coming-of-age present for the Removalist's favoured relatives.

One heir came to mind. His grandmother had expected him to become a priest. His reign had been lengthy, and his name had been grand: Ricardo Barononi. He had played a game with her: she must confess her sins and plead for his forgiveness.

Memories from long-ago were harder to ignore today. With a sigh, she leaned towards the window. There had been no vehicles on the road. A helicopter had flown overhead a few hours ago, and returned the same way a few minutes later.

She reviewed the information she hoped would give her a surprise advantage. Each evening, Destiny retired when the girls went to bed.

Alcohol and drugs were taboo while she was on duty.

And she was always on duty.

She often lay awake, staring at the ceiling, planning her escape. Sometimes she dreamed of the forest clearing and the man who slept there. The thought of spending time with other adults teased her with limitless possibilities.

To compensate for the nightly boredom, her days were productive. Destiny smiled. All the housekeepers from her past had been "Mrs Smith", but this one was the easiest to manipulate.

The housekeeper had taken Destiny on a tour of the three-storey house. The girls' dormitories were together on the highest floor. Her nine girls shared two rooms.

Her bedroom was across the hallway. There was accommodation for more girls, but Mrs Smith said Destiny must "prove her suitability".

The girls' sitting room on the ground floor opened onto their dining room, beside the kitchen. Each day, the girls and their Mistress ran up and down narrow winding stairs. The grander staircase remained unused.

The guest bedrooms and the formal reception rooms occupied the middle floor. One of those dining rooms was the venue for this evening's meeting with her "Masters".

Since Destiny's arrival, the household had been free from outside interference. The days passed without guests to entertain. Neither the Removalist nor any of his associates visited. The girls thanked her for the respite.

Why were the Masters keeping her waiting?

The temptation to go searching for them grew. She glared at the door. There were cameras in the hallway. She suspected there were also motion sensors on the stairs. The girls told a cautionary tale of a past resident caught out of bed by a guard.

The girls said the guards changed regularly.

But the same faces had been here since she arrived.

These big men lived in a small cottage near the gate. A high wall surrounded the property. The three guards always stared at the girls when they played in the extensive garden.

Destiny avoided them. Mrs Smith's sternest warning was about the guards. "Your predecessor was a foolish girl. See that you learn from her mistake."

"What mistake did she make?"

"She was too friendly with the guards. They brought her alcohol and other treats. She invited them into the house."

"What happened to her?"

"The Master ordered her termination," Mrs Smith replied. "Her disappearance upset the girls. I had to lock them in their rooms until you arrived. I think the Masters set a trap for her, to see how much freedom she would give the men."

"Why do you think that?"

"The guards went unpunished. Once she was gone, they left the girls alone." Mrs Smith waggled her finger at Destiny. "Don't feel sorry for her. She was here to keep the girls safe, not to enjoy herself."

When Destiny had questioned the girls about her predecessor, they became unusually quiet.

Ivy led her to the window. The teenager pointed to where Mrs Smith's husband worked in the garden.

"She didn't leave. She's under the roses."

Destiny had returned to Mrs Smith with the girls' theory.

"If you don't want to join her, make protecting the girls your priority."

Her reaction must have mollified the older woman.

"Be patient and put your insatiable curiosity aside. You're a clever woman. The Masters richly reward loyalty. When guests fill this house, you will have everything you desire."

Everything – except her freedom. Why did these thoughts haunt her?

She flounced onto the bed, willing the house phone to ring. There was a direct line from each room to the housekeeper's office.

Tap. Tap. Tap.

Destiny jumped. The housekeeper preferred to use the phone. The girls were secure in their rooms. What if one of the guards had come to test her? She looked for a weapon. She snatched the small nail file from the dresser as the door opened.

Quin grinned when he saw her defensive stance. "Is that how you greet me after a long absence?"

He wore a white tuxedo and bow tie, teamed with a black shirt and dress pants. She remembered his age, and the final clue fell into place. Quin was the current Young Master.

Her heart sang. She already knew how to manage him. Freedom was within her reach.

Destiny shoved him towards the door. "You should have waited for me to invite you in. I don't have time for an impudent wretch like you. I'm having dinner with someone important."

He laughed. "And I'm not important?" He bent back her fingers until she dropped the nail file.

She slapped him as hard as she could.

Quin rubbed his cheek before seizing her arm. "As much as I'd like to continue this game, my father doesn't like waiting."

"Your father?" She froze. "Your father is the Removalist?"

"That's my grandfather," Quin said, wrestling her towards the main staircase. "He's downstairs too. We're having a small family reunion so I can properly introduce my sweetheart."

"Introduce me?" she spluttered, elbowing him.

She continued her tirade as she stormed down the stairs. "Don't call me 'sweetheart'! You sent your *grandfather* to kidnap me."

This unexpected complication could ruin her plan.

She changed tack. "Do you know the restrictive lifestyle I've been leading? I haven't been this sober since I was a child!"

He caught her again, a few steps above the second-floor landing. "I like what sobriety has done for you."

"Don't mock me. If you don't remove these restrictions, you'll get nothing from me."

His laughter ceased, and she sensed his fury.

He released her so suddenly she toppled down the stairs. Her brief tumble brought her to her knees on the landing.

With her head bowed, she remonstrated with herself.

A strange breeze ruffled her shoulder-length hair, and a chill ran through her body. When she lifted her head, Quin had vanished.

An iridescent blue haze shimmered around her. The mist swirled, shifting to reveal a figure in a familiar forest clearing.

The man knelt, his lips moving in a silent petition. Then he raised his head.

Destiny stared directly into Samson's sorrowful eyes.

He prays for you.

Destiny covered her head with her arms, blocking out the vision.

Arms wrapped around her. When she opened her eyes, it was Quin who crouched beside her. She was back on the landing – the forest had released her.

Destiny faked a smile. "Well played. That's how I expect my Master to behave."

His troubled visage cleared. His kisses expressed his delight at her changed mood. He pulled her to her feet and guided her towards her future.

Past Enemies

ಬ ✿ ಆ

Isaiah 62:1b WEB - I will not rest, until her righteousness shines out like the dawn, and her salvation like a burning lamp.

ಬ ✿ ಆ

Destiny paused in the doorway. The small reception room was elegantly decorated in muted tones. Between the dining table and the door, a wooden coffee table had prime position. Four men gathered around a chessboard, set with exquisitely carved pieces. The men wore traditional black tuxedos. Quin's brother Matteus sat in an upholstered chair, facing the door. His opponent sat in an identical chair on the opposite side of the board. The dark-haired man didn't turn. As Quin brought Destiny closer, the spectators lost interest in the game.

Matteus frowned, before moving a chess piece. He shrugged, shaking his head as he rose to greet her.

"Destiny," Quin began, "you already know my brother Matteus, and our cousin Cosima." Both men nodded. Quin hesitated before the elder man. "My grandfather says he needs no introduction either. You called him the Removalist when he came for you."

"Our beautiful liar has finally joined us," the grandfather said with a sly smile. "You almost convinced me my grandson had broken my trust."

Destiny narrowed her eyes. "Quin didn't tell me you were his grandfather, but he gave me enough clues that I could guess your identity.

"I've heard many stories about you. If I'd thought them even half true, I'd have prepared a more believable answer. Will I continue to call you the Removalist, or do you prefer another name?"

The Removalist seemed amused.

"Remolind Vanito Barinov, at your service, Mistress Destiny," he replied, with a low bow. "My friends call me Remo, but to a *chosen* few, I'm Grandfather."

Destiny dropped into a curtsey, secretly vowing never to call him Grandfather again. "Quin has a different surname."

Remo laughed. "My grandson told me you were bright. You have my wife to blame for the confusion. She came from an ancient Italian family. She said my name suggested links to the Russian Mafia."

The remaining man kept his focus on the chessboard. Everyone waited. His hand moved. "Checkmate," he declared with great satisfaction. His voice was deep, powerful – and familiar. Finally, he stood to face her.

Only Quin's proprietary arm around her waist kept her upright. The chess player had lost none of his imposing stature with the passing years.

She prayed he would not remember her.

"This is my father, Rick," Quin said. Ricardo Barononi's grin widened, revealing perfect white teeth. She glanced at the other men, noting the family resemblance. Why had she not noticed before?

Rick reached for her hand. He kissed it and then tugged her closer. Quin released her unwillingly. Now she stood face-to-face with her enemy.

"I have waited a long time for you, Jezebel," Rick said, placing a hand behind her head and ruffling her hair. "I like what you've done with your hair."

His use of the name he had given her long ago made her dizzy. His eyes were empty of any sign of recognition. Relief battled with her wounded pride. He chose her when she was twelve, to celebrate the birth of his second son Quin.

Rick lifted her chin, examining her face. "You seem familiar – perhaps your photo's been on my wall for too long."

She could not trust her voice.

"You evaded me in Sydney. That took me by surprise. Your performance at the airport was spectacular. It was more notable because my Melbourne cousins thought they had broken your spirit. Your captivity here is a necessary precaution."

He spun her around. "You're an excellent acquisition. My son has good taste. It will be interesting to see if he can keep you."

Quin took this as an encouragement. He reclaimed her, holding her tight.

His father smiled – and she trembled. "Did you know of my attempts to liberate you from your mountain hideout? I almost felt sorry for Samson – he thought he was saving you from sin."

Destiny didn't take the bait.

"Did Samson know you would destroy him," Rick asked, "to gain your freedom?"

He laid his hand on his son's shoulder. "I've warned Quin. But he assures me he is strong enough to control such a rare and precious treasure."

Quin stiffened. He squeezed her so tight, she struggled to breathe.

"It doesn't matter how you came to this house. My patience has borne fruit." Rick smiled. "My son did well in choosing your new name. It's perfect for the future I've prepared for you."

Years of pretence had kept her secrets. Destiny returned Rick's appraising stare. "If I had known who was pursuing me, I might have made myself easier to catch."

He studied her for a moment before gesturing to the opposite seat. "There's time for a game of chess before dinner. I always play black."

Matteus abandoned the upholstered chair. Quin sat in it and dragged her down onto his lap while his father arranged the chess pieces for battle.

"I must disappoint you again," Destiny said, "for I refuse to play. You appear to be a man who hates to lose. I don't want to ruin your dinner by beating you. I've caused you enough displeasure already."

Quin gasped. His arm tightened around her waist. The other men laughed.

"Are you sure you want to concede without a single move?" Rick asked.

Destiny reached forward. "Positive," she said, toppling the white king.

Rick's powerful hand seized the white queen. He strode to the dining table and placed the chess piece beside a silver chalice. "Quin, bring your rebellious queen here. It's time for her to play another game. I call this one Confession."

The son hastened to obey. Destiny sat at the end of the table, with a subdued Quin on her left. Matteus sat beside his younger brother, with Cosima opposite him. She faced Remo. Her heart raced when the patriarch winked at her. Rick took the remaining chair on her right. His black eyes locked onto her face.

Destiny rotated the white chess piece between her fingers. His forgetfulness gave her the advantage. It was time to make her first move. The queen dropped from her hand.

She examined the intricate carvings on the silver chalice. Rich blood-red wine filled it to the brim. Destiny inhaled the heady aroma. All the other guests had white wine in crystal glasses. They drank freely as they watched her. With a sigh, she pushed the goblet away.

"You need to drink," Quin said.

"This is a test," Destiny said. "I'm not permitted alcohol."

"While you're a guest at this table," Remo said, "you're free of those restrictions."

"Ah." Her hands remained folded on the tabletop.

"You're right about a test, but not the form that it will take," Rick said. "Hold out your hand."

She obeyed.

Rick brought from his jacket a small paper envelope. "Every game needs a prize, and this is what you will win when you play." He placed the envelope in her hand.

She studied it before breaking the seal. A dozen coloured pills fell onto the white tablecloth. Every one bore the familiar chess piece symbol. They included four red ones. "Black Bishops. How do I play?"

Rick reached into his pocket again, retrieving another envelope. This one had a black border. "Eat this wafer and then drain the chalice."

The envelope held a thin white disk, again stamped with the black bishop symbol. The wafer lay in the palm of her hand. His favourite game had become more sophisticated with the passing years.

"I've prepared this especially for you," Rick said. "You've proven yourself a skilful liar. You've also demonstrated a stronger resistance."

The seconds turned into minutes. Quin broke the impasse. He took the wafer from her and pressed it to her lips. "Sweetheart, open your mouth. If you refuse to play, I'll have to kill you."

Her muscles tensed, ready to shove him away. Instead, she closed her eyes and let him place the disk on her tongue. A cold shiver ran through her. The sweet wafer began to dissolve.

Quin pressed the stem of the cup into her hand and raised it to her lips.

Her stomach flipped, and she opened her eyes to the dream world again. Destiny was alone, barefoot in a green meadow filled with wildflowers. In the distance, she heard running water. She walked until she came to the edge of a river. The blue water sparkled in the sunlight.

"Drink."

Destiny spun towards the woman who spoke. Here was the Melbourne girl whose abduction had been the catalyst for all this trouble. The last time she had seen Evie, that girl had been unconscious. Remembering her evil intentions towards Evie, unfamiliar shame swamped the dreamer. Terror quickly followed. If Evie was here, did that mean her protectors were coming?

"You have nothing to fear," Evie's gentle voice said. The woman held a gem-encrusted goblet, similar in shape to the one in the real world. "Fill this cup with life-giving water from the river. Your enemies have given you a powerful stimulant to loosen your tongue. When you drink this water, you will be able to control what you reveal to them. Choose your words wisely; tell them only what they already know."

Kneeling beside the river, Destiny filled the goblet. The water was like liquid fire in her mouth, but she emptied the cup. Weeping from the pain, she fell forward. When she recovered, the vision was gone.

She knelt on the floor beside the table. Quin dragged her upright. "Sweetheart—"

"Don't call me 'sweetheart', you foolish boy." She grabbed the back of her chair. The chalice stood upright on the table, empty except for a small residue in the base.

"He wants me to confess," she muttered to herself. "Confess, confess – I've played this kind of game before." She tipped the chalice, using her fingers to chase the final drops. "Was this a sacrament? Does that make you a priest?" she asked the father. "I've known many priests. They talk of sin and responsibility. I deserve punishment – is that what you want? Should I fall on my knees before you?"

She let go of the chair, stumbling forward, before changing her mind. "Wait. It wasn't the father who gave the sacrament."

She spun back towards Quin, falling into his arms. She giggled as she twirled him around the room. He danced as if he had two left feet. "Foolish boy." She placed her palm on his chest and thrust him from her. "You have so much to learn."

"Did your brother send you to me?" she asked Quin, leaping towards Matteus. "Does he expect me to teach you? I don't think Matteus knows how evil I am." She leaned around the brother's chair and applied enough pressure with her fingers. "I enjoy inflicting pain."

Matteus gripped her wrist and pushed her from him. She used the momentum to propel herself towards the grandfather's chair. The older man rose to his feet.

Grandfather waited for her to regain her balance. "Sit down."

"Yes, Gran'father," she sang in a childish voice, dropping onto his chair. "I promise I'll be a good girl now." Another fit of giggles burst from her. She snatched his wine glass and drained it.

"Have you ever been a good girl?" Grandfather asked.

Destiny laughed until she gasped for breath. "You know me so well, Gran'father," she wheezed.

"Oooh," she cried, straightening her shoulders and grinning at Rick. "This is a powerful brew. Whoo-hoo! You've chosen the wrong Mistress to look after the girls in this house. There's nothing kind or gentle about me, and I can't stand weakness. I'll teach them to be like me."

"There's still more for you to confess," Rick said. "Keep talking. I want all your secrets."

"You thought the boy told me about the Removalist," she giggled. She threw herself sideways onto Cosima's lap. "If Cosima and Matteus hadn't told Kimberley the Removalist was coming, I might not have joined the game."

"Then you don't deny taking Kim's children?" Cosima asked, pushing her into Quin's waiting arms.

"Why were you even there?" Quin asked, leading her back to her chair.

"You silly child," she laughed. "I was there for the boy."

Quin froze.

Deliberately turning from him, Destiny toyed with her fork. Her eyes drifted to the pills on the table as she focused on the printed marking. "Don't give in to temptation," she chided herself. "You haven't earned it yet, and you're already high." A giggle escaped her throat. She covered her mouth with her hand.

"You want me to confess," Destiny said to Rick, "or you'll put me in the rose garden."

Now it was his turn to be silent.

"You made these? You're smiling, so I'm right. You play chess – does that make you the Black Bishop? Those priests now approach me with fear and trembling. You call me Destiny, but you should call me Revenge or Destroyer instead."

"Is that why you married the saint?" Remo asked.

A dull ache awakened in her chest, but an excruciating pain in her hand drove it away. She looked down.

A small river of blood flowed onto the white tablecloth. How had the shiny fork become impaled in the back of her hand? Quin grabbed her. She didn't fight him, but Matteus came to help anyway.

"Why did you do that?" Quin asked her. "Why did you stab yourself?"

Matteus removed the fork and applied pressure. Cosima appeared with a small padded dressing and some tape. She kept still while they attended to her hand. She blinked, as perspiration ran down her face.

Every nerve in her body screamed, as if she was on fire. "I don't want to play this game anymore."

"It's not for you to say when the game is over," Rick replied. "Tell me what I want to know, and I'll give you the antidote."

"What antidote?" Quin demanded.

His father dismissed his question with a gesture. "Sit down, Quin. Destiny is right. You have much to learn."

The young man sulkily resumed his seat. He drained his wine glass and asked for a refill. Cosima complied.

"Why did she stab herself?" Quin asked, and his cousin shrugged.

All eyes turned to her.

"I think I may have made a mistake," Destiny conceded.

"How do you stab yourself by *mistake*?" Quin demanded.

She toyed with the edge of the dressing, then wrapped her fingers around the white chess piece.

She directed her words to the carved queen. "Perhaps this is a distraction. Did I stab myself to delay the interview?"

She set down the queen and picked up the chalice. Upended, the cup left another blood-red stain on the white tablecloth. "Does it matter if I don't answer?"

The white chess piece was again in her hand. "Maybe I thought I was hallucinating. Did I try to wake myself from the nightmare?"

She balanced the queen on the upturned base of the chalice and studied her arrangement. "Or perhaps the drugs affected my mind?"

A serviette appeared in her hand. With a flourish, she draped the fabric over the chess piece where it sat on the chalice. "Perhaps I didn't know what I was doing?"

"Which of those reasons is the truth?" Quin asked.

Destiny blinked at him. "All of them – none of them? I don't know."

She sat motionless – calm. The young man threw a startled glance at his father. Destiny diverted her attention to Rick. She waited for the Black Bishop's pronouncement. Rick pursed his lips and furrowed his brows. After a long time, he smiled.

Rick gave a signal, and Cosima left the room again. A few minutes later, the cousin returned, accompanied by a man wearing a chef's uniform.

The chef pushed a large trolley ahead of him.

"Your sweetheart has set me an intriguing riddle," Rick said with a grin. "I will consider my verdict after dinner."

ॐ ☼ ☙

Destiny smiled at Quin. He fussed over her, making sure she ate. She didn't complain when he denied her request for wine, nor rebel when he confiscated the packet of pills.

When dinner was over, the group moved from the table back to the chessboard.

"Will you agree to play me now?" Rick asked.

The chess pieces were ready. Quin sat her on his knee, and she leaned forward. With precision, she moved her first pawn. Rick studied her before making his countermove. The game progressed swiftly. Destiny moved each piece without hesitation. Finally, she declared, "Checkmate."

Rick scanned the board. "Where did you learn to play like that?"

"I don't like losing. I found a chess champion and *persuaded* him to teach me."

"Do you always get what you want?" Rick asked.

Destiny rose to her feet. "That's an interesting question to ask a prisoner. I'm tired now. I'm going to bed."

Quin caught hold of her hand.

"Don't you trust me to find my way?" she asked.

"It would be unwise for any of us to trust you," Rick laughed. "Tonight, you'll stay on this floor where we can keep an eye on you."

"I can't stay here," she protested. "My girls—"

"*Your* girls?" Rick's eyes narrowed. "Have we become your pawns? My son intends to tame you. He'll be a stronger man when he's done. Quin, take her away."

Quin swept her from the room. She was breathless when he bundled her into his bedroom.

"What about my girls?" she asked him.

"No-one will bother them tonight. Nor tomorrow night either."

An Afternoon Change

ಸ ☼ ಛ

1 Chronicles 29:11
For all that is in the heavens
and in the earth belongs to God.

ಸ ☼ ಛ

The girls were with Destiny in the garden when the helicopter flew low over the property. It disappeared behind the house. Everyone sat still. The engine of the minibus parked beside the rear gate roared into life. They gathered their possessions. That was the signal to begin a race to their private ground-floor sitting room.

Destiny dropped onto her favoured sofa. It gave her a good view of both windows and the entry to the kitchen. If Mrs Smith came looking for her, the housekeeper would find this Mistress ready.

Without invitation, five girls battled each other for her lap. The losers settled for the padded seats beside her. Pushing aside her feelings, she spread her arms around them. This mother-hen role did not come naturally. Since her interview with the Masters, her relationship with the girls had changed. Their smiling faces had joined the phantoms in her dreams.

The remaining girls sat at her feet, an uneasy tension uniting them. Ivy, the self-appointed leader of the group, paced the carpet beside the windows.

Destiny studied the group. All the girls had flower names because this was *Garden House*. Ivy, Fleur, Daisy, Rose and Cherry were her teens, while Daphne, Azalea and Violet were a couple of years younger. Holly, at eight, was the youngest, a tiny child who reminded Destiny too much of her past.

"Sit down, Ivy," Destiny commanded. "You're making everyone anxious. This might be nothing to worry about."

"It's bad news for someone," Ivy muttered, flopping onto the opposite seat.

"It might be Destiny's boyfriend paying another visit," Azalea said.

"And that's not bad news for her?" huffed Ivy.

"We get lollies and treats when he comes," Holly reminded her.

"Bribes to keep us quiet," muttered Ivy. "It's too soon. He was only here two days ago. He told Destiny he wouldn't be back until the next *Garden House* party."

"It could be new girls," Cherry said. "We haven't had anyone new for months."

"There won't be any new girls," Ivy snapped. "I told you the stories I heard at the last party. There's a police investigation, and a witness they need to silence before the Removalist can go back to work."

"That's good news for us," Fleur said. "If the police are chasing the Removalist, they might find *Garden House*."

Ivy snorted. "No-one will find us."

"You can't know that," Fleur snapped. "You don't know everything."

"I've been on more flights out of here than the rest of you," Ivy said. "There's nothing but trees in every direction, and only the one road in from the highway. The police will never find us."

"One of us could escape, and tell them," Azalea suggested.

"Shhh," Destiny said. "No more talk of escaping. That will only bring disaster."

"You say that because you're protecting yourself," Ivy said. "If Quin came to take you away, you'd be gone in an instant. You don't care about us."

A chorus of protests erupted from the other girls.

"You can't say that!" Cherry cried. "She's not like the other Mistresses. They only cared for themselves…"

"Destiny lets us all pile in bed with her, when we're having trouble sleeping," Fleur added.

"If she's so good, then why hasn't she found a way to save us?"

"I haven't tried to save you," Destiny said grimly, "because there are a lot of girls who are worse off than you. You should be grateful."

"But we're not free."

"There's more to life than freedom," Destiny said. "What you should focus on is learning to take care of yourself. When you are too old for this sanctuary, you have to know how to survive."

"Is that what you did?" Cherry asked.

"I never had it as easy as you," Destiny said sternly. "I had to fight to keep myself alive. I don't want any of you to have that kind of life."

The minibus rounded the corner of the house, disappearing towards the main entrance. All conversation ceased, as they strained to hear the muted voices in the hallway. The door to their study remained closed.

Whatever the trouble, it was not her immediate concern.

ဆဝ☼သ

Destiny knew as soon as the housekeeper arrived to clear the dishes after dinner that she carried a message.

"Destiny, send the girls to bed, and report upstairs," Mrs Smith said.

In a rush, the girls leapt to their feet. Destiny hesitated. Which of her questions was the more important? Before she could decide, a buzzer sounded in the adjacent room. A look of alarm flashed across the housekeeper's face. The older woman shoved Destiny towards the door.

"Hurry," Mrs Smith said. "He's waiting. Go now. There won't be time to change."

Destiny chased the girls up the narrow stairs.

"I'm going to lock your doors. I will visit you again if this is nothing more than a quick briefing. If you don't see me until morning, you'll know I'm staying downstairs."

"But you only go downstairs with your boyfriend," Cherry said. "And he comes for you."

Keeping her thoughts private, Destiny locked their doors. After checking her reflection in the hall mirror, she hurried downstairs. There was a light gleaming from the usual dining room. She entered quickly.

Remo sat alone on one of the sofas, an open book in his hand. He smiled, dropping the book to the floor. "Come and sit beside your grandfather."

Destiny obeyed, controlling her breathing.

"Aren't you even a little afraid of me?" he asked, tipping her chin.

She willed herself to remain soft and compliant. "Should I be?"

"No," Remo said. "I'm more interested in your mind than your body. I'm going to be a guest here for some weeks."

"Why?"

"Haven't you heard the rumours? I have to stay out of circulation until they eliminate the eyewitness."

"An eyewitness? From the myths that have grown up around you, I didn't think you appeared until there was no danger anyone would see you."

"There have been a few close calls over the years. I've been doing this job since before you were born."

"Do you remember all the targets?" she asked, afraid of his answer but desperate to know.

"I remember the targets who escaped me more than my successes," Remo admitted. "You were the naughty girl who interfered most recently." His arm snaked around her shoulders, and she squirmed. "That's why I visited you personally, to silence you if necessary. You were lucky that I listened to my grandson and agreed to save you for him."

"What about the eyewitness? Why didn't you silence her?"

"I made the mistake of leaving the woman to my helpers, and they let her get away. They thought it would be enough to torture her, then abandon her in a wilderness area. A storm was coming. They didn't expect her to survive."

The elderly man twisted her hair around his hand. He gave it a tug, watching her reaction. "Some women seem more determined to survive than others. I know that you're asking because you're hoping to be one of those who escape. This witness has gotten away from me twice."

She almost leapt up. He chuckled as she tried to cover her reaction.

"I told you," he said, "that I remember the targets who got away. Twenty years ago, there were two girls. The older one was as white as you. Her little sister was darker. The mother had agreed to hand them over to me, and I took them on a picnic into the local forest reserve. Back then, I took a more active role in the cultivation of talent. The girls called me Grandfather."

"What happened?" Destiny asked, locking her fingers together to keep her hands from clawing at his face. She pushed against the memory of a dark child who had adored her new grandfather. He mustn't know...

"The younger one fell asleep. The older girl screamed and woke her sister. Before I could silence her, she told the sister to run and hide. I didn't let the older girl go unpunished, but when I searched for the little one, she had disappeared."

He pressed her head against his chest and held her close. "I never expected that little girl to remember me."

Why was Destiny's heart still beating? How could she listen to this man? Her sister was alive!

"But she turned up twenty years later, during an important operation. I had three men working that target. They assured me the nosy teacher believed they were relatives. They brought me in to complete the transaction, but she'd called the police."

"You got away," Destiny said, trying to put some distance between them.

"I was almost caught. That made me angry. It was easy to find out where she lived. My men collected her. I wanted to be certain she wasn't an undercover operative, so I joined them in her interrogation.

"It should have been routine, but then she started screaming at me. She wanted to know what I did with her sister. There has only ever been one pair of sisters where one got away, so I knew who she was. And she knew me. That wouldn't have mattered, but she's an artist. Her sketches are good enough to convict me."

"Where is she now?"

"Witness Protection," Remo said with a smile, "but I'm not worried. The case won't make it to court. According to her official file, she's been a *very* problematic witness. The New South Wales agents are sick of her. They've had to move her several times because she keeps breaking cover. They've transferred her to Melbourne, along with all her evidence. Ricardo's about to eliminate her."

"If Rick's eliminating her, why are you here?"

Remo considered her. "You want this woman to succeed? Has she become a symbol of hope for you?" He released her suddenly and she fell sideways as he stood. When she pulled herself upright, he was approaching with two wine glasses. She accepted a glass of red wine. He studied her for a moment before he sat beside her again.

"You should choose your enemies more carefully," Remo told her. "Did you think you could keep Ricardo from finding out your little secret? You should have told him about the man who pursued you from Melbourne."

"What man?"

"The man who works for an ex-criminal called Romano. The man with connections to the Melbourne mob. The one who came after you because you threatened Romano's woman. Your enemy has taken an interest in my eyewitness. If he were to catch up with me, do you think he would agree to an exchange? Your life in exchange for mine?"

One final bluff. "I don't know what you're talking about."

"No?" he said. "I think I've changed my mind. You're such a beautiful liar."

Destiny brought her wine glass to her lips. What she would give for a mouthful of the mystical water from her dreams! She swallowed awkwardly, covering her mouth with her hand as she coughed.

"You claim not to know the name of my enemy. I'll whisper his name in your ear: Piper Maxwell."

Bad News Day

ॐ ☼ ॐ

Ephesians 3:16b WEB
May you be strengthened with power through His Spirit.

ॐ ☼ ॐ

Samson and his stepfather sat at the kitchen table, finishing their interrupted dinner. Grace was finally asleep – it had taken both of them to settle her. She grew more restless and confused with each passing day.

Samson's phone rang. He looked at the screen. "I don't want to answer this call. I thought sending Butch to live in Melbourne was the perfect solution. But that boy has turned Freddie's life upside down."

"What's he done now?" Old Jack asked.

"Remember I told you he put a teacher in hospital on Monday. They're still waiting to find out whether she's going to press charges. If Butch is charged, they'll throw him into the adult system, because of his temperament. Once he's there, we can't do anything to help him."

"Stop delaying and answer it."

With a groan, Samson accepted the call. "Okay, Freddie, tell me the latest bad news."

"It's not Freddie, an' it's not bad news," the teenager's voice shouted from the phone.

"Does Freddie know you're using his phone?" Samson asked.

Butch launched into his "good" news. "Yer not gonna believe who moved in next door, the teacher I was in trouble wiv. Everythinks ok."

"What do you mean, everything's okay?"

"Uncle Freddie likes her, I mean, *really* likes her. An' she needs friends, an' Evie and Romano gonna help 'er. Piper Maxwell too, except that's a secret. Don't tell Uncle Freddie I told yer, right? Evie says I'm expectin' too much, but this is it. Piper will beat the bad guys. Uncle Freddie's 'er knight-in-shinin' armour, then she rewards 'im by movin' in. You get t'organise Nikki's move to Melbourne. Problem solved."

"Is there anything else?" Samson asked, struggling with the jumbled details. Evie again, and Piper Maxwell too; but perhaps now he could stop worrying about Freddie's infatuation with a married woman.

"Oh, yeah. Piper Maxwell's mad about all the coincidences. He's talkin' conspiracy. He thinks Abby turnin' up next door's suspicious. And he's not happy that she an' Evie was talkin' about a river..."

"*Butch!*" Freddie's voice interrupted the teenager's story. "Who are you talking to?"

"I've gotta go," Butch yelled, and the call ended.

"Did that make any sense to you?" Old Jack asked Samson, who tried unsuccessfully to phone Freddie back.

Samson stared at the screen. "He must be dealing with Butch. I'll try again later."

"What was all that talk about coincidences?"

"I don't know, but if Evie Romano has anything to do with it, it must be important."

৪০ ✹ ୪

(Monday 6th November)

Samson stood in the open doorway, his phone hanging limply at his side. He had been on his way out to start the early morning chores.

"Who was on the phone at this hour in the morning?" Old Jack asked.

The two kelpies took advantage of the unexpected opportunity. They pushed their way past Samson, sniffing around the unfamiliar kitchen.

"Get out!" Old Jack shouted. They slunk out with their tails between their legs. He pushed the door shut and drew Samson to the table. "Was it Butch again?"

"No, it wasn't Butch," Samson said in a daze. "It was Evie Romano. Freddie's been arrested for murder."

"Murder!" Old Jack shouted. "That boy doesn't have it in him. Who's he supposed to have murdered?"

"Someone called Abigail."

Old Jack swore. "Isn't that the name of the teacher Butch said Freddie was sweet on?" He slapped his well-worn hat on the table and sank onto a chair. "What about Butch?"

"Evie said he's staying with her and Romano until our cousin Sigrid gets out of hospital."

"What cousin? There's nobody called Sigrid in our family."

"I know. Evie told me not to worry; Piper Maxwell's looking after everything. And if anyone from Child Protection contacts me, I'm to tell them that I haven't heard from Freddie."

"At least you won't have to lie. He hasn't told you anything."

"That's not what's bothering me," Samson admitted.

"No? What then?" his stepfather asked.

"Sigrid's not a common name. One of the people who helped me get Delilah out of Sydney had that name. That Sigrid worked for Piper Maxwell."

"Are you thinking whatever Delilah's involved in has something to do with Freddie's arrest? That's got to be an unlucky coincidence."

"But unlucky for who?" Samson muttered.

ဆုံ ☼ ဆ

Before lunch, Destiny walked with her girls on the lawn. Remo strode out of the house and headed in their direction. With a whisper, she sent the children running into the house by another entrance.

"You're happy this morning," she said.

"Ricardo has phoned and he's coming to collect me. This is my last day here. The witness is dead, and someone else has been framed for her murder."

She lifted her eyes above the tree line to the distant mountains. "Has Piper Maxwell stopped looking for you?"

"There's no evidence to identify me," Remo snarled, shaking her. "Piper Maxwell is chasing after ghosts. He'll never find me."

An Early Morning

ॐ ☼ ॐ

Genesis 28:15a WEB
I am with you, and will keep you, wherever you go,
and will bring you again into this land.

ॐ ☼ ॐ

Samson switched on the light, frowning at the time display on his phone. It was only nine-forty-five pm. He had been asleep for an hour. Why was he awake with a sense of urgency? The house lay still.

His mother was asleep in her bed. Samson paused in the doorway to Kim's room and prayed. She had disappeared after Butch and Nikki escaped from Brumby's Run. There had been no contact since the police interview about her missing children.

Samson moved to Butch's empty bedroom. This had been Freddie's room when his half-brother lived at *Mountain Rise*. Butch was still staying with Freddie's boss and his wife.

Samson leaned his head against the lintel as a feeling of dread loomed over him. His half-brother was still on remand, charged with his girlfriend's murder. Samson's efforts to contact Freddie had been unsuccessful. Old Jack wanted him to fly to Melbourne, but Piper Maxwell had told him to stay away.

Peace. Your brother walks in the light of My presence. He is safe. The hour of his deliverance is at hand.

I'm sorry, but I'm struggling to accept that. Please send me a sign to increase my faith.

Samson's chirping phone disrupted the nocturnal silence. He ran to his bedroom and looked at the unfamiliar number.

"Samson, it's me," Freddie said.

Samson rejoiced. "I'm so relieved to hear your voice, Freddie. But I'm having trouble hearing you. It sounds as if you're in a racing car."

"I'll put you on speakerphone," Freddie said. "We're in Romano's Maserati."

He listened to his brother's incredible tale, with the sports car's throaty roar in the background. They had denied Freddie contact with anyone outside the remand centre. Not even his lawyer had been able to visit him.

Then, without warning, they ejected Freddie onto the streets. He had neither money nor phone. Freddie said he'd walked through the darkened streets while a terrible storm raged around him.

Another coincidence? Samson had started praying, right when Freddie believed himself abandoned by God.

"I asked for a sign," Freddie said. "Romano swooshed to a stop beside me before I finished my prayer. Evie sent him to rescue me."

"How did Evie—"

Another voice spoke in the background.

Freddie laughed. "That's Romano. He said he didn't believe her and asked Piper Maxwell to confirm my release before he set out. Piper wasn't happy that Evie knew I was free before his agents received that information. We're going to pay Evie's prophecies more attention from now on."

"Evie sounds like a special woman."

"Amen!" Romano shouted.

"Amen," echoed Freddie. "I'll hang up now. Please tell Dad not to worry. God's got this."

After Freddie ended the call, Samson decided not to wake his stepfather with the news. He climbed back into bed, with his half-brother's final words echoing in his mind. *God's got this.*

ʚ ☼ ɞ

Brrp! Brrp! Brrp!

Destiny blinked awake to grab the handset. A surge of adrenalin made her jumpy. "Yes."

"Get up and prepare to receive new girls," Mrs Smith said. With a click, the housekeeper hung up.

"At this hour?" Destiny grumbled, already on her feet. She scrambled to dress.

There had been three other recent arrivals, each a separate daytime delivery. On the last occasion, one of the guards had accompanied Remo. The guard carried the unconscious teenager onto the dormitory floor. Destiny had been wary of the guard's wandering eye.

The key to the girls' bedrooms hung from a scarlet ribbon that Destiny wore around her neck. She slipped from her room, moving from door to door. When she finished locking the bedrooms, she hid the key inside her shirt. There was only time to switch on the light in a vacant room when she heard footsteps on the stairs.

There were three new girls. Destiny didn't hide her surprise. Remo smiled as he laid his burden on one of the single beds.

The two men who accompanied him did the same. Remo dismissed the other men. Destiny drew a cover over each girl while Remo watched from the doorway.

"Your presence here has increased the reputation of *Garden House*. Over the next few months, more experienced girls from other houses will supplement these new acquisitions."

Trouble Before Dawn

ಬ ☼ ಚಿ

*Isaiah 32:2 - A stream of water in a dry place,
and the shade of a large rock in a weary land.*

ಬ ☼ ಚಿ

Samson and his stepfather sat side by side under a starry sky. Two fire tankers were getting ready to leave *Mountain Rise*. Samson held his head in his hands. "I'm sorry."

"This isn't your fault." Old Jack reached out, patting his stepson on the shoulder before his hand dropped. "We both knew this was coming. You've not had enough sleep for months."

"I should have installed the lock on the kitchen door. I've had it sitting in the pantry since Christmas. If I'd done that, Mum wouldn't have been able to get into the kitchen."

"The damage is already done. Be thankful she was in the dining room when the alarms began screeching." Old Jack looked across to the ambulance. "Your mother's badly frightened but otherwise unhurt. She's forgotten most of it already. I'm sure they're only taking her to give us some respite."

Kurt Jensen walked towards them. The captain of the rural fire brigade came with him.

"Did Grace explain what she was trying to do?" Kurt asked.

"Cooking Christmas lunch," Samson groaned. "I'm still trying to work out how she fitted the roasting tray into the microwave."

The policeman considered that scenario. "You were incredibly lucky," he said. "If the fire trucks hadn't been coming back past Kidman Road from another fire, you'd have lost everything."

"Samson's God knew what He was doing," Old Jack said. He walked off into the darkness. The others stared after him.

"What did he mean by that?" Kurt asked.

"The Farm Stay people came before Christmas," Samson said. "They said we needed to upgrade the kitchen if we wanted their accreditation. Old Jack told me to get the work done, but I said we didn't have the money. He asked about all the times I've said God provided what we needed. He wanted to know if God was suddenly bankrupt. I didn't have an answer to that. It looks like I've lost this argument. We're definitely getting that new kitchen now."

He stared at the blackened hole where the kitchen window used to be. The headlights from both Kurt's police vehicle and Samson's LandCruiser provided enough illumination.

"Were you insured?" Kurt asked.

"The bank insisted, but I'm not sure it's enough. Even if I had the money, where would I find a tradesman?"

"This time I'm with Old Jack," Kurt said. "All you can see are the problems. You need some sleep. Once you've had time to think things through, you'll find a way forward."

"I hope you're right," Samson said. "It feels as if my prayers are going nowhere."

A cough interrupted Samson's confession.

"I'm not sure how comfortable I am," the brigade captain began, "as an answer to prayer. But my nephew's a qualified builder. He's coming to Meredith Crossing for an extended stay. He asked me if I knew anyone who needed some work done."

Samson laughed. It seemed as if a heavy weight fell from his shoulders.

৪৹ও

(4 am Tuesday 2nd January)

Tonight, the dream seemed determined to break Destiny. One by one, her scene-changing strategies failed. This did not bode well for the New Year.

Destiny stood in the familiar clearing. The storm raged. The wind in the trees increased her terror. Her failures disheartened her. The shadowy trees crept closer. She dropped to her knees and closed her eyes. Her whole body trembled with fear. Here came the familiar swoosh of the falling forest giant. Yet the expected crash never came.

Instead, she heard distant children laughing and calling to each other. Destiny raised her head. The sound came from the path that always tempted her into the undergrowth. She refused to go that way.

The voices faded. Her whole body ached with the effort to remain where she was. An uneasy silence settled over the land. She held her breath. Suddenly, a high-pitched scream filled the air. A chorus of cries issued from the forest, followed by a terrible wailing. With a groan, Destiny thrust the closest branch from her face and prepared her pursuit.

In an instant, her surroundings transformed. It was like she'd stepped through a portal into a better world. The dense forest glowered at her back, but its power had diminished. Thousands of stars shone overhead in the brightening sky. Destiny stood at the rocky verge of a river wild and powerful. The dancing waves shone with a glorious blue luminescence.

To her right, the river roared over a steep precipice. Iridescent spray from a massive waterfall shot high into the air. She pulled back from the edge. The river was too wide here, and she could see no way forward or back.

As she pondered this new scene, she heard her girls crying in the distance. They were on the other side of the river, waving and calling to her.

"Destiny, Destiny!"

"It's only a dream," she scolded herself. She stepped off the rocks into the river. The strong current caught her, sweeping her off her feet towards the waterfall. She tumbled down into the unknown. It seemed that she fell forever, before plunging deep into a broiling pool of warm, sweet water.

Coughing and spluttering, she reached for the surface. Once she had orientated herself, she searched for the girls. They were still standing at the top of the waterfall, screaming and calling to her. The girls wrapped their arms around each other and rushed the water's edge.

"No!" she screamed.

The force of their descent pulled them apart. They each sank deep below the waves. Destiny battled the turbulence until she reached the closest one. The swirling water threatened to sweep them further down the river. She pulled the first child from the waves and shoved her into the shallows. When the girl crawled up the sloping riverbank, Destiny turned back for another one.

All night, Destiny laboured to bring the girls safely to land. She pulled them from the waves. But each time she thought the rescue complete, they all appeared back in the water.

When morning came, the dream released her. Destiny threw herself out of bed and ran barefoot to the girls' rooms. Her fumbling hands battled with the ribboned key. Six sets of bunks crammed into the first room were fully occupied. The younger girls slept here. There were plenty of bedrooms, but they were more comfortable crowded together.

Destiny went through the shared bathroom into the next room. Here there were four sets of bunks. All but one bore a sleeping girl. During her inspection, one of them stirred, alarmed by the early visit.

"Go back to sleep," Destiny whispered, returning to the hall.

Destiny didn't check the remaining rooms. The empty bed was a reminder. Eight of the teenagers had left *Garden House* to attend a New Year's Day party. They wouldn't be back until later this afternoon.

With a sigh, Destiny returned to her room and showered. Half an hour later, the girls called to her. This early rising did not alarm her. They were often anxious when the older girls were absent.

It took all her patience to keep them occupied during the long day. Mid-afternoon, the group languished on the lawn, weaving flowers through their hair. She gave in to their demands to include her in their game. Their rough hands should keep her from falling asleep.

She was wrong. In an instant, the dream stole her away. She stood in the grassy meadow at the bottom of the waterfall. The girls from the garden slept at her feet. Each one wore a flowing white gown, with flowers in her hair.

She checked to see if any of them were missing.

A voice called to her from across the river. "Destiny." A group of girls stood on the other bank.

Destiny recognised them immediately: the eight girls who had gone to the party. She walked to the river's edge.

It was outspoken Ivy who called to her. "Don't cry for us."

The group walked towards the forest.

"Wait!" Destiny cried, but smaller hands prevented her from following. She tried to break herself free only to discover she was back in the garden.

"Destiny," one of the girls cried. "You fell asleep."

"We've been trying to wake you," Azalea added.

"Destiny, we have to go inside. Come on!"

Her head was heavy. The girls dragged Destiny to her feet. An unfamiliar van sat outside the main entrance. The three guards were talking to the occupants. One of the guards pointed in her direction. Destiny began to run, eager to get the girls inside.

As soon as she closed the door to the girls' sitting room, the opposite door opened. Mrs Smith appeared, hands clasped in front of her, her lips drawn into a terse line. "About time. I was about to send Mr Smith to get you. Take the girls upstairs and lock them in. The Master will phone you."

The girls ran towards the stairs. Destiny chased after them. The unease leftover from her dreams intensified.

With the girls secure in their rooms, Destiny sat on her bed. The phone rang. With a trembling hand, she picked up the receiver.

"There was a raid," Rick began without preamble. "I have dispatched extra personnel to *Garden House*. They won't be staying in the house, but I want you to be extra vigilant while they're on the property."

"Why?"

"Some of them expect extra privileges."

Destiny drew in a quick breath and immediately regretted it.

Rick laughed. "The safety of your girls will depend on your vigilance. I have lost too many assets today. I would be loath to lose anyone else."

"What do you mean, you've lost assets?"

"Piper Maxwell liberated fifteen girls, including all eight from *Garden House*. But his victory came at a cost. He sent in one of his agents, and she didn't survive."

CHAPTER 38
(Sunday 14th January)

Timely Warning

ॐ ✦ ॐ

James 4:14b WEB - For what is your life? For you are a vapour,
that appears for a little time, and then vanishes away.

ॐ ✦ ॐ

The door flew open, smashing into the wall. Destiny's unannounced arrival brought all but one Master to his feet. She crossed to the coffee table, upending his chessboard. Carved pieces flew in different directions. Rick rose, his temper matching her own.

Matteus and Quin stepped to her side, but neither dared to touch her. A steady stream of blood trickled from her nose onto the plush carpet. Remo watched from afar, while Cosima turned towards the dining table.

"What happened to you?" Quin asked.

Cosima approached with a serviette. She snatched it from him, dabbed her injuries, and then dropped her hand again.

Destiny never took her eyes from Rick. None of her passion tempered the ice in her voice. "If that man touches one of my girls again, I'm going to kill him."

She spun around, not waiting for a reply. Matteus stood between her and the door. He brought her back. Quin wrapped his arm around her and held the serviette to her face.

Rick remained standing. "Explain yourself."

Destiny pushed Quin's hand away. "I've told the one you call Barbie to stay away from the girls, but he said he's family and I'm just the hired help. I've tried keeping them indoors, but today they were too restless. That man cornered one of them. She screamed, and I confronted him. Barbie said if I wouldn't let him have one of the girls he'd make do with the 'nursery maid'. Before I could retaliate, he knocked me to the

223

ground." She sniffed, dabbing her nose again. Her chin lifted. "I haven't come snivelling for myself – I'm nobody's victim, but the girls thought I needed their help. I don't know what would have happened if Mr Smith hadn't chased him off with a shovel."

A heavy silence followed.

"I warned you there would be trouble if you allowed Constantino Barbara to stay here," Remo said.

Rick sat back in his chair. "Take him with you this afternoon and remind him of the rules. That should give our 'nursery maid' time to calm down before Barbie's return."

The grandfather hurried from the room.

Rick beckoned her closer and examined her injuries. "Go and clean yourself up. I'm disappointed to see you in such a state. I hope you've learned a valuable lesson."

"Yes," she muttered. "Mr Smith is getting me a shovel."

Matteus laughed.

She didn't linger, walking from the room. Behind her, Quin began a passionate protest at her treatment.

When she arrived on the dormitory wing, she unlocked one of the girl's rooms. The door refused to open. She called out. The girls replied by moving the furniture they had used to barricade themselves in. *Good.* She straightened her shoulders. It was time to have a serious talk to them about self-defence.

ಙ ✿ ಚ

(Tuesday 16th January)

Two days later, Destiny and her charges sat in their dining room. The door leading from their sitting room opened without warning. Destiny leapt to her feet. She snatched up the thick wooden pole from beside her chair and tested its weight.

"That's not the welcome I expected," Remo chuckled as he crossed the room. He carried a tiny child, no older than three. She had blue eyes and golden curls. "Take her."

Destiny dropped the shovel handle to accept the child.

The child sucked her thumb while clutching a ragged toy rabbit. One of those tiny hands grasped a fold of Destiny's shirt. "Are you my new Mummy?"

Destiny's face flushed. She glanced at Remo. He shook his head and frowned. The closest girls slipped from their chairs. They wrapped their arms around their Mistress.

"If Destiny's going to be her Mummy," Holly said. "She can be our Mummy too."

"I'm nobody's Mummy." Destiny tried unsuccessfully to pass the new child to one of the older girls. When this failed, she shrugged and sat in her designated place. "Does this one have a name?"

Remo smiled, and Destiny's breath caught in her throat.

"Buttercup – she's only going to be with us for a few days," Remo said. "Then she will transfer to her new Mummy and Daddy. There's no need for you to prepare her for life at *Garden House*."

She nodded.

He hesitated, scanning the room. "Be careful what she sees and hears while she's with us."

For the rest of the day, Destiny carried the child in her arms. Her shoulders ached, but her heart fared worse. Buttercup refused to allow the other girls to carry her. The toddler continued to call Destiny "Mummy".

This was not Destiny's greatest concern. When she took the girls out into the garden, Azalea hissed. Destiny's attacker was back. Barbie stood with his arms crossed, only two hundred metres away. He offered her a suggestive salute.

Destiny retreated with the girls into the house.

That night, the new child refused to sleep in her designated room. Buttercup whimpered and wailed. "Don't leave me, Mummy."

"I'll have to take her to my room," Destiny told the other girls. "I'm not allowed to sleep in here."

Finally, Buttercup fell asleep in the middle of Destiny's king-sized bed. As a concession to the child's fears, she left the bathroom light on and the door ajar. Destiny took a long, hot shower to ease her aching muscles. She dressed in a modest negligee with the ribboned key resting against her skin. Exhausted, she lay beside the child. At least this new duty had saved her from spending the night downstairs.

She tried to relax her tense muscles. If she was lucky, her physical exhaustion would reward her with a dreamless night. The child stirred, nestled against Destiny's body. The hours dragged on, neither slumber nor vision to distract her.

It must have been after three a.m. when the nightmare arrived. Bright sunshine flooded the clearing. Destiny became more alert. Pretty butterflies fluttered on the gentle breeze.

There on the ground, a small child sat on a tartan picnic rug. The dark, curly-haired child gazed at Destiny with large brown eyes. "Rufie, Rufie! Where have you been? I thought I'd lost you."

Before Destiny could respond, the child wrapped her arms around her. The dreamer sank to her knees, and the little one clung to her. Destiny sobbed and rocked the child. "Shhh, Bubba. Ruthie's here."

The pair lay down on the rug. She must have fallen asleep in the dream.

"Mummy!"

Destiny gasped. She sat up and tried to free herself from clinging arms. A different child had wrapped herself around her.

Buttercup was persistent. "Mummy, I'm scared. There's a monster in the hallway."

"There's noth—"

Wait. Were there heavy footsteps in the hallway? Was that a door handle rattling? Destiny reached for the house phone. An alarm should ring downstairs when she lifted the receiver. She rocked the whimpering child, hoping Mrs Smith was a light sleeper.

The footsteps in the hall became louder. Someone muttered outside her door. Destiny dropped the phone handset onto the bedside table. She leaned over the bed, attempting to conceal the child beneath the covers. Buttercup protested loudly.

"Shhh!"

The door burst open. The intruder stepped into her room. His silhouette revealed his identity – it was Barbie, the guard who had threatened her.

Buttercup shrieked. Destiny snatched up the child, yelling, "Get out! You're not allowed here."

"I've come for your key."

"You'll have to kill me first."

"That will bring me pleasure." Barbie lurched closer.

He trapped her in the narrow space between the wall and the bed. The whiskey on his breath made her nauseous. She leapt across the bed, holding Buttercup in her arms. The shrieking child slowed her escape. He caught her legs, dragging them both towards him. Across the hallway, the other girls banged on their locked doors. Their shouts intensified Buttercup's distress.

The child's screams enraged the drunken man. He heaved them both towards the wall. Destiny twisted her body, but could not protect Buttercup from the force of the impact. The child became silent mid-cry. Her limp body slipped from Destiny's arms.

"No!" Destiny threw herself at their attacker. "Murderer!"

She cursed Constantino Barbara, delivering targeted blows. In the cramped space, he could not evade her wicked hands.

But then the attacker changed the rules. Unable to defeat her with his hands, he produced a hidden weapon. The stabbing pain he delivered opened the door through which she made her escape...

℘ ✿ ℃

Destiny's eyelids fluttered. The white ceiling and the beeping hospital equipment confirmed her location. How did she get here?

"You're awake at last," a voice said. "Your grandfather hasn't left your side since you came back from theatre."

Her eyes lingered on the young woman's face.

Remo's figure appeared beside the nurse. He loomed over Destiny's bed, his arms reaching to embrace her. Her lips parted in protest, but his large frame concealed her alarm.

"Shh," he whispered, holding his fingers to her lips. "Don't talk. Your grandfather's here to take care of everything." His arms tightened, forcing the breath from her lungs. Tears escaped at the awakened pain. When he released her, she lay trembling with her eyes closed.

Several days passed in a drug-induced haze. Each time she awoke, one of the family sat in the chair beside her bed. Quin had been there at least once. He was responsible for the large bouquet of red roses beside her bed.

Even Rick had visited. Her hand slipped under the pillow. He had delivered a handmade card, signed by the girls. Rick said they were missing her terribly. He promised Destiny she would be home with them soon. She closed her eyes, fighting the tears.

Remo was her most frequent visitor. He kept silent vigil, refusing to answer her questions. The only exception was to tell her that Buttercup's body lay buried in the garden. Did she believe his testimony? Had Constantino Barbara forfeited his family privileges, and been dealt with?

The nurses said she was lucky. Not many victims survived such a frenzied knife attack. She endured their ministrations, pretending to be weaker than she was. They commended her for her bravery. Then early one morning, her patience bore fruit. Destiny awoke alone.

She threw off the covers and lowered her bare feet to the floor. Gasping from pain, she chastised herself. This might be her only chance. A rose-patterned robe lay over the chair beside her bed. It matched the brief negligee she was wearing. She moaned as she slipped her arms into the robe.

Destiny shuffled to the door and cracked it open. Outside her room, two men stood talking with a nurse. All three turned in her direction.

"Back into bed," the nurse said, directing Destiny with a firm hand. "I was just explaining to Mr Wolfe that you aren't well enough to leave." The woman efficiently tucked Destiny's legs under the sheets. "I'll get you something for the pain, and then I'm going to call the doctor."

One of the men remained in the room. He sat in the chair closest to her bed. "The Removalist was right," he chuckled.

Destiny's hands twitched.

"The old man told me to prepare for a fight. He said you'd fly at the first opportunity. I'm here to take you to a more secure cage."

"Who are you?"

"Clayton Wolfe."

The nurse re-entered the room. She approached the bed and prepared the injection. "This will make you sleepy."

After writing her notes, the nurse left the room.

"Did you wonder why nobody asked for your story?" Wolfe asked. "I'm here to legitimise your cover story. You're officially in Witness Protection now. No-one will ask any questions when you disappear. And there's no trail if anyone comes looking for you."

"Nobody's looking," she murmured. "Where—"

"A safe-house, with a private nurse. You'll stay there until you're well enough for the long journey home."

When she opened her eyes again, an unfamiliar city skyline greeted her.

ও ✿ ଓ

(Wednesday 24th January)

Destiny's secret stash of pills lay under the Gideon's Bible, in the drawer beside her bed. The patient pretended to sleep. She eavesdropped on the nurse. That woman spoke often to the guards outside the hotel room. One man watched during the day, and another during the night.

The nurse flirted with the guards. Destiny waited for the right opportunity. Finally, the nurse grew bold.

"Are you sure she's asleep?" the guard whispered as the nurse drew him into her separate bedroom.

The woman's answer faded behind the closed door. Destiny snatched the nurse's spare uniform from the bathroom. In the stairwell, she changed into the dress, before making her way downstairs. From there, she slipped out the side entrance and onto the streets.

Back in her familiar environment, Destiny executed her plans. It didn't take long to earn enough money to catch the next bus out of town.

Freedom was her new name.

Today's Guest

Matthew 12:37a WEB - For by your words you will be justified.

An unfamiliar car sat outside the homestead. Samson hurried into the house. His mother's voice came from the lounge room. He froze in the doorway. A small, dark stranger sat on the sofa. Her eyes were blue – the colour of the dream river. His knees weakened, and he almost stumbled. She was nothing like Delilah, and yet the sight of her set his heart racing.

Old Jack frowned. "Go and wash, boy. We have our first Farm Stay guest."

He shook himself. While changing his clothes, he analysed his reaction. Something about this woman screamed danger. Why was he certain she was no ordinary visitor? Could it be that he was still troubled by the financial risk this new enterprise had brought him?

It had been a struggle to get *Mountain Rise* registered for paying guests. The fire insurance money had covered the kitchen repairs. But Samson had to borrow against his army pension to modernise the servants' bathroom. God knew how desperately they needed the extra income, but something didn't feel right. Samson threw up a quick prayer.

> *Why are you so concerned?*
> I don't like surprises.
> *Is that all?*
> I'm still doubting this Farm Stay thing can solve anything.

Trust me. The solution to everything that troubles you is within reach.

Everything? That promise ricocheted in his mind. Samson mentally reviewed the preparations he needed to make. Why had he put off getting the bedrooms ready? The only guest room with the bed made up was Delilah's room.

When he returned to the lounge room, Grace had the large silver teapot in her hands. Steaming liquid poured into the best china cups. "There you are, Mr Davidson," Grace said. "I want to introduce you to our guest, Miss – Oh – I can't remember your name, dear."

The young woman laughed. "Sometimes, I have trouble remembering it myself." She stood, extending a slender hand to Samson. "Alixanda Jadaranata, and you're Samson. The people in Meredith Crossing speak highly of you. I feel as if I know you already." She smiled, looking up at him with those blue eyes. She was tiny, even shorter than his mother.

He shook her hand.

"I do hope we can be friends," she said.

Samson dropped her hand and retreated a safe distance.

Old Jack snorted in amusement. "Samson's a bit shy around women. He married our last *guest*, and then she ran away."

Alixanda's eyes wandered around the room. Framed photos crowded every space. "That sounds like an interesting story."

"There's no photo," Samson said.

A shadow passed over the beautiful stranger. The smile remained, but her blue eyes lost their sparkle. Again, she reminded him of the dream river, wild in its shifting moods.

Old Jack moved towards a bookcase. "Samson's wrong. Butch took photos. Kim had one printed for the family album. She insisted we have a record of Samson's disastrous wedding."

His stepfather returned with a photo album. Old Jack shuffled through the pages until he found the one he sought. He passed the album to Alixanda. Samson peered over her shoulder.

Samson's mouth dropped open. The camera had captured his doubt and fear. The memories of what followed endowed the bride's cruel smile with more sinister meaning. He reached for the album as the colour left his face. The visitor turned to stare at him.

Samson let go of the book. "I'll go and prepare your room."

"There's no need," Old Jack said, retrieving the album. "I've already put Alixanda's bags in Freddie's old room – the one Butch used when he was here."

"What?" Samson said. "She's supposed to stay in the old servants' quarters."

"I know," Old Jack said with a weary smile. "But Grace took our guest on a tour. The young woman took a special interest in Freddie's room – she liked the view."

"Freddie's not going to mind if she stays in his room," Grace added. "I've already explained to Alixanda that Freddie's away."

Samson looked at the woman. She avoided his eyes.

Old Jack watched them both. "Grace explained to Alixanda how easy it is to get lost in this large house, and that settled the matter."

"I'd better organise dinner," Samson muttered, fleeing from the room.

Half an hour later, Alixanda appeared in the kitchen. "I'm sorry that my curiosity upset you. You must have been deeply hurt when your wife left."

"Who do you work for?"

She sat calm and still at the table. Yet those piercing eyes followed his every move. "What makes you ask that?"

"I saw your face light up when Old Jack said there was a photo."

"I haven't found anyone else who had one," she confessed. "Your local policeman said you had Jezebel's identification papers. Could I get you to show them to me?"

"Kurt told you?"

"Don't be angry with your friend. I made him promise not to tell you. I'm deep undercover. There's more at stake than you realise."

"Like what?"

"Your wife helped rescue your nephew and niece?"

He nodded, his hands gripping the back of a kitchen chair.

"Butch told me. But he didn't know about her later disappearance. Kurt said you've read the file?"

He nodded again.

"I have evidence that ties her disappearance to a string of child abduction cases. This stretches back over two decades. Your missing wife is a vital witness, and I intend to find her."

"Why should I believe you?"

"I knew your wife when we were children. Her enemies are my enemies."

She imprisoned him with those blue eyes, and he knew. He collapsed onto a chair. "You work for Piper Maxwell."

Alixanda smiled – an eternity passed before she answered. His heart beat so loud, he almost missed her whispered words.

"I'm also a witness."

"What kind of witness?"

Her eyes flashed. "God has sent me with a message: justice is coming. Expect a summons to save Ruth."

The message delivered, Alixanda left him alone.

Zero Hour

৪০ ☼ ৪০

Isaiah 19:5 -
The river will dry up, and the riverbed will become a wasteland.

৪০ ☼ ৪০

Samson returned from moving a mob of cattle to new pasture. The old bull had taken umbrage with the change and become bogged in the dam.

Samson was in no mood for company, but three cars crowded the compound. He dropped onto the padded bench inside the door to remove his muddy boots. The builder had transformed the old alcove into a functional mudroom. It housed spare boots and coats for those tourists who wanted a genuine farm experience.

He grimaced. There had been few paying guests. Even Alixanda's visit only lasted two nights. That strange girl didn't step outside the main building.

> I'm sorry, God, but I don't understand what You're doing.

With a groan, Samson straightened and entered the house. There were voices in the dining room. Old Jack and Kurt's father, KJ, sat at the furthest end of the large table, a bottle of golden liquid before them. KJ half rose, but Old Jack constrained him.

"Leave him," Old Jack said in an ancient voice, returning to his drink. KJ frowned. He pointed towards the hall doorway.

With a sense of dread, Samson hurried towards other voices coming from his mother's bedroom.

"Is that you, Samson?" Mrs Mac peered out at him, wiping her tears.

Mrs J rushed him with an awkward hug. The two women stepped into the hall to make space for him in his mother's room. Tim Campbell blocked Samson's view of the bed. The doctor looked up from an official-looking document.

"I'm sorry, Samson," Tim said. "We hoped your mother would last long enough for you to get home, but she died fifteen minutes ago."

Samson couldn't remember later what he said to the doctor, or what filled his mind as he sat beside his mother's bed. Her face was white, her hands soft and still. He left the room, and became lost in the hallway. Mrs Mac and Mrs J rescued him, taking him to join the men in the dining room.

The older men ignored Samson. Behind him, the women worked in the kitchen. Samson held something in his hands – a crystal tumbler. He drained the contents in one smooth motion. The liquid fire awakened other memories. His stepfather nudged the bottle towards him. Samson stared at the reflected light shining from within the bottle. It promised a false comfort. His hand uncurled from the glass and he pushed the bottle away.

"Go and phone your brother," Old Jack said. "Tell him to come home for the funeral."

Rising to his feet took effort. He headed to the tower where he could survey *Mountain Rise* as he selected Freddie's number. It was only four-thirty pm. His half-brother would be at work.

Freddie answered with a question. "What's happened?"

The words flowed out of Samson as if he was talking about someone else's mother. It had been ten years since Freddie had been home, yet his half-brother took the news as Samson expected. They both knew their beloved mother had slipped away from them long ago.

"Your father wants you to come home," Samson said.

"Of course. I'll go and tell Romano. Then I'll break the news to Butch and Nikki. I saw them go past about ten minutes ago, on their way home from school. This news will upset them. Nikki's been asking when she could return for a visit, but something always seemed to come up."

"It will help Old Jack to see his grandchildren. We don't know where Kim is, so this is going to be difficult. If you could get a few weeks off, that would help."

"I'm sure I can manage that," Freddie said, and then he hesitated. "Samson, I'll be bringing someone else with me."

"Someone?"

"I'm getting married. I've been meaning to phone you to let you know, but everything's complicated."

Samson closed his eyes, crouching on the deck of the tower. He rubbed his beard. "What kind of complicated?"

"You already know Alixanda. She came to visit you."

"Alixanda?" Samson echoed. He was about to ask more, but there was a burst of conversation on Freddie's end.

"Hang on. Butch just rushed in with Nikki. They're in a state." Samson understood fragments of the shouted conversation. He stopped breathing when Nikki screamed Delilah's name.

"What was that about Delilah?" Samson asked when Freddie's voice returned.

"I have to go," Freddie said. "I'll phone you when I know more. Butch says Delilah – we know her here as Jezebel – Delilah attacked Evie and Alixanda. Evie's going to hospital in an ambulance."

Freddie ended the call. Samson stared at the silent phone. He wept, his whole body shaking. He curled into a ball and fell into an exhausted sleep.

It was seven-thirty that same evening when Samson awoke, stiff and sore. After some initial confusion, he remembered why he was there. The emotional storm broke in him again. When he regained control, he stumbled downstairs. He showered, dressed in clean clothes, and returned to the others.

"There you are," Mrs Mac said, leading him to the dining room. "Sit down and eat." She placed a large bowl of soup before him.

Samson wasn't hungry but picked up his spoon. Eating might distract him from the sadness seated at the other end of the table.

When the bowl was almost empty, Mrs Mac hovered with a refill. His phone chirped.

"It's Freddie," Samson said. A strange background noise made it difficult for Samson to hear. He clarified the information twice.

"I have to go outside," Samson told his stepfather. "Freddie's managed to catch a ride in a helicopter. They expect to arrive in a couple of hours. They're going to need a place to land. I've got portable floodlights and generators to organise."

"Where are they going to land?" Old Jack asked. "You made sure there were no open spaces for a chopper to land near the homestead."

"The paddock behind the stockmen's huts will be easy to clear. I put smaller boulders there. It won't take long using the tractor. Once the floodlights are set up, I'll do the clearance work."

"I'll get the bedrooms ready," Mrs J said. "Your father said Butch and Nikki would be coming with your brother."

"Alixanda's coming too," Samson said. He looked at Old Jack. "You're not surprised. Did you already know she and Freddie were a couple?"

"She told me before she left."

"Why didn't you tell me? Did you know they're getting married?"

"I didn't know that," Old Jack said, taking another gulp from his glass. "Alixanda asked me not to tell you. She said you were already upset because she was investigating your wife. She didn't want to make the situation any harder for you."

"My *wife* turned up in Melbourne this afternoon." Samson waited for his stepfather to respond.

They stared at each other along the table.

Old Jack drained his glass. "Trouble?"

Samson nodded.

"Go and do what you have to do," Old Jack said, reaching for the bottle. "Don't worry about me. When this bottle's empty, I won't open another."

ಬಂ ✿ ಳಿ

(Friday 27th April)

The physical activity pushed Samson through his strange lethargy. After removing the obstructing boulders, he adjusted the placement for the floodlights. Then he drove the tractor back to the shed to collect his LandCruiser. After checking the generators, he assessed the floodlight positions a final time.

He slumped on the ground, his mind drifting.

The helicopter's whoop-whoop reached him before the lights appeared over the treetops. He shielded his eyes from the debris whipped up by the rotor blades. The helicopter bobbed up and down until the machine settled on the ground. It was not the small commuter helicopter he had been expecting. The whirling blades slowed but did not stop, triggering other memories from military campaigns. Four figures disembarked, crouching low and hurrying towards him. Samson hugged Freddie and reached for Alixanda's suitcase.

"Piper wants to talk to you," Freddie said, pointing towards the helicopter.

Samson hesitated. He fished his keys from his pocket and handed them to Freddie. "Take the LandCruiser. When I've finished here, I'll walk home."

"Are you sure?" Freddie asked, glancing behind him towards the helicopter. Alixanda placed her hand on her fiancé's shoulder. An unspoken message passed between them. Her touch erased the tension Samson read in his half-brother's stance.

Samson forced a smile. "Positive. Don't let Butch talk you into letting him drive my Cruiser."

Samson braved the turbulent air. Memories from other missions informed his cautious approach. His preparation for the coming battle would have to be sufficient.

Piper leaned out of the cabin, still strapped in the pilot's seat.

"Thank you for bringing my family here," Samson said.

"I'm not here for them. Get in."

An armed man crouched in the rear compartment. He also wore an aviator's helmet. Samson climbed aboard, securing the door behind him. The manoeuvre was still familiar despite the passing years. This machine was large enough to carry at least a dozen passengers with room to spare. The man nudged him with the rifle towards the closest seat. Dismissing the danger, Samson dropped into a different row. His companion grinned, and sat beside him.

The helicopter lifted off the ground before either of them were in their harnesses. The weapon rested within easy reach of the other man. A pair of headphones appeared in Samson's hands.

"I'm Oliver. You have questions – Piper's not listening. He's on a different channel, waiting for news from Melbourne."

"What's going on?"

"Freddie told you about the attack this afternoon? Evie's eight months' pregnant with twins. There have been complications with the delivery."

Samson's head drooped. "Is Evie going to be okay?"

"That's the news Piper's waiting for. If the outcome is bad, Piper's the first in a long line of people who'll want revenge."

Samson blocked out his immediate surroundings, praying for Evie Romano and her babies. How many more lives would be destroyed by Delilah – or Jezebel – or whatever her name was now?

He blinked. "Piper knows where my wife is?"

"Jezebel got away while everyone was dealing with Evie's emergency. But Piper put out an all-ports alert. She made it easy for us. She collapsed in Sydney, after she disembarked from a Melbourne flight. Piper's *friends* redirected the ambulance to take her to one of the city's private hospitals."

Samson stared into the darkness. "We're going to Sydney?" Distant lights confirmed his guess. "Why did Piper come for me?"

"Alixanda made him promise not to talk to Jezebel without you."

"Alixanda? What does this have to do with her?"

Oliver's easy smile disappeared. He glanced towards Piper and back. "You don't know?"

"Don't know what?"

"Alixanda has her reasons."

"Can't you give me more information?" Samson asked.

"All I can tell you is Piper was furious. Alixanda endangered her life when she stood up to him."

"Why isn't Alixanda here then?"

"Jezebel doesn't know who Alixanda is. It's been twenty years—" Oliver fell silent, frowning towards Piper.

The unanswered question acted as a barrier between them. Samson stared into the night, pondering the cryptic clue. Alixanda couldn't be old enough to have known Delilah-Jezebel two decades ago. She must have been a baby...

Something Delilah had told him gave him the answer. Only the harness kept him in his seat. "Alixanda's her sister! Why didn't she tell me? Wait – is that why she's with Freddie? Did she use Freddie to get to me?"

"Alixanda was in love with Freddie before—"

"Before what?"

Oliver shrugged. "Before she was Alixanda."

Samson stared at him. "Alixanda's not her real name? Does Freddie know?"

"They don't have any secrets."

Samson snorted. "How can anyone be sure with these sisters?"

"This isn't ancient history. Alixanda only told Piper on Tuesday. Your brother was there. Not even Piper could do anything with that information in two days. Then, suddenly, your wife's back, and Evie's in jeopardy again. If Piper had been present when this attack occurred, your wife would be dead. Maybe that's why he came to get you. Evie continues to tell everyone you're the only one who can save Jezebel."

Why would Evie say that? Piper had an obvious height and weight advantage.

Samson pushed that question aside. "There's something else I don't understand. Delilah – Jezebel – ran away from Melbourne and said she wasn't going back. She claimed her involvement with Evie's kidnapping was a one-off mistake. Why did she try again?"

"She didn't. This time Jezebel was after your nephew, and Evie got in the way. That kid's story doesn't make sense. Do you know anything about a suitcase filled with money? He said you told him to hide it and she wants it back."

Samson saw red, swearing long and loud. When he regained his composure, he apologised before falling into a silent reverie. Oliver left him to his thoughts for ten minutes before tapping his arm.

"Piper's said worse, and he never apologises. I've never met your wife, but she must be something special to elicit such an outburst."

Samson flinched.

Oliver continued. "Evie's abduction had a big impact on Piper, but he won't admit his frustration. Both Evie and her husband Romano have told him to let the matter go. His temper hasn't improved. Not even when Alixanda's personal connection unlocked his investigation."

"How *did* Alixanda work it out?"

Oliver threw a furtive look forward. He leaned closer to Samson. "Alixanda said you're like Evie. Do you believe God is in control of everything? And God moves people around, to get them in the right place so He can accomplish His plan?"

Samson shot a silent prayer heavenward.

"What Piper dismisses as chance and coincidence," Oliver said, "Evie calls 'signs and wonders'. She says God answers her prayers. He's using all of us to get the outcome He wants. That makes Piper very angry. He doesn't like the idea that someone else is in control."

"He's going to be angry for a long time then. The more you tell me, the stronger my agreement with Evie. God is at work here. What did Alixanda discover that unlocked everything?"

"Your local policeman showed her the background file he compiled on Jezebel. That was the key. Until then, Piper had no background information on Evie's enemy. It was too big a coincidence for two sets of sisters to endure the same childhood trauma."

The distant city lights grew brighter. Piper contacted air traffic control before heading towards a particular tower. The helicopter descended to the painted circle-H on a roof designated with a red cross.

"What happens when we get into the hospital?" Samson asked.

"You tell anyone who asks that you're her husband, grab her and get out again."

"Why the urgency?"

"She's been admitted under a different name. When the evening staff came on, two people recognised her from an earlier stay. Last time, she disappeared without the doctor's approval. Our source said that might happen again."

Night Escape

1 Peter 1:8 - Though you have not seen Him, you love Him.

Samson followed Piper across the hospital rooftop. Oliver remained with the helicopter, moving into the cockpit.

There was no welcoming committee to unlock the heavy door. This was no impediment to Piper. He tapped buttons on the security panel and gained immediate access. The elevator doors also opened at the press of a button.

The pair descended to the twelfth floor. The doors swished open. Before they could step out, a man pushed them back. Samson recognised him. This *Maximum Security* agent had helped him get Delilah away from Sydney.

Nelson leaned on the button that kept the elevator in place. "You're ten minutes too late. Clayton Wolfe's already here, and he knows you're coming."

Piper clenched his fists.

Nelson continued. "Wolfe's claiming you authorised his involvement. We're fortunate that he encountered Macy first. The other nurse would have blown my cover. Wolfe doesn't know I'm here. Macy didn't make it easy for him. She asked him for his credentials to prove he worked for Witness Protection. Unfortunately, the other nurse arrived and sent Macy on an errand. She gave him the room number, and went to phone the duty doctor to authorise Jezebel's release."

Nelson stepped into the corridor and pointed to the left.

"Where is Wolfe now?" Piper asked.

Nelson turned in the opposite direction, waving for them to follow him. "Room twelve-forty-three. Another man has joined him."

The lights were dim, and the visible corridor empty. There was a "You Are Here" map on the opposite wall. Piper signalled for Nelson to keep the elevator ready and waved Samson forward. They covered the distance to the next corridor, making minimal noise. A woman's scream broke the silence. Both men abandoned their caution, racing around the corner.

A stranger stood in the hallway, guarding an open door. "Clayton! Company!"

The sentry stepped into their path, pulling the door closed as he came. Piper dropped him with a sliding tackle, while Samson rushed into the room. A man leaned over the woman strapped on the bed. This must be Wolfe. He had one hand over the woman's mouth, and the other wielded a hypodermic syringe. The desperate woman sank her teeth into her attacker's hand.

"Stop!"

Wolfe looked at Samson. He raised his fist, and the needle plunged into her chest.

Samson was beside the bed in a heartbeat. He seized her assailant, raising him off the floor. In a smooth action, he disabled her enemy and launched him across the room. Wolfe crashed into the further wall.

Delilah screamed and bucked against the restraints. Samson pulled the needle from her flesh and dropped the syringe to the floor. Her screams stopped abruptly. Samson struggled with the thick straps that kept her body imprisoned on the bed.

Piper appeared beside him with a blade in his hand. With the final straps severed, Samson threw her over his shoulder, heading for the door. He glanced behind him, memorising the position of the crumpled body across the room. Piper hurried him along the corridor towards the elevator.

"What's going on?" a voice cried from one of the darkened rooms. The door was ajar.

Piper shouted, "We're with Security. Stay in your room!" The door slammed.

"Where are you taking that patient?" an angry nurse demanded.

Samson ignored her, pressing on towards the elevator. Nelson appeared in the corridor. He held up an identification badge. Her whole temperament changed.

"There's been an attack," Nelson said. "It's no longer safe for this patient here."

"But her grandfather and her fiancé are on their way," the nurse said. "What am I to tell them?"

Samson thumped the elevator button.

"This man is her husband," Piper said, retrieving something from his pocket. "When those imposters arrive, give them this." He pressed a sculpted object into her hand.

She puzzled over the chess piece. "A black queen? Is there any other message?"

Piper waved Samson into the elevator. "They won't need an explanation."

80 ✪ 03

Ruth.

Who's there? I've had many names, but I no longer answer to that one.

I, too, have many names. You knew Me when you were a child, and I have been waiting for you to remember Me.

Jesus? Why did You abandon me?

My child, I never left you. In your anger, you closed your ears to My guidance. At every opportunity, you hardened your heart and chose a darker path. I offered you deliverance, but you would not heed My voice.

I didn't know.

She fled from that voice into the familiar dream. The forest closed around her. She continued running until she had no strength. Weeping, she threw herself under a massive tree. When there were no more tears, she raised her head.

"Destroy me!" she screamed. "I'm not running anymore."

The threatening shadows pressed closer, the wind shrieked, and the storm raged. Then gentle laughter filled the air. The darkness vanished in a blinding flash.

Your enemy has deceived you, Child of Mine. Will you turn back to Me and receive My forgiveness?

৪৩ ✿ ૪૩

Samson and Piper claimed opposite corners of the elevator. The rescuer manoeuvred the unconscious woman into his arms, and faced into the corner so his body could shield her. Adrenalin still surged through him. He pushed aside the memory of the broken enemy he'd left downstairs. He watched Piper's reflection in the shiny metal wall, alert for the first sign of malice.

Piper ignored him. He talked on his phone as they ascended towards the roof.

Samson caught fragments of conversation. The first call had been to Oliver. When they burst onto the roof, the rotor blades were already spinning. The helicopter lifted into the air, the door open. Samson leapt for the rear compartment, rolling onto his back to protect the woman. Piper followed on his heels, and slammed the door.

Piper remained standing, clutching one of the seats. Samson checked her pulse – faint and irregular. He tried to pray, but his thoughts were stuck. He replayed, again and again, the sequence that ended with her attacker striking the wall.

The helicopter lurched sideways. Samson looked back. Men ran onto the roof. He saw flashes of light coming from their outstretched hands. Their pursuers were trying to shoot down the helicopter. Oliver skilfully evaded them. While the building dropped from view, Samson secured her into a harness. He busied himself with his own straps, trying to ignore Piper's presence.

A set of headphones landed in his lap. Piper wore his aviator helmet. "She's still alive?"

"Yes. What happens now?"

"We refuel and return to *Mountain Rise*. Alixanda's organised a doctor to meet us there."

"Who were those men?"

"Ask a different question."

Samson considered his options. "Has there been any news about Evie?"

Piper did not answer immediately. When he eventually spoke, the danger had passed. "Mother and babies are resting."

Samson turned his head away and covered his mike. "Thank You, God."

Piper gripped his shoulder. "Tell your God to make sure it stays that way. And He'd better keep Jezebel alive too. I need her information. All this will be for nothing if she dies before she tells me what she knows."

The angry man climbed forward to sit in the co-pilot's seat.

Samson allowed a spark of hope to push back his doubt and fear. His wife was alive. He was bringing her home.

Home?

He didn't even know if Piper would allow her to live. What a fool he was! How could he love this monster? And what would Samson do if – no, when – she ran away again?

There was nothing to tie him to the land now his mother was gone...

That thought stabbed him deeper than the loss of his mother. Wrapping his arms around Delilah, Samson fell into a troubled sleep.

ও☼ন্ঠ

Samson woke briefly when Oliver moved into the rear compartment. The helicopter had refuelled. Piper sat in the pilot position. Oliver strapped himself into a passenger seat.

The next time Samson awoke, Oliver pointed out the window. "You're home. Ready yourself for the landing."

This landing would be hazardous. There was nobody on the ground with the expertise to organise everything. The generators must have run out of fuel. The only light came from his LandCruiser's headlights. Alixanda and Freddie waited beside his vehicle.

Piper's piloting skills were impressive.

They put the unconscious passenger in the tray of the LandCruiser. When Tim Campbell arrived, it only took a few minutes to set up an IV drip. He passed his keys to Samson.

"I'll ride with her. Bring my car."

Samson shook his head, tossing the keys to Piper. "He can drive your car, and Freddie can drive mine. I'm riding with you."

The small convoy crawled along the track. As soon as they arrived in the compound, Samson gathered her into his arms. Tim walked beside him, carrying the IV bag.

The doctor held the door open, and Samson went into the house. He didn't hesitate, going directly to his bedroom under the tower. It was only when he pushed open his door that he jerked to a stop. "Who did this to my room?"

He placed the unconscious woman on the unfamiliar double bed.

"You're a married man," his stepfather's voice growled from the doorway. "It's time you behaved like one."

Echoes from a long-ago conversation whispered to Samson. He stared at his stepfather.

"God has given you this woman for your wife," Old Jack said. "She's your responsibility." Without another word, the older man walked away.

𝕏✲𝕏

Samson followed Tim out of the bedroom, determined to guard the closed door.

"What's your diagnosis?" Piper demanded of the doctor.

"The injected sedative has started to wear off, but her body is fighting a chronic addiction," Tim began. "Detox is going to take time. With the right care, she should make an acceptable physical recovery."

"When can I talk to her?" Piper demanded.

"Not for a day or two," Tim said. "She's confused and upset. She needs complete rest."

Piper glared at Tim. "Are you sure this isn't another deception?"

Tim shook his head. "Samson's convinced her condition is genuine. He asked her about Melbourne, and she didn't react. She didn't know who he was, and she can't remember her name."

"I want to see her for myself."

"It's too early to push her for information. It looks as if she's been living on the streets for some time."

Tim held up his fingers to count off his concerns. "There's the usual malnourishment that accompanies that lifestyle." He ticked off another finger. "Her drug-taking has progressed since she was last here. The track marks on her arms are new, and I'd say she has an expensive habit. The last time I examined her, I classified her as a perpetrator, but recently she's been a frequent victim."

"Anything else?"

"About three months ago, she survived a vicious knife attack. The wounds were professionally treated, which should be traceable."

"We've already found those records," Piper informed him. "The staff at the Sydney hospital recognised her. The hospital records said she went into Witness Protection."

"Then how did she end up on the streets?" Tim asked.

"Not everyone in Witness Protection is safe," Piper replied. "Alixanda can testify to that."

Alixanda stepped forward.

Piper glanced at her. "Your enemy Wolfe again. Cross him off your list. I've had confirmation from Nelson. Samson killed him."

All eyes flew to Samson, who shuffled his feet.

"There will be an inquiry," Piper told him, "but you won't be testifying. I filed an incident report, with a reference number attached to your permanent record. There are no charges against your name. This was an authorised operation. As one of my registered operatives, your actions come under my warrant."

"When did you regis—"

"Not now."

Alixanda stepped between them. Her blue eyes flashed as she rested her hand on Samson's arm. "Don't feel sorry for that man. He was part of the plot that killed my friend. And he framed Freddie for murder. Anyone under his *protection* was in jeopardy."

"Alixanda knows firsthand how that man abused his position," Piper said. "Wolfe is another enemy these sisters have shared."

"There's nothing more I can do," Tim said, retrieving his medical bag. "Time, good care, and lots of prayer are my prescriptions for what ails her."

"I'll walk you out," Piper said, taking the doctor's arm. He spoke earnestly to him as they departed.

"Don't worry," Alixanda whispered to Samson. "You heard the doctor give his prescriptions. You're an expert carer. God is good. He knows what He's doing. Everything you've endured so far is the perfect preparation for what you face now."

Samson forced a weak smile. He slipped into the bedroom to keep solitary vigil. He fell asleep kneeling at her bedside.

৪০☼ঙঃ

When the sleeper opened her eyes, a man lay with his head resting near her elbow. He knelt beside her bed. She studied his weathered features. A fragment of memory awoke. His name was Samson. He wore a wedding band—

Her mind recoiled from the countless memories.

Jezebel's lustful violence and corruption.

Delilah's greedy pride and deception.

Destiny's self-centred ambition and duplicity. She had abandoned those girls to their fate without a second thought.

Waves of horror and regret brought a flood of tears. Her sobs woke Samson, and he reached for her hand.

"Don't touch me!" she cried, rolling away to face the window. "I'm cursed! I corrupt anyone who has anything to do with me. Leave me alone to die."

The room was quiet and still. She must have imagined he was there.

Then he spoke. "God has a message for you, Ruth. He says He'll never leave you, nor forsake you. His love is everlasting. He wants you to come to Him for forgiveness."

"I'm not worthy of forgiveness."

"God loves you anyway," Samson said. "He has called you, and He's named you as one of His own. Won't you come and receive His love?"

"I don't want His love. Go away. Stop tormenting me. Can't you see I don't want you here?"

His next words came in broken gasps. "God loves you – I love you."

"I don't love you," she shouted, refusing to turn and witness his brokenness. "I never will. Take your love and your God. Get out." She added every blasphemy, swear word and curse she could think of.

His footsteps moved away. A door opened and closed.

Alone – again.

Her heart danced within her chest, regret and relief in equal measure swamping her as the world faded.

ℬ ☼ ℭ

Absolute darkness stretched in every direction. She hit out with her hand and encountered – nothing. She kicked her feet and thrashed about. Suspended in a void, there was nothing below, above, or beside her.

She opened her mouth and screamed. No sound came from her lips, and even worse, the darkness made no response. The silent nothingness went on and on, without respite. Every attempt to take command of her situation brought her no reprieve.

She had only her thoughts for company: Expect no comfort here. Welcome to Hell. You're finally where you belong.

Ruth.

That voice echoed in the void. It seemed to be everywhere, even inside her head. The darkness within and without writhed in reply. Shock waves of pain smashed her last defences.

Ruth.

Lightning broke the darkness, hot and cold flashes of memory. She threw her hands over her head and curled up small.

Ruth.

That voice would not go away. Finally, she answered. "I'm here."

Come.

Cruel mockery – there's nowhere to go, and no way to get there.

Somehow, she stumbled to her feet and took a step. In a blinding explosion, the darkness evaporated. She shielded her eyes from the dazzling light. The whole universe was on fire. She burned with it.

Ruth. Come!

Interrogation Hour

ಹಿ ✡ ಲ

John 8:32 WEB - You will know the truth,
and the truth will make you free.

ಹಿ ✡ ಲ

The practised deceiver lay still.

The beautiful girl seated beside her bed spoke first. "We know you're awake. There's no point pretending otherwise."

The pretender squinted at this stranger. "You were in Melbourne."

"Yes. My name is Alixanda." The girl pointed to the gathered witnesses. "These people know you as Jezebel or Delilah. It's time to account for your actions."

"Are you my defence lawyer?"

The foolish girl smiled, offering an open invitation with those strange blue eyes. She could have passed as a younger teen, but something about her shouted age and experience. "If it makes you more comfortable, I'll act as your defender."

"Do you want me to answer as Jezebel or Delilah?"

"Neither. To me, your only name is Ruth."

The schemer's breath caught in her throat. Somewhere deep within, the dream river awoke and called to her. She exhaled slowly. Taking on that name didn't mean she would surrender.

With feigned disinterest, Ruth scanned the room. She identified Samson, and his friend, Senior Sergeant Kurt Jensen. She also knew the doctor, Tim Campbell. Old Jack leaned against the wall near the door. When her eyes rested on Piper Maxwell, she pulled herself upright and smirked.

Here was a man who exuded power and authority. She had never met Piper Maxwell, but she had seen him from afar. He would be her prosecutor, judge and executioner, all in one handsome package. "Finally, someone of interest."

Piper didn't respond. Alixanda adjusted the pillows behind the pretender and straightened the bedcovers. The girl reached for a large black folder of the kind artists carried. She laid an A3 monochrome sketch on Ruth's lap.

A small spark of curiosity flared into life. "What's this?"

Alixanda smiled. "I'm going to show you some people of interest. Your task is to confirm or deny that you know them, and to provide us with names."

With a twisted smile, Ruth picked up the drawing. It was a composite image. The artist had captured the man, both as he had been two decades ago, and as he was now.

"I must warn you," Alixanda said, "we already know you have connections with this man. So, don't try to deny that you know him."

Ruth nodded, pleased with the girl's bold certainty – a worthy opponent. She kept her voice flat. "Remo. Some people call him the Removalist. If he turns up at your door, you're about to disappear. I've known him for decades. He last visited me a few months ago, while I was a patient in a Sydney hospital." She folded her hands. "He likes me to call him Grandfather, but his kisses are an invitation to a living hell." She picked up the image and addressed Piper. "Grandfather cultivated the evil in me, but I was a willing apprentice."

Alixanda placed a second drawing on the bed.

"You drew these?" the confessor asked, studying the girl for confirmation. "You have a special gift. These men must have been *brutal* with you if you can portray them like this."

The girl met her accusation with a disturbing silence. Those blue eyes darkened like a coming storm. Ruth felt as if she might drown in their depths.

"We're not here for Alixanda's story," Piper snapped. "Look at the picture and tell us what you know."

Ruth returned her attention to the drawing. "This is Cosima, but you already know that. Butch or Nikki would have told you. The Removalist is his grandfather."

Piper stiffened.

She lectured him, secure in her triumph. "The family resemblance is obvious when you *know* what to look for. Cosima continues the family tradition of separating children from their gullible parents."

Her finger pointed to the second man. "This man I've never met – he looks like another relative. But this one—" Her fingers twitched. "This one is a murderer."

"Does this murderer have a name?"

"Barbie – Constantino Barbara."

Alixanda leaned closer. "Whom did he murder?"

"I'm here to confirm or deny what you think you know. Nobody said I was to give you anything else."

Alixanda's eyes narrowed. Sifting through the remaining sketches, the artist made a selection. The girl placed three drawings, one after another on the bed.

The murderer and his unknown companion dressed in dark suits, menacing and demanding.

The same men depicted in a crowd of familiar others.

The murderer with a group of terrified girls – sufficient detail to explain their plight.

"Enough! I'll tell you." A solitary tear escaped. "He killed Buttercup."

A heavy stillness dropped into the room.

Ruth's hands scrambled for the hem of her shirt. She revealed the scars on her torso. "I don't know Buttercup's real name, but I tried to protect her. I should be dead too, but Grandfather took me to hospital. He promised me *this* one—" She snatched the offensive drawing and shredded it. "Grandfather promised me this monster would never hurt anyone again."

A shower of paper flew into the air.

"I'm a fool! He's still alive! I should have gone back and killed him myself."

Her emotional outburst breached a floodgate. Cursing her loss of control, Ruth covered her tear-stained face with the bedsheet. Two pairs of arms enveloped her. Alixanda whispered on her right, while Samson offered her comfort from the other side.

Ruth threw off the sheet and pummelled both intruders. The girl was a quick learner, but Samson wrestled with Ruth until he had her arms under control. She raged at his unexpected dominance.

"You're too late," she shrieked. "Do you know what I did? I ran away – I thought only of myself, and I left my girls – *my girls* – I left them with that monster. I should have gone back..."

Samson didn't move. Tears streamed down Ruth's face. She couldn't look at him.

"Your weeping gives me hope," he whispered, and he kissed her temple. His arms released her, and then he was gone from beside her.

Ruth's heart skipped a beat. "I'm not weeping. These are crocodile tears." She turned to Alixanda, who handed her a box of tissues.

"When did Buttercup die?" Alixanda asked.

"Mid-January."

"You might be worrying about nothing. Nobody has seen this man since January."

"But these sketches— Wait! A party was raided in January—" Ruth glared at Piper. "You were responsible." She retrieved the surviving drawings. "This man came to *Garden House* after the raid. Are these scenes from that party? Let me see those girls again!"

Alixanda deferred to Piper, who nodded. The girl brought out another group of sketches. Ruth snatched these new drawings from her.

"Do you recognise any of these girls?" Alixanda asked.

Ruth studied them. The first drawing was a whole group image. Twenty chairs across a stage, with clusters of girls in the background. The other sketches were close-up portraits, making it easier to identify them.

"Eight of these girls are from *Garden House*." Ruth pointed at the drawings. "That's Aster, Bluebell, Zinnia, Daisy, Fleur, Cherry, Rose and Ivy." Then she recognised someone else. "This is you! You were at the party!" Her hands grabbed Alixanda. "What happened to the other girls?"

Piper rushed forward. "Let Alixanda go."

There was no mistaking his threat. Piper pulled her away from Alixanda. His hand gripped her by the throat and lifted her above the bed. *This was her chance*!

The expected darkness did not come to remove her from this world.

The room buzzed with activity. The policeman shouted at Piper, pulling him away.

Ruth dropped onto the bed, pretending greater injury while she rallied her defences. Tim examined her, and she made a plausible recovery. When the doctor withdrew to talk to Piper and Kurt, Samson pulled her upright. After straightening the pillows behind her, Samson settled against them. His arm slipped around her shoulders. She glared at his boots where they rested on the handmade quilt. He ignored her. Instead, he watched Piper. Ruth dug her elbow into his side, but instead of giving her room, he shifted closer.

Alixanda rubbed the red marks on her arms as she whispered with Piper and the others.

Then everyone but Samson returned to their former positions.

"We didn't know you had a connection with the girls," Alixanda said. "I'm sorry that I didn't think to ask them if they recognised you."

"They know nothing about Jezebel or Delilah," Ruth said.

Alixanda selected one of the drawings. "This girl, the one you called Ivy. She talked about an adult prisoner at *Garden House*. A woman called Destiny, her friend and protector."

Ruth kept silent.

Alixanda sorted through her drawings. "She said Destiny belonged to one of these men."

Ruth smiled. "Quin – he's just turned twenty-one." Samson held out his hand for the page, and she slapped him. "Alixanda's drawn him with his brother Matteus. They're representatives of the younger generation. Honey traps for unsuspecting fools like Samson's sister, Kimberley. Are there any pictures of them with their father?"

The girl started sorting through the other sketches. "Butch only remembered their first names. He picked them out from the party drawings."

"Their father?" Piper asked, snatching the drawings from Alixanda. "Is this him?"

"Yes. He calls himself Rick now," Ruth said, "but when I first knew him, he was Ricardo Barononi. He was one of the Young Masters during my training. I hated him – and I loved him." She tossed the sketch aside and selected another. "I remembered every little detail. Yet he didn't recognise me. He didn't even make the connection with my name." The paper crumpled between her fingers. "Rick was the first person to call me Jezebel. He said I was his queen."

"How did you get away from him?" Samson asked, rescuing the paper.

"He lost interest when I matured and he sold me." Ruth lifted her chin in defiance. "I survived."

Then she looked directly into Samson's face. "Ricardo liked to dress as a bishop and make me confess my sins. Then he'd administer my penance."

He flinched.

"I promised myself I would never submit to a religious man again. And then I met you." She invested those final words with scorn, before turning to Alixanda. "You weren't going to show me these sketches. Who else did you want me to identify?"

Alixanda no longer faced her. She carefully returned the drawings to her folder.

Piper moved away from the wall and reached for the door. "We'll leave the remaining questions for another time. You've proven to be more useful than I expected."

"I don't want to stop," Ruth protested. "I want to tell you everything so you can deliver your judgement."

"There'll be no judgement from me," Piper said.

"But I want to be punished."

"Then find someone else to do it. Evie made me promise to release you. Against my advice, she has forgiven you."

"What about you, Senior Sergeant?" Ruth asked.

"I've seen the evidence," Kurt Jensen said. "Unless someone agrees to testify, it would be a waste of time bringing charges against you."

"So you're going to let me go free?"

"If living on the streets and abusing your body is freedom," Tim Campbell grumbled. "I'd say you're punishing yourself enough without anyone's help."

"There is another option," Piper suggested.

"No!" shouted Alixanda and Samson at the same time.

"You can't send her back," Alixanda said. "It's too dangerous. You promised Evie you wouldn't put Ruth at risk."

Ruth chuckled. "I'm touched by your sentiment, but I don't need anyone to stand up for me." She patted Samson on the thigh. "I can understand why *you're* defending me, but I don't see what Alixanda's getting out of it."

Piper silenced the artist with a frown.

"If Piper sends me back to the streets," Ruth continued. "I'm certain they'll take me to *Garden House*, either to restore me to my former position or to bury me in the rose garden."

I Knew You Then

ஐ ☼ ෪

Jeremiah 29:11
For I know the thoughts
that I think toward you, says the LORD,
thoughts of peace, and not of evil,
to give you hope and a future.

ஐ ☼ ෪

Ruth waited for the right moment. Alixanda sat too far away from the bed for Ruth to see what she was working on. The artist's hand flew over the page. Piper's agent gave all her attention to these drawings.

Occasionally, the girl's pen paused, and she closed her eyes. More often, the pause preceded the drawing's rejection. She ripped the page from the sketchbook. It joined the other loose pages carpeting the floor.

"What are you drawing," Ruth asked. Alixanda's hand paused mid-stroke. Those blue eyes turned towards the bed.

"I didn't realise you were awake. How long have you been watching?"

"Long enough. I've never seen anyone so absorbed in an activity."

"I get tired too easily, so I've learned to work as fast as I can. I haven't always had this gift, and I'm still afraid that it will suddenly leave me."

"You have a photographic memory? Is that why Piper recruited you?"

"No." Alixanda put down her pencil. "My drawings only became useful when Piper needed a miracle. God provided it through me."

Ruth chewed her lip.

The artist's restless hands hinted at a complicated story. "My enemies were persistent – they wanted me dead. So, Piper gave me a new face and another identity. I wanted to repay him and agreed to go undercover – we didn't find out Rick had set a trap until it was too late. Rick poisoned me and expected me to die. Instead, I went to a special place where I experienced things too impossible to explain. On my return, I had new eyes – they used to be brown. I see things differently now. And I can draw everything I see. I provided Piper with evidence, and now he is preparing his case."

"How long do the memories last?"

"Indefinitely. When I focus on something, the details come back to me as if I'm there."

"I'm not sure I believe you."

"I'll show you." Alixanda shoved the recently completed drawings onto the bed.

Ruth shuffled through them, marvelling at the detail. Alixanda had captured the recent bedside interview, frame by frame. Ruth gasped. Is this how she appeared to them?

The expressions of each player built up an almost movie-like record. Here was the sketch recording her thwarted attempt to get Piper to throttle her. Her hand trembled, and the drawings spilled from her hands.

"Are you okay?" Alixanda asked.

"Why do you care?"

The girl avoided her eye. She busied herself with the scattered pages. "I'm not sure you're well enough for me to explain."

"I'm a survivor," Ruth said. "There's nothing you can say that will hurt me."

Alixanda took a deep breath. "You're my sister."

Ruth had been wrong. The emotions that awakened within her mind were more powerful than she had ever experienced. Wave after wave of pain washed through her, flashes of longing smashing against the hard stone of her heart. "That's impossible," she spat. "My sister's dead."

Ruth turned her face to the opposite wall.

Alixanda wept. "Ruthie, it's me."

Ruth sprang up, desperate to be free of this foolish girl once and for all. She snatched up the artist's paper and pens and threw them at Alixanda. "Prove it."

The girl swiped at her tears and sniffed, before reaching for the tissue box. After drying her eyes. Alixanda scrambled to retrieve the fallen items. Ruth recognised the brightness of hope alight in the artist's eyes.

"Take your magic pen and draw something from my childhood," Ruth sneered.

Alixanda shuffled in her chair and then shut her eyes.

"What are you doing?" Ruth demanded, the rage building within her until it threatened to consume her. "Why don't you admit you lied?"

"I'm praying," Alixanda said. "I might only have this one chance, and I can't afford to make a mistake."

The minutes drifted. The restless girl was gone, replaced by a frozen statue. Ruth studied Alixanda, considering what evidence the artist might offer.

Ruth's impatience grew. Finally, the girl shook herself from her reverie. Selecting a pen, Alixanda sighed. The sketchbook opened to a fresh page. Confident lines appeared as the pen flashed across the page like a laser printer. Ruth leaned closer. Those random marks spread across the page. Nothing made sense.

"Is this how you always begin?" Ruth asked.

The artist shook her head. "Sometimes I work on a picture one feature at a time. But it's especially fascinating when God reveals an image like this."

"Come and sit on the bed so I can see."

Alixanda scrambled to comply.

"What are you drawing?"

"You'll have to wait. If I tell you before I'm finished, you won't believe me."

Ruth snorted. "At least give me a clue."

"God gave me this memory in a dream, when I was beginning to doubt that you ever existed."

"How old am I supposed to be?"

"I don't know," Alixanda said. "How old were you when I was born?"

"I was seven when my sister was born," Ruth conceded, her eyes fixed on the paper.

Samson appeared beside the bed. "What's happening?"

Ruth swore. She kept her eyes on the paper. "Alixanda's proving she's my baby sister."

"Ah!" he said, climbing up beside her.

"Don't put your boots on my bed."

"Yes, ma'am," he chuckled, and she heard a thud. A second thud followed. He wiggled his sock-covered feet for her approval. Then he wrapped his arms around her. "So what is Alixanda drawing?"

"I don't think she knows," Ruth muttered. "Do you have to sit so close? You're distracting me."

"Am I? Then, my afternoon mission's a success."

Ruth swung to face him. Samson pressed his lips against her mouth.

It must have been the surprise that made her tremble. What other explanation could there be? Ruth planted both hands on his chest, ready to shove him off the bed. Inexplicably, she allowed the kiss to linger.

"Would you rather I left the room?" Alixanda asked, her cheeks flushed. "The two of you haven't had any time alone—"

"No!" Ruth protested. "Finish your drawing. He's going to behave."

"What makes you so sure?" he chuckled. "I'm only responding to your original invitation."

"A good Christian husband waits until his wife is ready."

"That only works if the wife wants him to be good," he retaliated. "Is that what you *really* want? I'll be good if *you* promise to be good."

"If that's what it takes to get you to leave me alone, I promise."

"Excellent," he exclaimed, sealing her promise with a hasty kiss. Then he reached past her and grabbed the drawing. "Look, Alixanda's finished. You can't deny those are your eyes peeking from behind those chubby little hands."

Ruth stared at the drawing.

"How did you know?" she gasped. "That's the ring my mother gave me when my sister was born. I lost it long ago, but I've never forgotten it."

Alixanda wrapped her arms around Ruth.

Samson slipped from the room.

The two women wept together.

"I can't believe you found me," Ruth sobbed. "How did you manage it?"

"It's a complicated story," Alixanda said, "and you'll have to settle for the short version today. Piper says this is all a coincidence, but as soon as I met Evie Romano, I knew God was doing something special. You were right when you said those men tortured me. I accidentally stumbled onto one of their operations. The man you call Remo worked out who I was. He told me what he'd done to my sister. That would have been the end of the story if God hadn't delivered me from them. They left me for dead, but I survived."

"You're more like me than I imagined," Ruth said.

Alixanda smiled. "I wasn't out of danger. My injuries made it easy for them to trace me again – they ruined my face. They tricked Piper into finding me an apartment. Freddie and Butch were my neighbours – another coincidence. They expected Piper to take the blame for my death, but the attackers killed the wrong woman."

"Remo told me about a murdered witness," Ruth said. "From his story, I knew it must be you. I never knew what happened to my baby sister. It almost destroyed me to discover she had survived, only to fall into his hands a second time."

"Piper gave me a chance for justice, and I wanted to repay the favour. I set out to find the kidnapper who took Evie. Following your trail to Sydney was easy once I knew where to look. But discovering you'd hooked up with Freddie's brother was a surprise. Piper's operatives identified him from the hotel. They'd reported helping him, but no-one made the connection. I'm curious about how you picked Samson up at the airport?"

"That's another of your coincidences," Ruth replied. "I needed to change my name, and I chose Delilah at random. Samson was waiting for some other Delilah, and I grabbed him before he realised I had conned him."

"But you were the Delilah he was waiting for." Alixanda laughed. "And he's the right man for you. I'm amazed – after years of separation, we fall in love with two brothers."

"I'm not in love with Samson," Ruth protested. She glanced around. Was he still in the room?

Alixanda chuckled, snatching her pen. The artist captured Ruth's response to Samson's surprise kiss in a quick sketch. "You can't deny this."

Ruth stared at the image.

"Don't look so worried," Alixanda said. "God doesn't want His children to be alone, and He makes plans. Because of our shared trauma, he's prepared men who have a strong reliance on God. Samson's perfect for you. Not only does he obey God, but he's proven he can defend you."

"You've almost convinced me," Ruth said, folding the drawing and hiding it under her pillow. "Keep going with your story."

"When I discovered Freddie and Samson were brothers, I questioned my mission. How could I deliver my future sister-in-law to Piper for retribution? That's why I went to see Kurt Jensen before I came to *Mountain Rise*. The file he'd compiled on you included the information you told Samson before you ran away. Those details matched so perfectly with my memories. I knew immediately that Samson's missing wife was my Ruthie."

"There are so many near misses in your story," Ruth said. "A wrong decision here or there, and we would never have known we were sisters."

"There's one thing I'm desperate to find out," Alixanda said. "I've never known my birth name. Do you remember who I am?"

"Pass me a piece of paper," Ruth said, "and don't look until I'm done. I can't remember your father's name. But our mother said his first and last names started with the same vowel. So both your names start with the same letter." She wrote quickly before folding the page.

Alixanda opened the page. Her eyes grew wide. "Really?"

Ruth nodded.

The girl looked again: "'Alice Andrea'. That's so close to who I am now." She began to giggle. "Piper's not going to be happy."

"Is Piper still here? I'd like to see his expression when he finds out."

"I'll draw his reaction for you."

Happy Day

❀

1 Peter 1:9
Receive the result of your faith,
the salvation of your souls.

❀

Ruth stirred a saucepan on the stove. She wore one of Samson's shirts, with the sleeves rolled up, over a pair of jeans.

Old Jack appeared in the kitchen doorway. "You look like the perfect country wife."

"Don't believe everything you see. You're back early."

"I've come to see if there's anything I can do to help."

"I think everything's ready."

"Is that one of Grace's recipes?" he asked as he approached.

"Mmmhmm," Ruth murmured, "but something's not right. Here, taste this. Tell me, what's missing?"

Old Jack took the spoon. "More salt."

He passed her the salt cellar that sat beside the stove. He looked at the crowded benches. "There's enough here to feed an army. You do know Mrs Mac and Mrs J will be bringing more food when they get here?"

"Samson told me," Ruth said. "But he said anything extra could go in the freezer. He thinks there may be days when neither of us will have time to cook, and we'd better prepare."

"Where's everyone else?"

"Freddie went to Sydney to pick up the Melbourne guests."

"Why didn't Piper fly them in?" Old Jack asked.

"Something about babies and helicopters not being compatible? I think Freddie was happy to have the long drive to distract him from the wedding preparations."

"And the others?"

"Samson's gone to check *Valley View*. His investors will want to tour their potential investment."

Old Jack walked to the window and stared up at the mountain. He remained silent for a long time.

"It's not too late if you've changed your mind about the new partnership," Ruth said.

He shook his head. "Where's Alixanda?"

"She went to Meredith Crossing to pick up the wedding flowers. Butch and Nikki went with her. They said they wanted to get some last-minute decorations. They're still nervous about being alone with me."

"How long until everyone's back?"

Ruth put a lid on the saucepan, before glancing at the clock. "We have another hour. I'm leaving that to simmer. There's time for coffee if you want one."

She made two cups of coffee and joined him at the kitchen table.

"What do you know of Piper's proposal to get these people to invest in *Mountain Rise*?" Old Jack asked.

"Freddie speaks highly of Evie and Romano," Ruth said. "Romano's cautious with his money. If he decides to invest, he'll expect to have a say in all the major decisions. I don't know much about Evie's sister, Sofia, or her husband, John. Except he's the celebrant for Freddie and Alixanda's wedding. They're all Christians. They won't make a decision without God's permission."

"Why do you think Piper came up with this deal?"

"Who knows with Piper? He keeps his plans to himself."

"Why does he want Samson to rebuild *Valley View*, as well as take over the Jensen spread?"

"He's put in planning applications for a private girls' boarding school on the Cassidy land. I have my suspicions about the girls who will be staying there. He's been talking about *Forest Heights* becoming a retreat for ex-servicemen. It wouldn't surprise me if he's recruiting extra security."

"Piper's name wasn't on the documents I signed with the bank." Old Jack put down his cup. "Samson wouldn't tell me where he got the money to pay off the overdraft. I'm guessing you had something to do with that. Why would you give him money for *Mountain Rise?*"

"I'm still dealing with my addictions," Ruth said. "While that money remained in my control, my old lifestyle tempted me. That's a daily battle I don't want to face any more."

"So you're going to stay? I've asked Samson why he's sleeping in the visitor wing. He said you made him promise to leave you alone."

Ruth rose to stir the saucepan. "You know what kind of woman I am."

"You're having counselling. And you're going to church with Samson." He walked across the kitchen and stood beside her. "Isn't that why you're going into the river this afternoon?"

She waited for him to finish.

"I've talked to Samson," Old Jack continued. "He's explained how this baptism ceremony signifies dying to the old life and getting rid of the past. When you emerge from the water, you're a new creation."

"That's the theory," she said, her eyes downcast. "I'm not sure it will work with someone like me."

Old Jack raised her chin. "I don't think the ceremony brings the transformation. That's just for show, to tell everyone the job's done. It's the changes in your life that prove the old you is gone. I can see it in your eyes, and in the way you move. I've seen the hundred little things you do when you think no-one's watching. You used to be cruel, malicious and selfish. Now you're always putting others first. I've never believed in miracles, but you're living proof. God's forgiveness is real. Don't miss out on your new life, because you can't forgive yourself."

"You talk like a true believer," she sniffed, rubbing her eyes. "It's not too late for you either."

He stared at her, and she couldn't read his expression.

Then he snatched up his battered hat. The outside door slammed behind him. Ruth watched him stalk across the compound. She bowed her head, praying through her tears.

୫୦ ✿ ୧୫

Ruth paced beside the car. Old Jack hadn't come back.

"We can't wait any longer," Alixanda said.

Samson had gone down to meet the local guests by the river. Freddie was meeting them there with the interstate visitors. Butch and Nikki were already in the car.

"I'm sorry I upset Old Jack," Ruth said. "He was so kind, and I should have kept quiet."

"This is between Old Jack and God," her younger sister said. "Butch says he's taken his horse, so he could be anywhere."

"Hopefully, he'll be back for the wedding."

"If the wedding was in Melbourne, as we originally planned, Freddie's father wouldn't have been there anyway. We have to trust that God knows what He's doing."

"It's easier to think of all the things that could go wrong," Ruth admitted.

The twenty-minute drive down the mountain passed too quickly. Samson helped Ruth from the car.

There were cars parked up the hill on either side of the bridge. People lined the riverbank. Ruth trembled, recognising some of her former clients among the crowd. Everyone who lived anywhere near Meredith Creek had come to see her baptism.

The Melbourne visitors stood on the bridge. There wasn't time for more than a quick introduction. Evie held one of her babies, while her husband carried the other twin. Ruth threw another thankful prayer heavenward because both little boys had survived.

Piper Maxwell waited in the background. With his arms across his chest, he leaned on the further rail. Two pairs of bodyguards flanked him. Evie's protectors, Jenny and Sigrid, were intimidating women. Thomas and Patrick shadowed Evie's sister, Sofia. The sister's husband, John, was trying to keep his sons, Matthew and Peter, from falling into the water. Sofia's son Marco was chatting with Butch and Nikki.

"The water's moving faster than I'd like," Samson said, leading Ruth through the crowd. "You'll have to step carefully if you don't want a premature swim. I'm coming in with you to make sure you're safe."

"I'm coming too," Alixanda said. "I want to be the first to welcome you into Christ's family."

"Are you ready?" Samson's friend Caleb asked.

Ruth nodded. She met with Caleb twice a week as part of her rehabilitation. She felt safe with this man. She slipped off her coat and shoes. She wore a long white gown. She felt underdressed in front of all these people. "Let's do this."

With Alixanda holding one arm and Samson the other, Ruth entered the water. Caleb was a few steps ahead of her. He walked until the water was waist-high. It was colder than she expected. The smooth river mud squelched between her toes as she stepped on the rounded stones.

Caleb called out in a loud voice. "Thank you for coming today to witness our sister's public declaration of faith. She has not come to the waters of baptism lightly..."

He continued with a brief explanation of the sacrament's history. Caleb was retelling the story of Christ's baptism when a shout came from the road.

"Wait!" Old Jack rode his horse down to the riverbank. "Don't start without me." The horse kept coming until he was beside them. He slipped off the horse into the water. Samson helped him regain his balance.

"Well, Caleb," Old Jack shouted. "Get on with it. This water's too cold for my old bones, and the sooner you drown me, the better."

An excited buzz rippled through the crowd. Caleb recovered from the unexpected interruption. "Jack Kidman, do you come to these waters to be baptised in the name of Jesus Christ?"

"Yes."

"Do you repent of your sins?"

"Do I have to confess them first?"

Old Jack didn't wait for confirmation. "I'm an alcoholic, and I've refused to face the truth about my addiction. I'm a proud and selfish man. I was a cruel husband and a despicable father. When my eldest son died, I turned against my other sons. I drove Freddie away, and I've treated Samson like a slave, never thanking him for all that he's done. I spoiled my only daughter and excused her wicked behaviour."

Old Jack paused and threw his arms heavenward.

"God, You know everything about me. I haven't been to church since my wedding day. And I've made fun of those who believed in You. I can't ignore the example of my sons, who have loved me despite my faults. In front of this crowd, I'm telling You, God – it's time for me to change. I want this new life Samson's been telling me about. Come and make me new."

He turned to Caleb, who declared, "I baptise you in the name of Christ."

Caleb didn't have time to assist the older man, who threw his arms out wide and dropped down into the water. Samson and Caleb fished him out. He laughed at their concern.

"New life," Old Jack cried and then winked at Ruth, before he stumbled up the riverbank. Freddie met him with a blanket. Old Jack embraced him. A cheer rang out from the assembled crowd.

On the bridge, a woman's voice began to sing: "Amazing grace, how sweet the sound..." One by one, other voices joined Evie in the familiar hymn.

Ruth blinked away tears. It was her turn. She kept her answers to a simple yes.

Caleb told her to cross her arms across her chest, and he held her firmly. "Bend your knees," he said. As she obeyed, he lowered her backwards.

She gasped at the cold. Water flooded her mouth and nose. She couldn't feel Caleb's hands, and she floundered.

Daughter!

In an instant, the emptiness inside her filled with power. God really did love her! She shot upward from the water. Ruth squealed with delight. Alixanda appeared beside her. The two sisters danced and sang in celebration. Samson and Caleb yielded the river to them.

Ruth imagined a thousand voices singing. The song was new, and as she listened, the words bubbled up inside her.

She began to sing: "Jesus Christ has set me free, the curse is broken. With a roaring flood, God's Holy Spirit sweeps away His enemies. See, the river comes from the throne of God, the Father of All. The rushing waters bring power and life to all who come to Him for deliverance. I am free! I am alive!"

As the words echoed among the trees, Ruth released her sister. She threw herself at Samson, knocking him backwards. Her lips found his mouth beneath the water, as they sank to the bottom. His arms clung to her, and she melted into his embrace.

When she ran out of breath, Samson delivered them from the water.

"I love you," Ruth whispered, as he helped her to the riverbank.

Alixanda and Caleb had already left the water. Freddie and Mrs Mac waited with towels and her coat. Ruth beamed at the welcoming committee. She threw her arms around the matronly woman.

Mrs Mac wiped a tear from her eye. "It's sure been a day for surprises."

Butch and Marco were eager to tell them what they had missed, while they were under the water.

"Evie pushed Piper off the bridge," Butch laughed.

"She didn't mean to—" Marco protested.

"The railin' busted 'n' down 'e went—"

Marco interrupted him again. "The water's deeper on that side—"

"He went under for a bit—"

"Then he exploded from the water and launched himself towards the bank."

Butch grinned. "Piper was so mad he stole Uncle Sam's Cruiser!"

But Marco was determined to have the last word. "I don't think he'll be back for Freddie and Alixanda's wedding."

"Speaking of their wedding, we'd better hurry home to get changed." Ruth dragged Samson by the hand through the spectators. "Alixanda's shivering and I'm cold. Samson, you'll have to squeeze into Alixanda's car with me. I'll sit on your knee."

"Is she always this bossy?" Marco asked Butch.

"Nah," Butch said. "Only when Uncle Sam's too busy laughing to tell her to behave."

Ruth stopped suddenly.

Her earlier euphoria drained away. Samson stole a kiss before scooping her into his arms. He carried her to the car, wrapped in a blanket. He was more concerned for her welfare than his own damp condition. Ruth closed her eyes and tried to pray.

Eager to get home, Alixanda raced her car up the hill to the homestead. They were almost at their destination.

Samson whispered in Ruth's ear. "Ignore Butch. God made you strong and independent, and that's what I love about you.

When you commit to something, you do it with your whole heart."

"I still have so much to learn."

"Then here's a lesson for today," he said, kissing her. "You've made your feelings towards me clear."

"Because I kissed you? It wasn't our first kiss—"

"Every other time your kisses wounded me," Samson said. "Today you surrendered your heart to me and became my wife."

"Oh," she said, a strange warmth spreading within her. "I'm a slow learner. Can you repeat that lesson..."

Timeline

June 30 (#1 *White Rose of Promise* begins)
*August 5 (Chapter 2 *Which Promise This Time?*)
　　　　The beginning of Jezebel's adventure, to escape her
　　　　enemies she changes her name to Delilah,
　　　　Introducing Samson
August 6　　　Samson takes Delilah home
　　　　Introducing his family: Kimberley, Butch, Nikki,
　　　　Introducing Old Jack and Grace, Tim and Kurt
August 24　　　Old Jack's birthday dinner
　　　　August 25 (#2 *When Promises are Broken* begins)
August 29　　　Delilah's enemies attack
September 4 - 8 The storm and the aftermath
September 28　Introducing new enemies
October 3-5　　Samson's family drama, Destiny disappears
October 12　　Destiny meets her captors
　　　　October 30 (#3 *When Freedom is Promised* begins)
November 1　　Destiny discovers a clue to her past
January 14-16　Another enemy for Destiny, then freedom
April 13　　　Samson has an unusual visitor
*April 26 (Chapter 1) Destiny resumes her Jezebel identity
　　　　(Chapter 40) Samson is recruited to save her
April 28　　　Delilah/Jezebel faces her accusers,
　　　　her past is uncovered, she changes her name to Ruth
May 26　　　Ruth and Samson's story ends

Which Promise This Time? starts with a prologue, and then
　　　　jumps back to reveal the adventure that brought
　　　　Jezebel/Delilah to her transformation

Character List

<u>Key Characters from the series to look for in this book:</u>

Jezebel (34) - Books 1&3, **main character Book 4**, fugitive
    aka Delilah, aka Vixen, aka Salome, aka Mystery,
    aka Destiny, aka Freedom, aka Ruth

Samson Davidson (45) - **main character Book 4.**
    Grace's son, Jack's step-son, Kim & Freddie's
    half-brother, Butch & Nikki's uncle

Evie Romano (Books 1-7) - Sebastian Romano's wife,
    Marco's aunt, Sofia's sister

Sebastian Romano (Books 1-7) aka The Boss aka Romano -
    Evie's husband, Freddie's Melbourne employer

Jenny Prescott (Books 1-7) - Main Character Book 7.
    Maximum Security deputy commander,
    Evie Romano's bodyguard

Piper Maxwell (Books 1-7) - Main character Book 7.
    Maximum Security owner, Romano's friend,
    Operation Phoenix Commander, Valentino's cousin

Sofia Fontana - Main character Book 2. Evie's sister,
    Marco's mother

Valentino Horatio (Book 1-4) - Main character Book 2.
    Piper's cousin, Jezebel's Melbourne enemy

John Edwards - Main character Book 2. Evie's friend,
    church pastor, Matt & Peter's father

Ricardo Barononi (Book 2-7) aka Rick - Piper's enemy

Alixanda Jadaranata (26) - Main Character Book 3.
    Freddie's fiancée, artist, *Maximum Security* operative

Freddie Kidman (28) - Main character Book 3. Samson's half
    brother, Kim's brother, Butch & Nikki's uncle,
    Alixanda's fiancé, Romano's employee

Oliver Johnston - Main character Book 5.
    Piper's friend, *Maximum Security* operative

Kurt Jensen (46) aka Senior Sergeant - police officer
    Main Character in Book 6,
    Samson's childhood friend

Sigrid Ericson - Main character Book 6.
    Maximum Security operative, Evie's bodyguard

Character List (con't 1)

Jezebel-Delilah's Associates:
The Black Bishop - Jezebel's enemy
Clayton Wolfe - Witness Protection Officer, Jezebel's enemy
Constanino Barbara, aka Barbie - Delilah's enemy
Cosima aka Uncle Cosi - Matteus & Quin's cousin,
      Rick's nephew,
Delilah Jones - an alias for Jezebel
Destiny - the new Mistress in charge of the *Garden House* girls
Garden House girls: Aster, Bluebell, Zinnia, Ivy, Fleur, (14)
      Daisy (14), Rose, Cherry (13), Daphne, Azalea (10),
      Violet (10), Holly (8), Buttercup (3)
Loki (deceased) - Jezebel's Melbourne boss
Matteus - Quin's brother, Cosima's cousin, Rick's son,
Quin, aka Young Master - Rick's son, Matteus's brother,
      Cosima's cousin
Remolind Vanito Barinova, aka Remo - Rick's father,
      grandfather to Cosima, Matteus & Quin
Rick - an alias of Ricardo Barononi (Book 2-7)
Mr & Mrs Smith - Gardener & Housekeeper at *Garden House*
The Removalist aka Grandfather - Delilah's enemy

Samson's Family and Associates:
Aiden - Kimberley's friend, lives in Brumby's Run
Butch Cassidy Kidman (15) - Kim's son, Nikki's brother,
      Samson & Freddie's nephew, Grace & Jack's grandson
Caleb Read - Pastor, Samson's childhood friend
David Davidson (deceased 35 years) - Samson's father
Grace Kidman (62) - Jack's second wife, mother to Samson,
      Freddie & Kimberley
Jack Kidman (79-80) aka Old Jack - Grace's second husband,
      Kimberley & Freddie, Samson's step-father
Jack Junior (deceased) - Jack Kidman's son from first marriage
John Jensen (deceased) - Kurt's younger brother
Kimberley Kidman (31) aka Kimmy aka Kim - Grace & Jack's
      daughter, Butch & Nikki's mother, Samson's half sister
KJ Jensen - Kurt's father, Jack's friend, lives at *Forest Heights*
Mrs J - KJ's wife, Kurt's father, member of Caleb's church
Michael Cassidy (deceased) - Butch's father
Nikki (Nicole) Kidman (12) - Kim's daughter, Butch's sister,
      Samson&Freddie's niece, Grace&Jack's granddaughter
Mrs Mac - Jack Kidman's relative, member of Caleb's church,
Tim Chappell - doctor, Samson's friend

Character List (con't 2)

Evie's Associates:
Edwards Boys from book 2 - Matt (9), Peter (7)
Lilly Henderson (5) - Marilyn and Dave Henderson's daughter
Marco Fontana (14) - Evie's nephew, Sofia's youngest son
Marilyn Henderson - Evie Romano's friend, Lilly's mother

Piper's Connections:
Abigail Golding - an alias for Alixanda
Alice Andrea - a girl from Alixanda's past
Macy - *Maximum Security* operative
Nelson Felmingham - *Maximum Security* operative
Patrick Sims - *Maximum Security* operative, Sofia's bodyguard
Ruth Foster (32) - aka Ruthie, Alixanda's missing sister
Thomas Demistrani - *Maximum Security* operative
        Sofia's bodyguard
Xanda Jadaran - *Maximum Security* operative

Locations used in this story
Bottom Pub aka Meredith Crossing Riverfront Tavern
Brumby's Run - fictional town near Meredith Crossing
Forest Heights - Jensen homestead
Garden House - secret location
Kidman Road - leads to the Kidman homestead,
        crossed by a river prone to occasional flooding
Melbourne - capital city in Victoria, Australia
Meredith Crossing - fictional township in NSW
        remote mountain forested foothills & a wide valley
Mountain Rise - Kidman homestead
New South Wales, state in Australia (NSW)
Newcastle - closest city to Meredith Crossing
Romanos - automotive workshop, home to Evie and Romano
St Jeromes Boys School - Melbourne private school
Sydney - capital city in NSW
Top Pub aka Meredith Crossing Motel
Valley View - Cassidy homestead
Victoria, state in Australia (VIC)

River Wild Series

Book 1 (2019) *White Rose of Promise*
Book 2 (2019) *When Promises Are Broken*
Book 3 (2020) *When Freedom is Promised*
Book 4 (This book - 2020) *Which Promise This Time?*
Book 5 (2021) *When Promises Are Forever*

These books can be read in any order. Each story stands alone, but some of the characters make an appearance in every story.

Available at www.chrissygarwood.com

White Rose of Promise

A prophetic dream she can't remember. A shameful past she can't forget. An impossible future she dare not cherish.

Maria Evangelina Fontana* comes home from twenty years in exile. She is looking for reconciliation but her family refuse to acknowledge the secret that keeps them apart. They cannot accept that the lost years have changed her forever. Her hope for a new beginning fades.

Sebastian Romano has no time for women and abhors weakness. The wealthy businessman is uncertain why he offers Ria* a way out of her dilemma, but it is too late to change his mind. If only he had understood the risk.

Ria's innocence turns his orderly world upside down. Her faith challenges his values as she steps into her destiny. He thought he was done with his violent past, but his enemies have found her. Romano watches helplessly as the prophecy unfolds...

When Promises Are Broken

A family curse, an evil plot, an unlucky coincidence. Three destinies entwined.

Sofia sits in angry isolation at the wedding reception, unspoken secrets and broken promises her only consolation. No-one will listen, and now it is too late. Her innocent sister has married a very bad man.

Pastor John Edwards is puzzled by Sofia's animosity. Her emotional outburst drives him to prayer. When a sinister stranger warns him to keep his distance, he wonders if it is already too late.

Valentino makes clear what he wants from Sofia. He is rich, handsome and available. So why does she question his motives and reject his advances? He laughs at her assertion that trouble pursues her, but then he disappears...

When Freedom Is Promised

An unlucky coincidence? A fiendish plot? Or a sacred design that promises freedom?

Bad things happen to good people. Abigail is on the run, anxiety and fear her constant companions. She must survive to testify and needs a place to hide. Her new identity comes with the assurance that her enemies will not seek her in Melbourne. Could it be the answer to her prayers?

Freddie's nephew has disrupted his orderly life. After a decade cut off from his family, his loneliness awakens. But the angry teenager's violence is only the beginning.

When the boy and Abigail collide, her cover is blown. Her relentless enemies are coming. But Freddie is in their way. Can Abigail forget past betrayals and learn to trust this gentle stranger? Will Freddie risk everything to set her free?

When Promises Are Forever

Sara Messinger has a crush on her boss, Nero Mariani. When she meets Oliver Johnston, a *Maximum Security* agent, he warns her to be careful. Oliver knows that Nero's family business is not what it seems. Has Oliver's warning come too late? Nero's influential family want to find him a replacement wife, and Sara seems like the perfect candidate.

Fantasy River Series

Phoena's Quest: First Spark
(Christmas 2020)

The quest begins with a first spark. It flares in isolation, untended and unknown. Too late, the darkness tries to smother it...

The Westernbrooke Academy for Young Noblemen has always been Phoena's home. An orphaned servant without a past, the teenager lacks magical talent and protections. She is often targeted for magical experiments. After years of torment, she longs for invisibility. The other servants think her luck is running out.

Lord Karilion, the Academy's best magic-user, has beaten all challengers. The wealthy heir is also the champion swordsman. Viscount Baraapa, secure in second place, has no magic but his scientific mastery outweighs that disadvantage. The foreigner, Lord Oramis, threatens the balance when he refuses to be tested. What is the Ambassador's son hiding?

The quest selects its champions: a servant girl and three noblemen who think winning her loyalty is a game. And there's a dragon in the back garden...

Other titles in this series:

Phoena's Quest: Second Flame
Phoena's Quest: Third Fire

Acknowledgements

This book could not have been written without the support and encouragement of many people.

Firstly, I am grateful to God for inspiring me, for giving me the time and the persistence to bring this story into life.

My writing adventure has not been a solitary one. God provided me with a supportive team - determined to ask the right questions, demand the next instalment and keep me moving forward. Thanks to Gillian Perrett, Naomi McGlone, Belinda McGuire, Donna Bullen, Tim Berry, and Eva Bitterova for your help with *Which Promise This Time?*

I am thankful for you, dear reader. I am especially grateful for your gentle reminders to keep writing because you want to know what adventures are in store for your favourite characters.

A special thanks to Belinda Pollard, publishing mentor and editor, for taking me under her wing and for the professional advice that has helped make this book better than I could have imagined.

Last but not least, thanks to my patient husband Tony, for his constant encouragement, and ongoing support.

Chrissy

A Note From the Author

Greetings from Tasmania, Australia.

Thank you for reading my book. This is the fourth title in my *River Wild* series. I hope you enjoyed it as much as I enjoyed the writing process. If you are able, please leave a brief online review, as this will help other readers find my work.

If you would like to receive updates on my progress with other titles as they are released, please visit www.chrissygarwood.com and complete the form. Links to social media can be accessed from my webpage.

Publishing a novel was a childhood ambition, one that I set aside for decades. I added wife and mother, student, childcare educator, visual artist and chaplain to my list of achievements before I was ready to return to that writing dream.

In that time, God has brought me through many challenging experiences to help me appreciate the riches at my disposal.

But the adventures my characters endure are works of fiction – a small grain of inspiration, a mountain of imagination, and months of hard work to bring it all together.

When I first lost myself to the rediscovered joy of writing, my horizons expanded. My fictional world has become populated with characters who whisper their stories to me. They are impatient for me to give their adventures a narrative to activate the transformations which will lead them to a Happy Ever After ending.

I have learned a lot about myself and my ambitions while pursuing the writing dream. The confidence I am gaining as a storyteller is enriched my character. I believe it is making me a humbler disciple of Jesus Christ, a more determined encourager, a better friend.

Chrissy